For Love
and
Loyalty

by

Diana Rubino

For Love and Loyalty

Cover Art by *Debbie Taylor*

The Wild Rose Press, Inc.
PO Box 708
Adams Basin, NY 14410-0708
Visit us at www.thewildrosepress.com

Publishing History
Previously published as "One Too Many Times"
First Faery Rose Edition, 2014
Print ISBN 978-1-62830-462-6
Digital ISBN 978-1-62830-463-3

Published in the United States of America

Richard shook his head.

"I never brought a lady flowers, I don't pour honeyed flattery over them like Ned, I don't recite poetry like George, I don't cook gourmet cuisine. All I can do is spread bananas on pizza."

She smiled and sipped at her wine. "It's romantic if your intentions are sincere. I enjoyed your banana pizza more than any gourmet meal I could get at LaGrenouille."

"Sincere?" He buffed the Wensleydale Ring on his shirt. "Mayhap. I don't put forth any false fronts. Nay, there's naught false about my front." He took a quick glance downward. Her eyes couldn't help but follow.

"That's my idea of romantic," she assured him. "Not flowers or poetry or flattery. Just sincerity. That other stuff is just veneer, and it wears quite thin after a while."

His gaze pinned her and she took another sip to ease the tension. "Simply speak your heart. Share your heart. That's what romance is all about—to me," she said softly.

He reached over, took the glass from her hand, and placed it on the table in one swift, graceful movement. "Then may we share some tonight?"

The hearth glowed, seductive music floated through the lounge—the perfect ambiance. But now that the moment was here, the reality of it nudged her in a stern warning:

Don't.

Praise for *FOR LOVE AND LOYALTY*

"This is the book to read when you want pure entertainment. Funny and a bit outrageous, these wonderful heroes are willing to take a chance on changing history to put things right."

~Susan Mobley, Romantic Times

~*~

"What do you get when you take 3 members of the 1463 Royal family and transport them to the present? You're reading one of Diana Rubino's books, you get laughter. Rubino has taken characters from two worlds, combined their differences and blessed us with a book that I feel would make a very enjoyable, funny movie. This is one that Mel Brooks needs to read."

~Martha Cheeves, A Book and A Dish

~*~

"I love the detail the author put into the past and present, making the story richer and more fulfilling. My favorite character was the wizard, sort of a bumbling magic man with an unusual story to tell."

~Theresa B.

~*~

"What I liked: Comedic, romantic, and historical. This is what Diana Rubino brings with her story.This book is a solid tribute to Rubino's novelist skills...for those who us who love to read romance, but with a touch of everything. I really enjoyed reading this tale and it takes place in a very absorbing time. The characters, dialogue, time period, time traveling, are all things that make this book so special. Rubino knows how to write and she surely shows it in this comedic medley."

~Denise, The Pen & Muse

Dedication

To Foery MacDonell,
my star sister

Acknowledgments

The Richard III Society, and its fascinating members. http://www.richardiii.net/
My expert Ricardian friends for the many hours of brainstorming.
Bonnie Schutzman for her creativity and letting me 'borrow' Nicky and the band.
Claudia Fallon, my meticulous, dedicated editor, also great fun to chat history and time travel with.
Photo credit: Phil Stone and the Richard III Society.

Chapter One

Wensleydale, the Yorkshire Dales, August, 2012

SÉANCE headed the first email in Julianna's in box.

Hello, Julianna, just firming up our date & time; tomorrow at eight, Middleham Castle again, correct? Maybe King Richard will stick around a bit longer this time. Cheers, Trev.

She tapped out a reply: "Confirmed. Don's hauling the firewood. Remember, no loud clothes: Hawaiian print shirts, neon orange socks, you know the deal. We don't want to scare him away. I'll wear my Wensleydale Ring again. Let's hope it still carries some energy to attract him. JLH." Before logging off, she visited the Richard III Society's website, to see if any more reviews got posted.

She clicked on the Library section and there it was.

Red Blood, White Rose, by Julianna Hammond, gives a unique perspective on the Wars of the Roses from the viewpoint of a double agent...three weeks on the bestseller list, and quite deservedly. We look forward to many more tomes by Miss Hammond, a member of the Richard III Society's Board of Directors.

"Yes!" She punched a fist in the air. "From the

Times, woo-hoo!" She logged off, put the kettle on, and got back to work on her next book, a collection of medieval home remedies.

****

Westminster Palace, August, 1476

King Edward IV threw back his bedcovers in the morning sunshine. "Rise and shine, sweetcrupper." He gave his blonde bedmate a playful slap on the rump. "Wakey wakey."

He glanced round his bedchamber. Ah, privacy! No grooms, gentlemen of the chamber, or throng of lesser servers. They cleared out at midnight, not to return till sunrise. To Edward, a king's biggest perk was privacy—a precious commodity at court. Droves of nobles, advisors, and servers observed his every act, from using the close-stool to creating the laws of the land. But midnight to morn was his time alone—or as alone as he wanted to be—this morn with Jane Shore, his favorite 'turn' as he affectionately called her.

"Janey, you must rise..." Pulling on his nether stockings, he turned toward the rumpled four-poster bed, but she'd already slipped out without a sound. A smile played upon his lips. Ah, the dream mistress—fell on her back when he wanted her, and vanished when he didn't. Pity she wasn't fit to be queen consort.

A familiar rap on the door brought him to his feet and across the plush Oriental rug. He opened his door to his youngest brother Richard, current heir to his throne.

"Are we alone, Ned?" Richard peered in, his blue eyes darting about, purposely avoiding the disheveled bed.

"Of course, Dickon. Enter, take a swig of wine."

Edward quaffed from the pitcher, ignoring his personal tankard. "What gripes you this morn?"

"Sorry to trespass on your, er... morning activities so early, but I need some brotherly advice before the world descends upon you." Richard stood erect, bedecked in velvet chausses and velvet doublet displaying his White Boar emblem. Beringed fingers held a sapphire-studded hat.

"Come sit by me and tell me all about it." Ned perched at the edge of the bed and patted a space next to him.

"Could we go to the window seat instead?" Richard gave the rumpled royal bed wide berth as he headed for the oriel window.

Ned chuckled, shook his head, and joined his brother. "Now, tell me what ills you, but remember, I'm only the king, not the royal treasurer." That was a running joke when any of his siblings came scrounging for a handout.

"Anne and I had a terrible row last eve. She said she's finished with me. 'Twas all my fault," Richard poured forth his sorrow, as if reciting confession. "I tried to keep it from her, but—"

"Tried to keep what from her?"

"She knows about Kate Haute, the other lass I've been...." His voice trailed off, he lowered his head and shuffled his feet.

"So she knows you fancy Kate." He guffawed. "I wrote no laws that preclude fancying two wenches. Anne'll learn to live with it."

"There's more to it than that, Ned. There may be a third person involved."

"Another wench?" He slapped Richard's thigh. "I

knew you had it in you somewhere, Dickon. Keep it up, lad!"

"Nay, 'tis not another wench. Kate believes she may be carrying my child."

He shook his head and wagged a finger at his little brother. "For God's sake, Dickon, Kate Haute is the daughter of a fishmonger. I said she was fit to give you a snog, not a whelp."

Richard scowled at Edward's ribald quip, as always. "Nevertheless, Ned, if there is a child, I want to give that child my surname, as he'll never be legitimized. And a title when he's older. But meanwhile, Anne feels I betrayed her. She's been saving herself for our wedding and..." He turned his gaze outward. "Ned? Did you ever bungle so badly you wish you could go back and do it all over again?"

"What mortal hasn't?" He gave his brother's nose a tweak. "But we're just that, Dickon, mortal. We can't undo what's been done. If Kate really is breeding and Anne can't accept that your attention need be divided from now on, she's too selfish for you anyway. You don't need her."

Richard twisted his rings. "Mayhap I should go to that wizard George always goes to. He cooks up grand love potions."

"Bah." Edward gave a dismissive wave. "George couldn't live a decent love life if Julius Caesar were running it for him. Alas, our pater didn't pass on his common sense to all his sons. You don't need any supernatural help, Dickon. Love holds enough logic-defying properties that potions only undermine. Naught can change what's in Anne's heart. Except time. Time mends wounds better than any codswallop cooked up by that wizard prat, to whom I wouldn't give a groat to shovel a dungheap."

Richard looked into his brother's eyes. "Ah, but that is you, Ned. You rule over your love affairs as you rule over the realm—expertly and majestically."

Edward shook his head. "Bosh. I've a breakable heart just as any other man—and mine, as theirs, is mendable. But love—love is magic. Mayhap that's why I'm so intrigued by it. It never fails to surprise me." He gave Richard a wink and a reassuring nod. "When you're sure Kate is breeding, make sure she is well provided for. My possible future nephew shan't want for anything just for being whelped on the wrong side of the sheets."

"Your heart is bottomless, Ned." Richard stood and gave his brother a small but respectful bow.

"And think before you act in future," Edward added as he headed for his shaving bowl. "That'll eliminate the futile yen to go back and do it all over."

"Of course, you're right, Ned. But as men, there are times when not all the blood is in our brains." Richard departed with a wry smile and left Edward to attend to his toilette.

****

George Plantagenet, the middle brother, pranced round the realm with every expectation of sitting on England's throne someday. He wanted that throne so badly. It teased him like a wanton splayed atop his bed—but just beyond his reach. Ah, the throne...every time Ned vacated that carved, cushioned, dilapidated old heap of bark after a state event, George sneaked up and placed himself upon it, wriggling in nice and comfy, to fancy all of England cowering, bowing, and groveling before him.

Ned hadn't coveted the throne. It had been thrust upon him after their father died in battle. His followers begged him to reign, lest the feeble Henry VI and his snaggletoothed wife return. Ned accepted the crown with his usual aplomb, merely duty-bound. Never had Ned displayed a lust for power, or thrilled in giving orders. He had no desire to manipulate markets or unite lands. Being the realm's almighty ruler didn't faze him. To Ned, it was simply a job to attend to, a business to run. The profundity of it, the glory, the magnificence, eluded him. Instead, he capitalized on the position to further enjoy life's sensual delights. He reveled in luxury and in sharing it. "'Tis a big game to me," Ned once said, for certes a gracious winner.

But to George, kingship stood a rung below sainthood—that one stab at immortality he was willing to kill for.

If only it weren't Ned.

George, as did Richard and their sisters, idolized his eldest sibling. After their father perished, Ned became the family patriarch, their healer, protector, and provider.

George blotted out the memory of his slain father, the Protector of the Realm, his head hoisted atop Micklegate Bar to rot in a paper crown. But the Plantagenets were now legally royal, George's only consolation.

Immediately following Ned's lavish coronation, he'd made George Duke of Clarence and Richard Duke of Gloucester. As respected Knights of the Bath and the highest ranking, they became the most eligible bachelors in the kingdom.

Richard was smitten with Anne Neville, their frail little cousin. George fancied her sister Isabel, heiress to a sizable fortune. But still he prowled the bawdy houses like a common whoremonger, in disguise if too near court, affecting a Cockney accent that never betrayed his royal station.

But on this chilly morning, his problems loomed much graver than how many years stood between him and the throne. It was so cold, his codlings shriveled like walnuts. At least he hoped it was the cold. Muttering every Anglo-Saxon curse he knew, he pulled his cloak tighter and tied his mount to the post outside the Grand Wizbar's wattle-and-daub cottage. Shivering in the dampness of the English spring, he sprinted up the path.

He was impotent, constipated, hung over, and he'd soon burst if he didn't get help. He pounded on the door. "Come on, you bugger, wakey wakey!"

Still uttering his mutterings, he found himself pounding on the Grand Wizbar's head.

"Sakes, George, can't you do anything quietly?" Ulch rubbed his head and swung the door open for the Duke of Clarence to enter.

He twirled round to entreat his most trusted soothsayer. "Ulch, you must administer something—an antidote—I don't give a toss if I have to pour it down my gullet. I'm desperate."

"What is amiss, George?" Ulch sounded genuinely concerned.

George took a deep breath and winced as a stomach cramp doubled him over. "It concerns Mary, the witch's daughter."

Ulch helped him to a three-legged stool. "Which

witch? Not Horse Face Hortense?"

"Nay, her sister, the name escapes me, pity her face doesn't. She's so ugly, they haven't come up with a name for her yet. Don't want to insult any reptiles, I reckon."

"So what of you and Mary?" Ulch folded his hands across his chest. "She's guarding her maidenhead, and you want a love spell to make her want to marry you?"

"I don't need a love spell to make her marry me." George let out a whoosh of relief as his stomach relaxed. "My bald-headed hermit's already promised her that."

"Nay, you didn't breed her...aw, George." Ulch shook his head and took a swig of ale from a horn.

"Well, I ain't here because I enjoy your company, mate." George stood and paced the creaky floorboards. "The old warthog put spells on every part of me except my little toes, and I trust she'll get them with the gout. I need help, Ulch." He pressed his hands together in entreaty. "She'll have my head for certes—one of 'em, anyhow."

"Let her have the one on your shoulders. You don't use that much." Ulch took another quaff of ale.

George cocked his head. "I didn't come here to play sillybuggers, mate. I need something to ward her malodorous hocus-pocus off me. And if I throw in a few guineas extra, make the whelp come out looking like Henry Tudor, or—anybody but me." He threw his hands up, and they fell to his sides with a smack.

"Follow me." Ulch led George through his workshop area to a dark alcove dripping in gemstone pendants. Suspended on various-length cords from the ceiling beams, the stones sparkled in divers sizes and shapes: hearts, pyramids, teardrops, eggs. Some even resembled dripping icicles. The charms dazzled George as they shot multicolored rainbows across the walls.

"Crikey, Ulch, these gems are brilliant. I've always fancied sparkle, shimmer, and glitter." He wiggled his fingers, adorned with rings to rival these hanging jewels. "I wear more baubles than the king. Ned reckons 'tis gaudy and vain for a ruler. But now that I've become royalty, I want the entire realm and all who visit to know it." He polished his thumb ring, a bright citrine, on his doublet.

"Aye, I noticed...and who with sight hasn't?" Ulch rolled his eyes.

"Looks like the sultan's tent in here, Ulch." George palmed an oval blue stone, gazing at multiple reflections of his eye staring back at him. "These whatnots work magic or just twirl round looking pretty? This one would look grand with my apple-green doublet." Gazing into its depths calmed his stomach.

"Of course they work magic. They're charged with positive energy." Ulch rubbed an amethyst twixt his fingers. "These purples are amethyst." He strummed a row of stones like lute strings. "They guard against drunkenness." He cocked a brow. "May want to invest in one sometime." He strode over to the wall. "However." Sweeping his hand left to right, he indicated a row of polished gems in an array of vibrant shades. "Adventurine for luck, red jasper for inner strength, sapphires for the sweat. These"—he pointed to the row hanging twixt them—"are toad-stone, to be hung at the girdle for dropsy." He pointed to each group of stones as he spoke. "Rhyolite, petrolite, and coprolite. Each with its own unique properties."

George's eyes bugged out. "Hey, this coprolite looks grand. Matches my coloring perfectly. What's it for?"

"I'll tell you when you're in better form." Ulch turned toward the other wall and pointed to a row of glittery golden chunks. "Here's the one for you."

George's jaw dropped with wonder. Ulch plucked one off its strap and handed it to George. Turning it over and over, he marveled, "'Tis for me, Ulch. This leapt up and smacked me in the very face!"

"If only it could. 'Tis pyrite. It offers protection, just the kind you need. My spell shall increase its power to perform as an antidote. Taking care of your slattern and offspring is your problem. I have a deep-seated belief in paternal obligation, being an orphan meself." He pointed at the stone. "But one of these will ward off the old gash's malevolent spells. 'Twill protect you from any kind of harm. Not only will you be immune to her spells, you'll be protected from life's everyday maladies and obstacles. Pain will elude you. Illness will dribble off you like water off your greasy body."

George enclosed the chunk in his fist. "How about the ones she's already heaped on me? She's got me so bunged up, I can't get anything up *or* out."

Ulch bit his tongue to keep from grinning. "This charm will annul all she's inflicted on you, present and future. But 'twon't take effect till you've had it forty-eight hours, so at that moment, make damn sure your arse is seated firmly on the garderobe, for all hell will break loose. And I don't mean that lightly."

"Another forty-eight hours of this?" George groaned. "Make it twenty-four, Ulch, I beseech you. We've a banquet tonight, one of Ned's twenty-course feasts, and it'll be squirting out me ears."

Ulch shook his head, his lips compressed into a thin line. "Forty-eight's the best I can do, George. These antidotes take longer than the average spell. I'm negating someone else's power, you know. But once it takes effect, you'll be protected. It's a powerful charm. Like any great effort, it can't start working immediately. It demands patience. Just like waiting for the finest mead to ferment. Fret not." His voice lightened. "It'll pass in the blink of an eye. And your"—he cleared his throat—"other nether parts should spring back into life about that time, too."

George rolled the charm twixt his palms. "Grand. I'll use the garderobe by the scullery maids' chamber then."

"So that is the amulet you want?"

"Hmm, I'm not sure yet. 'Tis such a hard decision. But I must learn to be more decisive for when I'm on the throne..." George swept his eyes over the row of pyrite baubles and chose the biggest, chunkiest, gaudiest one. It also turned out to be the most expensive. Coin changed hands, then Ulch went back into the shadows and slipped the amulet into a pouch. "Remember, forty-eight hours. And it's got to be in your possession always, in order to protect you. So don't let anyone borrow it or it'll be guarding them instead, and you'll stay clogged as ever."

"Aye, Ulch, thanks indeed." George opened the door and breathed deeply as the invigorating wind rustled his red-gold hair. A stirring warmed his loins already. "Forty-eight more hours, Percy." He cupped his crotch, mounted, and waved to Ulch. "Cheers, mate. Next time you see me I'll be a lot emptier."

"Whoa, George! I won't be here for a while. I'm attending the annual vernal equinox ceremony up at Wyndehenge. I return Tuesday fortnight."

"Jolly good. Cheerio then." George galloped away, as eager to let loose on the garderobe as he was to let loose on the next heedless wench.

Court currently resided at Westminster Palace, and when George approached the gates under that eve's full moon, the sounds of clinking glasses and tankards grew louder. Raucous laughter rang out above the minstrels' playful music. Dismounting, he tossed the reins to a stable boy and hurried to his apartments to change into proper raiment. Shucking off his cloak, he felt in the pocket for his new amulet. There it was, nestled in its pouch. He slid it out, wanting to hold it up to the candlelight and watch the colors whip round the chamber. But his jaw dropped as he stared at the object in his hand. It was not his ornate, glittery charm. It was an elegant polished stone of pink, a perfect circle, with a tiny hole in the middle. But to him, it was useless, utterly useless, down to the hole.

"That pribbling puttock, he gave me the wrong one!" George spat out a string of Flemish curses and flung the stone across the chamber. It rolled in a circle, wobbled and keeled over like a drunken sailor. "Dainty little pink—looks like something Richard would go for."

Richard, his youngest sibling, slight of build, of swarthy complexion, and nut brown hair, the royal fop—never a hanging thread from his expertly tailored doublets, or a trace of stubble on his chin. He bathed and shaved twice a day, color-coded his shoes and hose in neat rows, and lined up his coins in columns like soldiers. His every appointment, down to those with the privy, recorded in meticulous detail in a leather-bound, gold-inscribed journal. Richard drove everyone loopy with his fastidious manner, his pared nails, and especially his aversion to the vulgar. Whenever a ribald joke drifted his way, he made his cabbage face—akin to sniffing overcooked cabbage—verbalized his disgust with a "How uncouth," and glided off, leaving the earthy Ned and the lusty George shaking their heads.

"Dick needs his wick dipped," George always said, getting a one-shoulder shrug from Edward, juggling more important matters than whetting Richard's carnal appetite.

Yet George loved the lad fiercely, and part of him didn't want to see Richard conducting himself like him and Ned. Richard's lady love was Anne, who was keeping Richard at bay till the wedding bells clanged. He didn't think Richard minded waiting. He was too busy wielding his swords and practicing at the quintain, the effort culminating in a brilliant military career. George and Ned could be raking wenches with the French army at the foot of their beds, and Richard would be there to defend them.

George walked across the chamber and retrieved the amulet. As hard as he'd flung it, he hadn't made the slightest chip in the smooth, shiny stone. Mayhap it was a rare and valuable gem, and that beetle-headed wizbar had sold it for a song. No doubt in his cups—Ulch did look rather onion-eyed when he answered the door.

George then decided to give the charm to Ned as a peace offering. They were currently on uneasy terms since he caught George indulging his most forbidden fantasy: shagging one of the royal dog-walkers in his favorite trysting place—the throne of England. Besides, Ned could use protection from harm that he never bothered about, like enemy factions, and the ever-returning pox.

George decided to make the sacrifice for his beloved brother and seek relief from his ills the conventional way.

Exiting his chambers, decked in court finery, he went to summon the royal physician. He was beyond desperate; he'd try anything, even the brews cooked up by Dr. Rotgut, as they affectionately called him.

****

Julianna locked up her three-hundred-year-old cottage and headed for her annual pilgrimage amidst the ruins of Middleham Castle. Middleham had been one of Richard III's boyhood homes and a favorite residence as king. Nestled among the Yorkshire moors, its remains lay at peace.

She tried to forget that another year had slipped by and it was now the five-hundred-twenty-ninth anniversary of King Richard III's death in the Battle of Bosworth. Every August 22, several Richard III Society members held a séance to summon the slain king's spirit. Lady Dorothy Warburton, a leading psychic, acted as medium. Richard's spirit appeared every time, splendidly attired in kingly raiment, a glittering crown atop his head. He would visit with them briefly, then return to the great beyond, leaving them speechless with wonder.

Julianna was the first to arrive at dusk. The others usually didn't arrive till after dark.

She spread her blanket on the ground, among the ruins of what had once been Middleham's great hall.

She sat cross-legged, closed her eyes and imagined life in this magnificent castle five centuries ago. Marble floors gleamed, torches blazed, minstrels played merry tunes in the gallery, courtiers feasted on rich foods and flowing wine. But with the castle's inhabitants long dead, all lay still.

A car engine's hum broke the silence. Doors slammed. She rose to greet her fellow pilgrims, three men and two women, carrying blankets and fire logs.

"Where's Dorothy?" she asked.

"She couldn't make it." Susan, the Society's librarian, spread a blanket on the ground.

"Then who's going to summon the spirit of Richard the Third?" Julianna helped carry the logs.

"We were hoping you would." Trevor, the research officer, arranged the wood for a small bonfire.

"Me?" Threads of doubt crept through her. "But I've never done this before. I'm no psychic medium."

"You're the closest to King Richard spiritually," Trevor said. "You're the longest-standing member among us; you've written books about him. If anyone can summon him, it's you. Just give it a try, and really concentrate. We'll all concentrate, like we always do. Just say what Dorothy says. You know, 'we hereby summon your spirit,' so on and so forth."

Shaking with apprehension, she forced a smile. "I'm flattered you're so confident in me, but I don't want to let you down. I've seen ghosts before—you know about Galahad, the playful poltergeist in my house, and others I didn't get around to naming. But I've never summoned any of them. They show up when they feel like it."

"You can do it," Dorothy assured her, leading her

toward the forming circle.

"All right." She gave a resolute nod. "I'll have a go at it. But don't be surprised if nothing happens. Dorothy's the one with the magic touch."

"Oh, don't be so doubtful, Julianna," Don, the Society's treasurer, assured her. "The king's spirit comes back every year. Maybe we don't even need Dorothy; he'll just come on his own."

"Well, don't get your hopes up," Julianna muttered. As she did every year for this special séance, she removed her Wensleydale Ring, a medieval gold band she'd found with a metal detector on a bridle path near the castle. She placed it on a satin cushion and sat across from it. The group joined her around the bonfire, clasped hands, and closed their eyes.

"Here on the anniversary of the Battle of Bosworth, the day England lost its honorable, brave, and noble king, uh—" she faltered, clenching her fists. "Uh— brave and noble king..."

"What's wrong, Julianna?" Trevor whispered.

"I forgot the rest of it."

"Now we summon his spirit..." He helped her out.

"Right! Now we summon his spirit, so that he may know he is still revered and respected. Come forth, King Richard! Come forth and make yourself known."

Since she'd botched it, maybe he wouldn't appear. He was known to offend easily.

She peeked with one eye. The breeze didn't pick up as it usually did when he appeared. The fire didn't blaze any brighter. The others sat still, deep in concentration. No spirits yet. She heaved a sigh of disappointment. "Please appear before us, please come to us, King Richard," she whispered.

Chapter Two

King Edward tossed a few pounds on the table. The goldsmith beamed as he snatched up his fee.

"Are you sure it is to your liking, Your Highness?" He'd already asked this divers times.

"Aye, son, 'tis truly a work of art." The king nodded, in a buoyant mood, for he'd just spent the third night in a row with Jane Shore, a record for him with one harlot. As usual, their night had lasted till dawn, and he'd stumbled into morning Mass looking rather un-kingly. His subjects paid his appearance no heed—they were just happy to be in his joyful presence.

Edward truly loved people and treated everyone as his equal, from dukes to lepers. Women he adored—no matter what their size or shape, or if one mound was larger than the other. He reveled in feminine company and fortunately for him, he needn't seek it out. His tall commanding stature made wenches literally swoon at his feet.

But the kingdom was impatient with the bachelor monarch. He needed a consort at his side. Yet he couldn't take some slapper to queen just to please the masses. He would scarce admit it, but he sought a love match. So, whilst maintaining his carefree bachelor image, he put every wench he wooed to his rigid test. None had passed yet. They were all too eager to please him. He liked to chase and pursue till driven mad with desire. Only such a wench was worthy of England's crown.

He caressed the charm George had given him, now a pendant suspended on a gold chain with *Comfort et liesse*, his official motto, meaning "comfort and joy" engraved into the stone in gold leaf. He slipped it over his head.

"'Tis regal looking. Good work, lad." With a benevolent nod, he dismissed the goldsmith, who bowed out of the audience chamber looking like he'd never straighten up. Edward chuckled. "Cease all the fawning, I'm only Ned Plantagenet." he always wanted to say, but had to catch himself in time. Hard as it was for him to believe, he was the King of England. But somehow it didn't mean all that much, as long as an abundance of good wine and feminine company awaited his command.

At the end of the busy day, Edward yawned, winked at the shapely French courtesan splayed for his pleasure, and shucked off his shoes. He'd dismissed his Esquire of the Body earlier. He disliked having anyone dress him, and as far as undressing—that was the job of a wench with long, nimble fingers. He slipped off the new pendant and tossed it into his jewel box. With a groan of anticipated bliss, he made for the bed and the warm, luscious performer awaiting his Highness.

The next morn, the main beam in the king's vacated bedchamber collapsed. Plaster sprayed in all directions. Fallen beams crushed the furniture, shattering glass and splintering wood everywhere. Only one item survived intact, like it had never been touched—the jewel box containing the protective amulet George had given King Edward. While the king presided over his realm, his staff summoned workmen to repair the damage. The wreck took place exactly forty-eight hours after the Grand Wizbar told George his protection would take effect. Meanwhile, George swallowed a potion from Dr. Rotgut and hurried to his privy.

"Crikey, what happened here?" King Edward swept through his apartments for a change of raiment.

"Wonky beam collapsed, your Grace, a structural defect in the building construction," his groom of the chamber informed him. "I fear your bed and nightstand are destroyed, and alas, your wardrobe chest is in a frightful way."

He winked at the groom. "I mind not, I shall use the north apartments. Better view. Inside, that is. No direct sunlight." Edward wasn't bothered; the palace was abundant with roomy, comfortable beds. He'd made sure of that. Although he provided his guests with comfort and privacy, he still bumped into ardent lovers coupling or tripling in the palace's many nooks and alcoves. He himself preferred the vastness of a feather mattress.

After donning a velvet doublet embroidered in gold thread, Edward rummaged in his jewel box and slipped his new pendant over his head. He lingered for a moment at the looking glass. The charm was rather comely, but it didn't quite flatter the rich purple of his attire. The shade of pink was a tad too pale. Nor did he believe all that mumbo jumbo about protective powers that George insisted it carried. Nevertheless, 'twas sweet of George to want to safeguard his big brother this way. The lad did have a heart after all.

He slipped the pendant off and returned it to his

jewel box. Mayhap he could wear it another time, when dressed more casually.

****

Richard stood still as his Esquire of the Body straightened his doublet and smoothed the velvet nap down. He nodded his dismissal and flipped open his jewel box. Before him lay the same old jewels in the same neat, orderly rows. He made a notation in his journal to visit the goldsmiths in Cheapside and see what was new and fashionable. But for tonight, he wanted to look especially regal. George was holding his betrothal banquet at his Chelsea townhome, and Anne Neville, the lady Richard had betrayed, was attending. He hadn't seen her since their row, and despite Ned's advice, he needed to apologize, although it wasn't protocol. It was simply the gentlemanly thing to do. George courted her sister Isabel for two years, finally earning her father's blessing. Hence, George's lavish betrothal feast.

Winding through the palace's passageways and rows of bowing guards, Richard reached Ned's private apartments. Entering the royal bedchamber, he observed the repair work in progress. Dismissing it as another of Ned's remodeling sprees, he headed for the jewel box and flipped it open. He espied a ruby ring, but lost all interest as his gaze landed on a unique piece: a polished round pink stone suspended from a gold chain, *Comfort et liesse* engraved into the stone.

"Ah, Ned." Richard smiled at his brother's choice of a motto. "Always pursuing comfort and joy."

He slipped it over his head and beheld the charm, already warm from his body heat. Unlike any other piece he owned or borrowed from the generous Ned, this stone accented his burgundy doublet. It nestled above his White Boar emblem. He'd never seen a gemstone quite like this before. Where had Ned gotten this? Mayhap another bribe from the Spaniards, always badgering him to raid the royal coffers for a voyage across the Ocean Sea, but Ned was financing his own navy.

Richard sized up his reflection in Ned's looking glass. If only he were taller, his nose less pointy, his chin less jutting, but he made the best of what he had. Tonight there was something different about him that made his eyes gleam. It was that stone. It seemed to glow, with an inner radiance of its own.

Ned wouldn't be looking for this; he was busy in the north wing with his newest doxy. Oh, why wouldn't Ned find a suitable noblewoman and take her to wife already? Earl Rivers's daughter Elizabeth Woodville was especially comely, despite her advanced age of twenty-six. "Ah, Ned," Richard sighed as he strode down the corridor. "Need to get the blood back into your brain."

The banquet was building to a crescendo when the guards bowed and parted to admit Richard. He glanced round George's great hall with a *tsk* of disapproval. What a bloody mess! Goblets and plates lay everywhere, as did cloaks and other garments not of the outer variety. He strode forth as the borrowed court musicians played a lively tune. Those who weren't twirling about the floor sat gorging or imbibing. He saw George entertaining a bevy of wenches, his bride-to-be nowhere in sight. Richard regarded his brother's deportment.

"He's so much like Ned." He sighed. Richard knew

how much George wanted to be in Ned's shoes, Ned's robes, and above all, Ned's crown. But Richard was his heir, although no one knew it. Richard himself had no desire to be king; he would ascend the throne only in honor of Ned's wishes. He saw how the kingship ravaged Ned, at times collapsing from exhaustion. Richard just wanted to live out his days in a quiet Yorkshire hamlet. But George as king? "God save us," he muttered under his breath.

He scanned the crowd for Anne, grabbed a goblet from a passing steward, and took a swig of wine. Several comely maidens batted their lashes in a come-hither gesture, but Richard ignored them all. He didn't need to be dunking his privy parts in vinegar all night.

"Dickon!" George's boom rose above the loudness. Richard embraced his brother, turning away from his ale-stale breath.

"Why, what a timely entrance, Dickon, we were just talking about you, weren't we, uh—" He waved in the direction of his nearest doxy.

"Cate," replied the slapper, reclining in a most conspicuous seat—George's lap. She stood, brushing herself off, adjusting her bosoms under her bodice.

"Right." George grabbed Richard's hand. "Well, Dickon, grab a doxy or two and join in. Don't stand there holding your rooster. I'll show you the ones I haven't had yet." George knew bloody well Richard didn't engage in random dalliances; why did he always insist upon trying to lure him in? One of the slappers put a goblet to George's lips and he slurped. Purple liquid ran down his chin, and Cate leaned over to lap it up, her breasts all but spilling out of her bodice. Then their mouths met. Richard looked away when it turned to a tongue-wrestling match.

He tapped George on the shoulder, knowing he had to come up for air sometime. "Where is Isabel, George? And for that matter, where is Anne?"

George pushed the wench away, and she stumbled backward. "Uh—don't tell anyone, Dickon. Not to spoil the jollity, but Isabel's a bit miffed. Seems she cares not to marry me after all."

Richard's mouth fell open. "What? After all that courting and begging and negotiating with her father? Whyever not?" Richard stood there, shaking his head in disbelief.

"Seems Mary Lyghtfote is breeding—and seems I may have helped."

"Ah, George, you bloomin' spiv." Richard heaved a deep breath. Bad enough Ned had two bastards; now George.

"Isabel got wind of it and called off the nuptials," George griped. "Isn't that just like a wench? But I didn't see any reason to cancel this soirée. Seems Hoghead Hortense is trying her damnedest to get me to make an honest woman out of her daughter." George took a thoughtful swig from his goblet.

"Why, of course not, George." Richard's voice lilted over his sardonic tone. "There was no earthly reason to cancel your betrothal party. Who would notice the one minor change, the absence of the bride?"

George wiped his lips. "And there'll stay no bride if I have any say, Dickon. The old Hortense slag's had me so bunged up, she had me coming *and* going. And now I'm warding off her guts-griping spells with some deflection of my own." He gave a resolute nod.

"All you needs do is hold up a mirror to her face,"

Richard commented. "Might not deflect the spell, but should scare the holy shite out of her."

"Better even than that." George chucked him under the chin. "Twixt the Grand Wizbar and Dr. Rotgut, I've got it all covered."

"Oh, not that fustilarian quack." Richard shook his head.

"But he cured Ned's catarrh!"

"Nay, I mean that wizbar lout. Don't tell me you fell for his hokum again," Richard chided his older brother, never able to talk sense into him.

"*Et tu*, Dickon? I tell you, I was desperate. And he's gotten me out of sticky wickets before. Remember the time I had the pox, after jumming that reeky—"

"Spare me the beslubbering details, George." Richard held his hand up. "I refuse to partake in a celebratory feast of such an impertinent sort, however grandiose."

As Richard turned to leave, George grabbed his sleeve. "What's that you're wearing round your neck? It just glinted in the light when you turned round—what ho, 'tis the amulet I gave Ned. He gave it to you?"

"Nay, I found it in his jewel box. I'm forever borrowing his baubles, he never minds. You gave this to him?" Richard lifted it to gaze at it once more. It was even warmer than before. "Your taste has improved a millionfold. I truly adore it."

"The wizard gave me an amulet to counteract a spell my latest doxy's mother cast upon me. But when I opened the pouch I saw he'd given me the wrong one." George pointed at the round pink stone. "'Tis just as well you have it, it suits you far better than either I or Ned. Goes with your rosy cheeks." He reached forward and pinched Richard's cheeks.

Richard stepped away from further pinching reach. "Thanks, brother." He released the amulet, and it fell back against his doublet. "But I'm a disbeliever in spells and their dubious antidotes. I shall wear it simply for show, as was my original intention. So enjoy your festivities. I'm off."

"Nay, do stay!" A young doxy with flowing hair and full lips clutched Richard's arm. He plucked her hand off him like a piece of lint.

"God's truth, George, they swarm like flies in here. Wherever do you find them all?" Richard smoothed down his sleeve.

"You get more flies with honey, Dickon." George ruffled Richard's hair, another of his brotherly gestures that rankled.

The Earl of Suffolk approached Richard and George. Richard wanted to discuss some business with him, but Suffolk opened the conversation on a rather lower note, asking Richard if he'd ever heard the one about the English soldier and the camel. "An English soldier was on crusade and needed a shag really bad. The sultan offered the use of his camel. 'Take the camel, all the soldiers take her,' he offered. The soldier looked at the camel chewing her cud, walked around her a few times, then, since he was horny as a hound, he whipped out his rooster and started giving the camel a jumm. The sultan observed this and asked the soldier, "What on earth are you doing?' 'You said to *take the camel!*' the soldier said. The sultan shot back, 'I meant ride her into town!'"

They whooped and howled. But Richard shook his head, not the hint of a smile curving his lips. "What's

25

so funny about jumming a camel? I think it would be most repulsive."

Suffolk blinked in bemusement.

"'Tis a bloody joke, Dickon, for Joe's sakes," George said over a guffaw.

Richard took another sip of wine, glad he had the prop to hide behind.

"He sees no humour in epicure of the carnal sort," George explained to Suffolk. "Thinks it's strictly for promul—promflu—" He slapped himself across the cheek. "I'm willing to wager he's never even given his gooser a name, have you, Dickon?" He jabbed Richard in the ribs.

"Call it Dick. Should be easy to remember," Suffolk suggested, wiping his wine-stained lips with his sleeve. "Imagine having to remember all your friends' dicks' names as well as all your friends' names?"

"So how you hangin', Redcap?" George addressed Suffolk's nether region.

"That's Lord Redcap to you," Suffolk shot back, elbowing George, wine sloshing over the rim of his tankard.

This was all too much for Richard. "I'm off. I shall see you, er—gentlemen, on the morrow. Enjoy yourselves this eve—the four of you."

George spat out a stream of wine as Suffolk whooped. "Good one, Dick!" But Richard was already out the door.

He climbed atop his mount for a solitary ride. Twilight cloaked the realm, and the breeze refreshed him after that crowded party. Passing through the city gates, he took a deep breath of the clean air, free of London's odours. He galloped over the moors, watching the moon rise over a copse of trees. Stars twinkled from the velvet canopy above him. He wanted to be alone, to think.

In a clearing that afforded a view of the sky, nestled between the earth and the heavens, he gazed up at the stars, listened to his breathing, felt the beat of his heart.

But his heart beat a sad tattoo. He wondered how Anne fared since he'd hurt her so. Oh, why couldn't life offer second chances? After all, man was only human.

The pounding approach of hooves startled him. Two shadowy figures charged toward him. He reined in to give them clearance, but they surrounded him, leaping from their mounts. They pulled him from his mount, tearing his doublet.

Highwaymen!

"I have nothing you want—" The only object worth anything was the pink stone amulet. He had but a few groats on his person. Would they kill him just for a bit of coin and a hunk of stone? He slipped it over his head as they forced him down and brandished daggers, glinting in the moonlight.

"This is all I have, take this—" Richard gasped.

They slammed him to the ground. He blacked out, but felt no pain.

He knew not how long he'd been out. But when he opened his eyes, the robbers were gone. So was his mount. He lay alone in an open field. The moon still shed soft light upon him. He stood and dusted himself off, feeling for injuries. He took a deep breath. His ribs felt fine; nothing had broken in that fall. The amulet still hung round his neck. They hadn't even robbed him! Mayhap they'd been after the horse.

Still dazed and disoriented, for he didn't know what direction was which, he started walking the way he'd been facing. Looking up, he could see the stars, but they were fewer in number and not quite as twinkling, as if some had burned away. He recognized a few of the constellations, found the Big Dipper's handle and the North Star just beyond it, and turned to walk in the opposite direction, back toward the City.

Piles of stone ruins loomed in the distance. He wasn't aware of any ruins here. The nearest Roman remains lay much farther out. Mayhap the robbers had knocked him unconscious, dragged him a distance and abandoned him here—but where was here?

He walked farther. Strange lights glowed to the west. As he approached the ruins, a smoky aroma filled the air. Orange tongues of a bonfire danced before his eyes.

He quickened his stride, eager to get help and secure transport back to Westminster. Reaching the ruins, he saw some folk sitting round the fire. They turned, caught sight of him, and stared. In turn, he regarded their bizarre raiment—plain shirts, short sleeves, bare feet.

A beautiful woman approached him and stood before him. He stared and she stared back, silent, stunned.

Chapter Three

Richard knew he had to be dreaming. His dreams usually carried him to unfamiliar locales like this, surrounding him with otherworldly beings who frightened him into waking, as a familiar stench or noise assured him he was in his own realm. But even rapid blinking didn't blur or obliterate the sight before him—this ravishing woman, her complexion free of pockmarks, red hair cascading round her shoulders and straight white teeth displayed in a brilliant smile.

"One of those medieval actors." Her strange accent sounded vaguely Cornish, her gaze enraptured him, but her eyes shone with an intelligence he'd only seen on older women. She held out her hand. "Hi. I'm Julianna Hammond. You're just in time for our séance. Glad you could make it."

A sweet fragrance emanated from her. He couldn't help feeling aroused as she clasped her long slender fingers round his, still atremble from the highwaymen's assault, the tumble from the horse, and now this bizarre encounter. He kept his eyes averted; her knees showed, as did her feet! Not even George's orgies demanded a dress code of this sort.

He jerked his head to give consciousness one more try, squeezed his eyes shut, and opened them again. But it was still before him: the ruins, the fire, those strangely garbed folk, and the beautiful vixen. If it was a dream, it had gone on long enough; it had to end soon with the gong of the church bells. So he let his mind lead him. How harmful could it be? If it took a nightmarish turn, he could force himself awake.

She led him to the group, who hadn't taken their eyes off him since he'd stumbled into this bizarre landscape. "Whose spirit are you summoning?" he asked.

"King Richard's," she replied. "I thought you already knew about it, and that's why you came here. This is something we do every year at this time."

"I'm Trevor." The man to his left offered his hand and Richard took it, limply, not returning the firm handshake that further confirmed his suspicions. No, he wasn't dreaming. Richard inched back, bumping into the woman. "So sorry!" He turned and found the safest spot, just outside the circle.

The rest of the group regarded him with a mixture of wide-eyed awe and bewilderment. But no one said a word; they merely clasped hands as Julianna's fingers closed round his. Trevor, on his other side, grasped Richard's hand loosely, to his relief. They all closed their eyes and bowed their heads as Julianna continued her summons of the king's spirit: "We beseech you, King Richard, our noble king who was so defiantly betrayed and brutally slain at Bosworth, to appear before us. Come forth and make yourself known." Her voice resonated with intensity and emotion. "We beseech you, your Highness, to appear before your humble subjects."

King Richard? Bosworth? Richard knew his history. Neither Richard the First nor the Second had ever engaged in such a battle. These people were clearly misinformed. He couldn't sit by and watch them blunder so.

He pulled his hands free and stood, brushing the dirt off his hose. "Forgive my rude interruption, but you've been sadly misinformed of our heritage. There has been no battle with the name of Bosworth. Richard the First died of an arrow wound, and Richard the Second was starved to death in prison."

Now all eyes fixed upon him. Bodies leaned forward in anticipation of his next revelation.

He noticed a gold band resting on a cushion at the center of the group and stepped closer to get a better look.

"We're trying to bring back the spirit of Richard the Third. Every year on the anniversary of the Battle of Bosworth—you know, where he was killed—we summon him and his spirit joins us for a short while."

One of the other women added, "You should know more about him than any of us. You're practically the spitting image of him."

"You're right, Pippa, the resemblance is uncanny." Julianna leaned forward and retrieved the ring. "You are an actor, aren't you? Cause if you aren't, you ought to be."

His gaze returned to the gold ring. It winked up at him in the fireglow. Something about it looked familiar. "May I examine that ring, please?" he addressed Julianna. "It bears an uncanny resemblance to—oh, but it couldn't be."

She placed the ring in Richard's palm. Seeing the notch in the surface, he blinked in astonishment. The gold was tarnished, but it was unmistakably his—the ring he'd lost three years ago. It had slid off his finger into the mud, and he'd never found it. "You recovered my ring!" He slipped it on his third finger, where he'd always worn it. Still a perfect fit.

"What do you mean, your ring?" Julianna made a move to retrieve it, but he held his hand up, out of her reach.

"'Tis mine. I lost it nigh on three years ago." He buffed it on his shirt. "See the notch here? That happened whilst I was fencing with my friend Francis Lovell."

"You couldn't have lost it three years ago. I found it five years ago." She plucked it from his fingers and placed it back on the cushion.

"I think it's about time this bloke told us who the hell he is," Trevor spoke up, kneeling before Richard, as if afraid to stand up to him. "Cor blimey, you don't believe you're King Richard, do you?" He turned to the group. "Maybe he's one of those loons," he said out the side of his mouth.

"No, I am Richard Plantagenet, and I know not of whom you speak when you refer to this Richard the Third. Was he—" Then it hit him. He shook his head, fighting back raucous laughter of relief. Just as they thought he was an actor, they were playacting! He'd attended many a show of this sort. Ned summoned traveling minstrels for these performances all the time. They created the most outlandish episodes and acted them out—comedic farces, Greek and Roman myths, and of course, the ever-popular Camelot. But this was an exceptional exercise of the imagination, pretending this was an alternate course of history. And they wanted him to play the king! Richard the Third. He'd never heard the words spoken out loud. They rang ominously in his ears. He especially didn't like the way they'd plotted out this king's demise, in this Bosworth battle. Where pray tell was Bosworth anyway? He'd never heard of it.

"Your game is amusing indeed. But your plotting leaves much to be desired. Death on a battlefield? Indeed. Were I king, the entire realm would support me, including the lords of the south. Your plot reeks with imagination but its outcome is absurd. And the casting isn't exactly to my liking, either." He examined the results of his ring-buffing. Some of its familiar glow returned.

"Acting? No, we're not acting, mate," Trevor replied and slugged from a bottle. "We're trying to bring back—"

"Trev!" The Pippa woman screeched and all gazes turned to her. "Don't you know who this gentleman is? It's really King Richard! He's come back, but this time in solid form! Just look at his countenance. Who else could it possibly be? You've all seen the facial reconstruction of the skull. If this isn't the king, it's his twin brother, and we know he had no twin."

The group gasped in unison. One by one they stood and paced toward him as if in a trance, mouths agape. Two of them tentatively touched his doublet with their fingertips. He felt someone stroking his hair and turned to see Julianna, her eyes wide and unfocused, her lips parted as if to speak but no words emerged. He looked round him, more confused than ever now. People had this kind of reaction to Ned, but never to him. Was he this popular here? He hadn't been aware of it. He felt a pleased grin playing upon his lips "My God, I don't believe it. He does look like the facial reconstruction."

Trevor's eyes roved over Richard's features, as if studying a complicated text.

"He does," Pippa added, her head moving slowly as if following a swinging pendulum. "All the other séances, we couldn't touch him, we saw right through him, he was a ghostly mass of ectoplasm. His face was a blur. Now he's—solid."

Pippa approached Richard, slid a pair of wire spectacles down her face, stepped up to him and nearly nose to nose, made his eyes cross. He blinked and stepped back, recreating his invaded space. "Except not so troubled. He looks almost happy now. And a bit more fattened up."

"Fattened up, indeed. I've not one spare ounce of flesh on my body." Richard ran his hands over his lean hips.

"Your spirit must be at rest, finally," one of the men declared, grasping Richard's hand between his palms and pressing it possessively. "Oh, I'm so glad we could help you. You poor man, what your being has suffered over the years."

Richard shrugged. "It hasn't been that bad."

Julianna nudged her comrade out of the way. "What have you people been smoking? You actually think this is Richard's ghost?" She laid a hand on his arm and gripped it. "There's no way. I've seen more ghosts than you can shake a stick at, and he's as solid as the rest of us." She glanced over at the beer-bellied Trevor. "Well, almost." Again she faced him and picked up his hand. "Where's all those rings you wear in the portraits? And the hat with the pin on it and the teardrop pearl and the fancy neck thingy?"

As he took a breath to reply, she carried on, "You

did a fair enough job with the black wig and the big ears..."

She brushed a lock of hair off his shoulder. "Oh, no gold stud in the earlobe. We all know Richard loved to flaunt his bling," she challenged, stepping back and sizing him up from head to toe. "The costume is authentic, down to the pointy shoes, but the accent...that's hardly Yorkshire."

"I do take umbrage at that vituperation." He stomped his left foot on the ground, balling his fists on his hips. "I certainly am Yorkshire born and bred. 'Tis you who betrays that Cockney impediment." He curled his lips into a wry grin.

"Cockney, ha!" Julianna fluttered her lashes and gave him a wink. "I'm as Cockney as the queen herself. I'm Cornwall born and bred, thank you very much."

She seemed to enjoy this bantering. He certainly didn't hide his amusement.

"Well, since you obviously went far out of your way to entertain us, we'd love you to stay for the séance. But I have to hand it to you, out of all the re-enactors and stage actors and—of course Olivier notwithstanding, he was downright campy—your Richard impersonation's the best I've seen in ages. Did you glue on those eyebrows the way they did at the facial reconstruction? They're a bit more caterpillary, but an honest effort."

He licked a finger and drew it across his left brow. "Every strand of body hair is my very own, you saucy wench." He tugged on his hair. "I would never don an item as epicene as a wig. I'd be laughed straight out of court. 'Specially by George." He held up his hands. "I simply chose not to don any fine jewels this eve. Just this stone adornment." He pulled the pink amulet out from under his doublet. "And 'twas a wise choice. Those robbers would have had my head for jewels when they accosted me."

"What robbers?" The folks looked in every direction.

"Who accosted you?" Julianna asked him.

"We did have some UFO abductions near here last year," Trevor said. "What did they look like?" He turned to Richard, eyes wide as saucers. "Were they short and gray with big heads and slitty mouths?"

"Oh, shut'chyur silly gob, Trev," Julianna chided him.

"You speak with an insolent tongue," Richard remarked, cocking one of those caterpillary brows, as she put it. "Is this how the peasants address one another?"

"We're hardly peasants, mate." Trevor stood and looked down at him from an imposing height. "If you came here to insult us, you can go back to whatever repertory theater you came from and take some more acting lessons."

"Don't antagonize him. He's only playing sillybuggers." Julianna nudged Trevor aside. "You must still be pretty shaky if you had muggers after you. We didn't see or hear anyone around here. How did you get here? Did you drive or walk from the village?"

"What are muggers? And what is a USO?" He tried to calm down by taking a few breaths. "These unfamiliar words sound more disconcerting than you folks' garb and your blithering pribble about spirits."

"UFOs. Unidentified flying objects." Trevor pointed straight up. "You know—aliens."

"Now how would he know about aliens, Trev? Get real, will you?" Julianna reprimanded him. Her insolence startled Richard; no one in court circles would have tolerated such a sharp tongue. Is this how the peasants address one another?

"They didn't have aliens in the fourteen-hundreds."

"They had them in the Bible, Miss Best Selling Historian!" Trevor snapped back.

Someone whistled shrilly. "Will you two stop arguing in the presence of His Highness King Richard?" Pippa yelled at both of them, and they contritely clamped their mouths shut.

"No, I woke up down the road..." He rubbed his head and looked round at the ruins, the scantily clad folk, the strange chests full of brown bottles. "Look, I was riding my horse, highwaymen accosted me, I fell off, got knocked out cold, and woke up..." He gestured at his surroundings. "My horse was gone, so I just started wandering...and here I am. But where is here?"

Julianna took his hand and brought him closer to the circle. "Here is Middleham Castle. North Yorkshire."

His mouth hung open. A stab of fear pierced his gut. "But Middleham is splendid, palatial." He raised his arms and spread his fingers. "This is in ruins!"

"Well, of course it is." Worry lines creased her forehead. "Middleham's been in ruins for centuries. This is—Good God." She grasped his forearms and stared into his eyes. "Did you just come from the past? I mean, this is the year two thousand twelve. We started to summon Richard's—your—his spirit, but is it possible you could have time traveled and you're here—alive?"

37

He looked down at the amulet and lifted it off his chest. It glowed, warming to his touch. "Why, it is possible... it came from a wizard. It has magic properties, but I never knew it could transport one through time."

She turned to the group, wide-eyed at this exchange. "Hey, you guys, I believe we really did summon the real Richard. Not his spirit. Him. In the flesh. Somehow this amulet around his neck connected with us and brought him here from his time."

A collective gasp reached his ears.

She faced him, hands clasped. "We're so sorry, Rich—er, your Highness." Julianna bobbed a quick curtsey, lifted his hand to her lips, and kissed it, lingering a bit longer than protocol demanded. But still, it was a bit shorter than Ned demanded.

"No need to address me as such." Richard shook his head, offering her what he hoped was a pleasant smile. "I'm but a nobleman. My lord will do."

"No, when you're with us, we'll address you as your Highness, nothing less." He felt a slight tug as she tried to pull her hand from his, but he didn't want to let go. So he didn't.

"Nay, I won't have it, just address me as Richard," he replied only to her, and their eyes locked for a long moment.

"You feel so real—Richard," she breathed, and he was too overwhelmed with confusion and fatigue to question any more of this group's queer remarks. He'd even given up trying to figure out just why he'd been thrust into this story, or scene, or alternate existence, or whatever in the Lord's name it was. Fate brought him here for a reason, though he did not know what that might be, and was too frightened of the answer to try and guess.

"I feel real to me as well." He finally freed his hand, running it over his head, feeling no hot stickiness of blood, no bumps, no gaping wounds. He reassured himself that he hadn't been hurt in the fracas with the robbers or in the fall from his mount. His body felt as always. It was his mind he no longer trusted.

"Are you going to be staying with us for long, your Highness? I stand before you as your humble subject Pippa Lewis, sir." Pippa dipped in a low curtsey and needed the assistance of another to rise, who now stepped forth and swept a reverent bow.

The others introduced themselves, bowing or curtseying, in the formal fashion of a receiving line. Then they stood back in an orderly row and regarded him with renewed awe.

"Please say you'll stay a while," Julianna beseeched. "Last time your spirit came and went so fast, we didn't even have a chance to tell you what the crazy Aussies did at the Mass!"

"Aussies?"

"He doesn't know what Aussies are," Trevor hissed out of the side of his mouth, bowing to Richard.

"Well, if he sticks around long enough this time, we can tell him—and about a lot of other things as well." Julianna stepped forward and dipped in another light curtsey. Richard bowed back. God's truth, this was worse than some of the court dances. "Can you stay, please, sir? We won't tell another soul—er, anyone else you're here if you don't want us to. We'll keep you completely to ourselves. You can stay with me; the entire top floor of my house is a self-contained flat. It's got a sink and a stove and—oh, never mind, I'll show you. My house is three hundred years old. You should be really comfortable there."

"I—I suppose." Richard nodded, too tired now to even converse. Enjoyable as this adventure was, he was ready for sleep, to awaken again in his own bed, his prized mastiffs at his side, a warm cup of ale on the table, familiar faces and raiment. But he couldn't help wondering when he'd ever again see a bit of bare leg such as this.

"So you will stay longer this time?" Julianna implored, leading him from the group toward a narrow path. A sprinkling of lights glowed in the distance.

"Maybe he can't go back till you release his spirit." Pippa ran her hand over Richard's sleeve, plucking at it as if he were a ripe fruit. "You're the one who conjured him up."

"We all conjured him up. It was the concerted energy fields of our collective wills," Trevor insisted, as the group followed Julianna, her arm linked firmly through Richard's. "Julianna was just the spokesperson."

"Well, I'm the only one who's got accommodation fit for a king," she replied smugly.

"Weren't you supposed to be letting out that flat for the week?" one of the group members in the rear asked.

"I'll cancel."

"Yeah, can't wait to see what excuse you'll use. You're going to say you've got Richard the Third staying there?"

"Nah, I'd better not. They're from Wales."

She went back her ring resting on the cushion,

picked it up and brought it over to him. "As this is rightfully yours, you shall have it back." She grasped his hand and slid the ring onto the fourth finger of his left hand, like a bride and groom on their wedding day.

They all took turns bowing, curtseying, and kissing the gold ring. After swearing each other to the utmost secrecy about their discovery, the crowd dispersed at the top of an incline over what appeared to be a village in the distance. The brilliant lights glittered. Mayhap they manufactured candles here, or were having a festival of some sort.

Julianna led him down the hill toward a cozy timber-framed cottage. "It needs some work. You know how hard it is to keep up something this old." She laughed as she turned a key in the lock and swung the door open. He hesitated in the doorway, peering in, half expecting George to leap out of the beams and yell 'surprise!' along with the rest of the court. But this was no joke, he realized as she tapped the wall, flooding the interior with bright light.

"God Jesu!" He shielded his eyes and watched in amazement whilst she turned a round knob on the wall. The light faded to a soft glow.

"I'm sorry. That better?"

He could say naught, only gaze round the small, well-furnished room. A large brick hearth faced him, above which hung a coat of arms he recognized as his own. Attached to the wall, displayed in order of size, was an array of swords and daggers, their polished hilts gleaming.

Rows of portraits covered the adjacent wall, some of which he recognized as former monarchs. Shelves lined the other wall, stuffed with books from ceiling to floor. Several plush seats faced each other around a leather chest that served as a table, covered with brass candlesticks, tankards, and more books. A tapestried rug covered the flagstones. The exposed beams looked as if they'd been replaced recently.

He stood, stunned at the mixture of the familiar and the frighteningly bizarre. Especially that dark square of glass sitting atop a writing desk with an instrument before it that bore rows of letters, numbers, and strange groupings of buttons printed with symbols, more lettering and numbering. "By God, what is that thing?" He pointed to it, and she led him over to her desk. She bent over, pushed a button on another strange looking contraption, and the most disconcerting hum filled his ears, nauseating him.

"That noise, it assaults my constitution so!" He clapped his hands over his ears and blinked with disbelief as the box began to glow with a blue light and large letters formed before his eyes: WINDOWS 7.

"It's all right, your hi—Richard. It's a computer. Here, now sit down. Make yourself comfortable."

Nay, he could never be comfortable again. He wanted to dash out of there and retch until he could bring up no more. Then sleep through all eternity. "Oh, to sleep, or to awaken, whichever I am, I want to do the opposite."

"You'll be fine, Richard, I promise. This machine won't hurt you. Look. It does all kinds of incredible things." She began pushing buttons and sliding another strange contraption that resembled a rat with a long skinny tail round the desktop. "I don't know if we can ever send you back, but as long as you're here, I want you to be as comfortable as possible."

"Here? And where is here?" He gestured at his surroundings.

"Here is Yorkshire. When is the twenty-first century."

"How many?" His eyes slid shut even before he finished counting.

Chapter Four

Blixworth, Northamptonshire, 1476

"God's truth, look at the size of that codpiece! He's certainly well equipped...for battle, that is." Lady Jacquetta Woodville let out an embarrassed titter as she watched her daughter fit a cloth-of-silver suit of armor to a doll she'd fashioned out of satin. Blond hair hung to his shoulders. Long lashes, hand-sewn in one at a time, rimmed expressive blue eyes. She walked over to take a closer peek into her daughter's world. Plunged into widowhood at twenty-six, Lisbet now occupied her own little realm among imaginary characters and their adventures. Sending her two young sons away to be educated, she found amusement writing romantic plays and acting them out with, Jacquetta had to admit, exquisitely crafted puppets.

"Actually, he may not be quite that well-endowed. He's rather vain and the codpiece is for show." Lisbet gazed longingly at her creation. Holding her soldier up, she caressed it like a lovestruck maiden.

Oh, my poor daughter! Jacquetta mouthed silently. *Will she ever rejoin the real world?* The physician hadn't helped, with his concoctions of felon fat and boiled tree rinds. Pshaw! Her daughter needed some real help!

"Lisbet, I need bring you to—"

"Ma mère, this is not another play puppet. Nay; he's going to help me win the man I've yearned for since Twelfth Night, with whom I have fallen hopelessly in love."

Where had we been on Twelfth Night? Jacquetta scanned her memory. Ah—court! Court? Who had captured Lisbet's fancy there? She'd shunned all the knights of the realm's attentions, snubbed a few earls and an Italian explorer. When they returned home, she'd retreated to her puppet theater and staged a production about Druids. She'd never mentioned a live, breathing man. "I can't recall seeing anyone at court who resembles this handsome knight," Jacquetta urged. "May it have been someone visiting from outside the realm?"

"Nay, ma mère. No mere knight nor foreigner. His name is Edward, and I shall seize his heart," she replied over a sigh, embroidering a tiny coat of arms upon his breastplate. "He is the bravest soldier in the realm, always putting his life on the line for the kingdom, yet that is not his only virtue. His heart is ever so generous. He rewards his friends and forgives his foes. This is no puppet, ma mère. This is a love spell, to make this handsome charm's live counterpart marry me."

Edward, Edward, Edward... Jacquetta couldn't recall meeting anyone named Edward...

Oh, no!

"Lisbet, you are in a dream world, surely." She placed a hand over her racing heart, truly worried for her daughter. The poor girl was delusional for certes! Jacquetta reached for her cloak. This was a case for a real alchemist, not that dotty quack she'd been to before.

"Aye, ma mère," her daughter's voice rang out across the chamber. "I intend to marry my lord King Edward and become Queen of England."

****

"She's gone over the top. I fear she's truly moonstruck." Jacquetta unfolded her linen handkerchief and sobbed as the Grand Wizbar sipped his homemade mead. "She thinks she's in love with the King of England, and he's going to marry her. And she's using a puppet to cast a spell on him."

"So, you've a loony for a daughter." The Grand Wizbar stuck a beeswax candle onto a dragon-shaped holder and lit it. "My newest invention," he boasted. "Bug candles. Attracts the biggest bugs round here." He rubbed his hands together. "Great for me real juicy potions."

Approaching her, he assured her, "Fret not, Jacque. Would you rather she aspire to something truly daft, like building a machine that flies? At least with puppet shows, the most harm she can face is a harsh critic."

"A machine that flies! Har!" Jacque had to laugh through her despair. "I come here asking for help and you spew forth the truly daffy. Can't you stay within the realm of the possible for once, Ulch?"

"Anything's possible in this universe, Jacque. I didn't become Grand Wizbar by being a debunker. Me mind's open at all times."

"Well, mayhap you should sew it shut, lest the rest of it leak out. I need something to restore my daughter to normal."

He wiggled his brows. "Normal for her, or for the rest of us?"

He had her there. "I just don't want the poor lass

setting herself up for heartache. Marrying the king? God's foot, she's already lost a husband. I can't have her thinking the bloody king's going to fall under her poxy little love spell and—"

"What ho!" Ulch raised his arm, and his sleeve swayed, knocking over a beaker. A pungent aroma escaped.

"Pew. That pongs." Jacque wrinkled her nose and thrust her handkerchief to her face. "Whatever is that, Black Plague pustules?"

"Just me eel pie seasoning. 'Tis a bit ripe, in'it? Now—what you said about a spell. What does the lass know of love spells? Naught. So instead of swaying her from this illusion of marrying the king, why not grant her wish instead?" He splayed his fingers. "With a real love spell? Cooked up by the grand master of them all!"

"I thought Merlin was dead."

Ulch narrowed his eyes and scowled. "Did you come to me to help your daughter, or to make frail attempts at waggery?"

"Of course I need your help. But—a real love spell? Can you truly do that?"

"I've been known to set a few hearts a-fluttering." He buffed his nails on his robe, its embroidered moons and stars reflecting the bug candle's glow. "Ever see Roger and Bruce—oops, bad example. Er—all right, me very first spell! Thirty years ago, 'twas upon the kindly old dairy farmer who owns Fiddleford Farm, and the Earl of Hereford's milkmaid. The lovebirds are still mad about each other to this day! Not only that, I get free double cream and curd cheese for life."

"But he's not exactly the King of England," she countered.

"Matters not. Love doesn't ask to see your bloodline. Love is blind. And sometimes I think it's deaf and dumb, too," he added with a shake of his head. "Love spells aren't my specialty. I decided not to specialize. Too narrow a market. But I've good references. And that's more than I can say for some of the quacks round here." He *tsk*'d and started flipping through a huge book of spells.

"I'll pay as much as I can afford, Ulch. I'll sell my gowns, my plate—anything to help my poor baby." A surge of sadness and motherly love filled her eyes with tears.

"Right then. I do offer a wide range of services to suit every money pouch." He handed her a list of spells and their fees. "And we can concoct a payment plan should your credit references pass muster. Ah! Time for me daily dose of lamprey liver oil. Pardon me."

She studied the list while Ulch retreated to his back room. When he returned, she pointed to a spell under the heading *Affaires de Coeur.* "Very well, this is what I want for Lisbet."

He took it and blinked. "Uncontrollable Lust with Brutish Passion for the Satisfaction of Animal Needs?"

"Nay, you dolt, the two under that. I want both a spell of Complete Unequivocal Surrender at First Sight, followed by a spell of Unconditional Tender Devotion."

"I can offer you the triple combination package—a third spell, Long-Enduring Marital Fidelity, for only another ten groats. 'Tis three for the price of two and a half."

She scowled. "Let's get her married to him first, shall we?"

"Very well." He nodded, and she plucked a velvet

pouch from under her chemise. His attention returned when she began counting out coins. "How long do you want this spell to last?" he asked.

"Does it not last for life?" Jacquetta looked up. "I didn't know love spells had time limits."

He suppressed a chuckle. "Not my life, my lady. How do you think I stay in business? They must all expire eventually, like everything else."

"You said the farmer and milkmaid are still in love after thirty years!"

"Aye, and I'm swimming in double cream till I croak. After that, who knows?" He shrugged.

"Hmmph." She snatched the list away from him and eyed the prices. "Very well, three months' time. That's all I can afford at the moment. Now the trick is getting the two of them together. Can you do that?"

"Dearie, I'm a wizbar, not a courting service. I shall utter the magic chant upon your departure. The Unconditional Tender Devotion and Complete Unequivocal Surrender at First Sight takes effect at King Edward's first sight of Elizabeth. His gaze will fall upon Elizabeth, and the spell will render him senseless. But he must see her first. Once he's seen her, he'll be precluded from attraction to any woman other than Elizabeth. But getting his eyes laid on the fair Elizabeth is your job."

"Bloomin' quack," she muttered under her breath, handing over her coins.

"Beg pardon?"

"Quaa, quaa—just a frog in my throat." She turned to leave.

"I can give you something for that—"

"Never mind, you already took me for skint." She

rushed out of his cottage.

"Sod ya, then, I'll drink it all meself." He proceeded to crack open a new bottle of aqua vitae.

****

Lady Jacquetta turned to her daughter in the litter carrying them to Westminster Palace. "Now remember, Lisbet, do not act in the least bit smitten with the king when you are presented to him," she urged. "Complete Unequivocal Surrender at First Sight will happen as soon as his eyes land upon your comely countenance, so do not let him reduce you to a twaddling twit."

Lisbet took in another deep breath. She felt her heart pounding through her cloak. Oh, finally, to be on her way to capture the King of England's heart! She gained this audience with his Grace because the king invited her father, Earl Rivers, to court, along with other soldiers who'd fought against him in the Battle of Towton. The king's forgiving nature was his finest virtue. Once Lord Rivers swore fealty to the king and the House of York, begging for good favor, the king responded with an invitation to court and a supplication to join the privy council.

His Grace didn't yet know that Lord Rivers's daughter was counting her final days of widowhood. If Lisbet got her way with the king, Lord Rivers would not only become a member of the king's council, but his father-in-law as well. Although the Grand Wizbar's love spell came out of a book, and the king was to fall in love with Lisbet at first sight, she brought the poppet she'd fashioned in Edward's image, just for comfort. It sat in her lap as she ran her trembling fingers through the silky hair. As her eyes focused on the blue marbles set into the handsome face, she wondered how the real king would act upon falling in love with her at first sight. Unable to calm her racing heart, she expelled a ragged, nervous sigh.

They alighted from their litter, and a page led them to the great hall. Courtiers mingled and servers bore trays piled with delicacies. Fires roared in the hearths. The minstrels tuned their instruments in the gallery. The mix of voices was light and pleasant, as no one was yet in his cups. The king had not yet arrived, and the dais was empty.

Lisbet remembered her last visit, his considerably late entrance after the main dish. With no blast of clarions to herald his arrival, he'd simply swept in quietly and strolled up to the dais as the crowd bowed and curtsied. Lisbet had been unable to tear her gaze away from him. Alas, she never had the chance to be presented to his Grace, for he'd slipped out just as furtively. But this time the fates were with her. She had the blessing of magic. Tonight would be the king's first bout with Unconditional Surrender.

A page led Jacquetta and Lisbet to seats at a long trestle table, above the salt cellar. Lord Rivers sat across the great hall with some other nobles. Lisbet waved to her father, and he blew her a kiss. The main dish of stuffed pigling, entrayle, lampreys in galytyne, and blackmanger was served. The wine flowed and the tunes played. But still no sign of his Highness. At the dais sat the nobles of high rank, but no women.

Lisbet couldn't eat a bite, just nibbled on some nuts and cheese. Jacquetta turned to her and urged her to eat.

"I hear he likes his women plump," she remarked.

Lisbet looked down at her slim figure. She couldn't imagine her bodice buttons straining or her promontories spreading.

Chairs scraped back, and the crowd clamored to its feet as the doorway filled with an imposing figure. A hush swept over the great hall. King Edward shone as if a light glowed from within him. Lisbet stood on trembling legs, gaping.

He strode forth, smiling and waving, motioning with his huge hands for everyone to sit. As he spoke with a courtier, his deep voice drifted toward her. His Highness was the tallest, trimmest, and most handsome man at court, as well as the best dressed. Gold threads in diamond patterns glistened on his velvet doublet. A gold girdle hugged his waist. Purple hose molded to his strong, lean legs. He was devoid of all jewels except for a simple pendant. A feather streamed from his rolled-brim hat. *Does he ever wear his crown?* she wondered. *When I am queen, I certainly shall.* Her eyes followed his every move up to the dais, as he swigged his wine, tucked into his meal, laughed with the nobles flanking him. Stewards constantly approached him, eager to please. He waved them off.

The moment arrived. She stood in the receiving line to be presented to the king, her future husband. She'd practiced curtseying so much, her knees wobbled, or was that from his nearness? She stood in line behind a chubby lass who turned round and introduced herself. "I am Elizabeth, the Earl of Devon's daughter. Oh, I am shaking so. I've never met His Highness before." The trembling lass wiped her sweaty palms on her gown, leaving dark streaks.

"No need." *She's more hysterical than I.* "He will simply greet you, you curtsey, then be on your way."

After the Devon lass curtseyed to the king and

stepped aside, Lisbet now stood before him. "Dame Elizabeth Woodville," recited a page. She dipped, her eyes roving down the length of his body, the cinched waist, the hose hugging his bulges, then back up again. This time she captured his gaze. He smiled warmly, then released her hand. His eyes were already on the person behind her.

Wait! she wanted to shout. *You're supposed to fall under Complete Unequivocal Surrender at First Sight!* But nothing in his behavior approached even mild interest. She stood, her satin slippers rooted to the floor, waiting for his eyes to shine like stars, his body to lean toward hers in ardent response.

Mayhap it needed an extra few moments to take effect.

"Your Highness—" she stammered, her voice small and childlike. With a wave of his long-fingered hand, he dismissed her. She had no choice but to step aside. What went wrong? She hung her head, mortified, her heart weighing her down like a stone. Gently nudged out of the way by the next guest in line, she scurried away.

****

The Earl of Devon's spinster daughter Elizabeth gasped in delight when King Edward pulled her to his hard, demanding body.

Using a page as a go-between, Edward summoned her to his privy chamber. Never had a man approached Devon's daughter, even paid her a wink of attention. She'd never been kissed or caressed, not by a stableboy, nor a leering drunk. She was plain, with a bulbous nose and thin, unkissable lips. Her body was corpulent, milk-fed, rotund.

A groom led her into the king's chamber. She stood before him, pale and shaking, unable to utter a word. He strode up to her and curled a finger under one of her chins. He couldn't tear his royal raiment off fast enough.

Now his magnificent warrior's body stood naked before her. Only the pendant remained, a delicate contrast to his manly physique.

She writhed under his expert touch as he ravished her. "Your Highness," she gasped, his face buried twixt her breasts, suckling them, bringing her to heights of dizzying ecstasy.

"Ned, call me Ned, shout out Ned when I enter your luscious body," he panted. "Ah, you are so beautiful; I've never wanted a woman the way I want you. Ah, my darling! Ah, Elizabeth! Ah, my darling Elizabeth!"

His insatiable desire for this wench's person was unlike aught he'd ever experienced. 'Twas obsession, that's what it was. He'd asked all about her, from the moment of her birth. Everything about her had riveted him.

After their urgent coupling, she sang and strummed a lute for him, and he wept with appreciation. He even pictured her at his side bearing a crown, but didn't dare take that thought any further.

So Elizabeth Wycliffe, of dairyland Devon, lost her maidenhead to the King of England, while Elizabeth Woodville sobbed her heart out. The love spell had failed her. All for one simple reason: the Devon maid was the first Elizabeth the king laid eyes on under the Grand Wizbar's love spell. For the first time in his libertine life, King Edward experienced Unconditional

Tender Devotion and Complete Unequivocal Surrender at First Sight.

****

George dismounted at the Grand Wizbar's cottage and secured the reins to a low-hanging branch. He pounded at the door with the moon-shaped brass knocker. "Come on, you bloody ruse artist, crawl out and answer it!"

After several minutes, he remembered the giglet had gone to some absurd ceremony up north, so he went round back and kicked his boot through a shutter, splintering the wood. He reached in, unlatched the window and swung it inward. Flattening his palms on the ledge, he scrambled over it and landed inside. Dusting himself off, he regarded the disorderly surroundings.

What a bloody mess. Shirts, doublets, and robes hung across chair backs, piled in corners and lay strewn over the floor. Glass beakers and vials stood upon tables, chairs, and shelves. He picked one up at random and touched the tip of his tongue to the brownish liquid inside. It tasted enough like ale, so he quaffed it, thirsty from the ride, his last privy stop five miles back.

Stumbling over discarded clothing and shoes, he made his way to the alcove that dripped with stone amulets. He headed for the pyrite section, snatched the stone he'd originally chosen and paid for, and turned to leave, but thought again and swiped the lot of them. "Now we're even, mate," he muttered, stuffing his pockets with the booty.

A high-pitched voice startled him. He turned and tiptoed through the cottage, peering out each window, trying to discern where it had come from.

"Sod off, bum bandit, sod off, bum bandit!" The words rang clearly, on the verge of anger, yet with a playful edge.

"Ulch, where the feak are you?" He peered under tables, under the bed, strained to see beyond the beams above. No sign of the measle.

"I can see you," the voice chirped, mocking him.

"Come out, ya scut, I've no time for sillybuggers." George now wondered if those amulets were for driving one mad, making him hear things. Next he'd be seeing things, and he had enough of that when in his cups; he didn't need it sober, too. He extracted one and tossed it on the floor.

As a fluttering assaulted his ears, he felt a stab in his back. "What the—" He twirled round, flailing his arms as a dark blur converged upon him. He stumbled back and crashed into a row of beakers. They shattered, spilling fluids all over the floor. "God's truth! A bloody talking bat!" He knew Ulch performed some baffling stunts, but making animals talk? And tattle?

"Hey! Don't tell him I was here. I just came back to fetch this lot. I paid for it all, honest..."

The bat, now nestled on a perch, sidestepped away from the blubbering intruder, his little claws clinging to the branch. He cocked his head and regarded George, not emitting another word, as if waiting for him to carry on.

"You don't believe me, do you? Here, take this—" He fumbled in his pocket for a couple of his horse's dried apple slices. He held them up, and the creature snapped at him, nipping the tip of his finger. "Puking little dizzy-eyed varmint!"

He sucked on the wounded digit, searching the

room for something to make this wretched creature's moment his last. Ulch had some syringes with bulbs attached; he could forcefeed the beast with one of these things. Instead he simply grabbed his dagger from his belt. The bat screeched, flapped his wings, and took flight, circling the room directly over George's head.

"Come back here so I can make a pie out of ya, ya onion face." As if on cue, the bat swooped down and squirted a stream of warm droppings onto George's head. George wiped it away with the first robe he grabbed from the floor, shaking his other fist at the bat soaring into the ceiling beams. The creature tittered from above, as George spat upon the floor.

"You breathe one word of this to him and you'll be my mastiff's dinner," he warned, but not another sound emerged from the creature, who swung on the rafter upside down and shut George out.

As George headed out, some glittering objects caught his eye. On a table next to the door stood a glass jar filled with sparkling stones. He emptied the glass into his palm. The size of his thumbnail, they shimmered in gold, his biggest weakness, after wine, wenches, and wars. A sharp odor emanated from them, but he dismissed it as a potion they'd been soaked in. He wondered what kind of magic they wielded. Whistling merrily, he swept them into his pocket and considered a string of further possibilities as he wiped his hands on a curtain, pulled the shutters tight, and let himself out.

****

"Ned, whereabouts is Richard?" George approached the dais. The meal was ended, and Ned's private fool was juggling eggs, warming up for his act.

There was the King of England, nibbling at the Earl of Devon's daughter. Never before had Ned sat a wench to his left—the place they all hoped awaited a future queen.

"Haven't seen him," Ned replied, lacing his long fingers with her pudgy ones. "Come to think of it, he didn't show up for the council meeting."

"Jesu, I hope he's not ill."

"Was he dressed warmly enough?" Ned asked.

"Aye, he was dressed rather regally: velvet cloak, silk shirt, the pendant I gave you—oh, shite!" He smacked his forehead. That bloody amulet; had it swept Richard away to never-never land?

"Ah, 'twas he who borrowed it; he's always pinching my jewels." Ned returned to the Devon cow and made kissing motions with his lips. Her chins jiggled as she tittered.

"Ned, that pendant, it truly has magical protective properties! I got it from Ulch."

"Who in hell is Ulch?" he thundered, looking up.

"You know—the Grand Wizbar."

"Oh, no." He wiped his mouth. "You wasted our coffers on the likes of him and his pissant magic?"

"I only gave him two guineas. I didn't pay too much." George's tone carried a bragging note.

"If you gave him two cow chips, you paid too much."

"You have to be a believer, Ned. He's helped me more than old Dr. Rutgut ever did. Last time I had the pox, he fashioned an amulet for me out of a gorgeous stone; called it Plantagenite. Had me pissing like rain soon after. Haven't had the pox since."

"I can only hope that's because you've outgrown

your warthog fetish," Ned said. "Don't you know vinegar and quicksilver are a lot faster—and cheaper?"

"Aye, but Plantagenite doesn't burn my ballokes off."

"Just go back to that silly wanker and get your money back." Ned waved a dismissing hand.

"'Tis far from blithery, Ned, and if I daresay," he leaned forward and whispered, "It wouldn't hurt you to carry one of these. You can sprout the pox, some of the apes I've seen you with. You need all the protection you can get."

"I like my women hairy, don't I, Bess, my mushpuff?" He nipped at Devon's ear, and George had to look away.

"Very well, I'll take one, just to humor you. You take one, too, Bess, my squidgie," and he slipped one between her breasts.

"Cor, this pongs!" Ned wrinkled up his nose, turned the pebble over in his hand, and dunked it in his goblet.

"Sometimes they do, Ned." George nodded knowingly.

"You sure this isn't Shoreditch hogshite?" Ned poked at another one with his knife.

"That color?" George examined it. "It can't be. It's a stone, older than the Garden of Eden!"

"If naught else, 'twill keep the flies off me," Ned said, turning and whispering something into Devon's ear. She dutifully rose, curtsied, and waddled off the dais.

Ned stood. "Give me twenty minutes, George, then we'll seek Richard."

"Twenty seconds is all I'd need," George mumbled

as the king swept by him.

****

Ulch entered his cottage and knew something was amiss. It was more of a mess than when he'd left. Kit was resting comfortably on his perch. "Who was in here, Kit?" He approached the bat with a cracker, which the creature gobbled up happily.

"Puking little dizzy-eyed varmint. Come back here so I can make a pie out of ya, ya onion face," the bat rambled several times.

Ulch didn't have to think any further. "Plantagenet! That flap-mouthed lewdster!" He noticed the empty glass jar by the door. "That silly sod, he took suppositories medicated with St. John's Wort!" Even he couldn't have put a spell on those hard little lumps; they were no more than cow chips dipped in gold leaf.

Kit snickered with glee.

Ulch returned to his gemstones and looked round. It was truly dark in here. He could easily have made a mistake, and confirmed his suspicion when he realized the rose quartz was gone. He'd slipped the wrong amulet into George's pouch. Even though he'd vested it with the same protective powers, he knew George would be back. That stone was elegant and understated, and those words weren't in George Plantagenet's vocabulary.

"Come, Kit, we'll have some repast."

"Puking little dizzy-eyed varmint. Come back here so I can make a pie out of ya, ya onion face."

Now Ulch had to spend the rest of his eve de-Georgifying the damn bat.

Chapter Five

"George, I swear, if anything's happened to Richard at the hands of this ratsbane, I'll personally have you infested with the pox!" King Edward roared as they dismounted before the Grand Wizbar's cottage. His retinue held back, positioned in a protective semicircle behind the royal figures.

"Bring the horses to water and get yourselves a repast at that inn we passed," Edward ordered his groom. "But don't dally; I don't plan to tarry here." He turned round and pounded on the wooden door.

The door swung open, and the Grand Wizbar stood there, stunned. He blinked several times, looking from Edward to George and back at the king again. He fell to his knees, muttering homage to his Highness.

"Enough already, now get ye up." Edward smacked him on the head with his glove and swept past.

"Why did you not tell me the king was coming with you?" Ulch hissed at George, already helping himself to a pitcher of ale.

"Richard borrowed the amulet and vanished, and Ned's more worried about him than I thought he'd be," he replied between swigs. "Thirsty work, travel."

Ulch stumbled over to the king. "Your Highness, what can I offer you? I am so sorry I've nothing fit for a king, just some aged plum wine and a few cakes I made from an old family recipe, unless the bat got to them."

"Nay, just tell me what that bleeding amulet did to my brother, or you'll be aging your plonck in the Bell Tower, and I don't mean the apartments with the view!"

Ulch flinched and even George felt his skin prickle; he hadn't seen Ned so mad since Henry VI's last uprising, led by his rump-fed wife, Margaret of Anjou. Margaret had actually propositioned Ned as part of her peace offering, adding insult to his already blazing fury. She was at least thirty years his senior and looked sixty. George reckoned if she'd looked like Helen of Troy instead of a warthog, they'd have at least done some negotiating.

Ulch dragged his most spacious cushion-backed seat along the floorboards. "Sit here, sire; I shall show you. Fear not; he is safe from any and all harm."

"I don't believe he can be anywhere near safe at the hands of a chiseler like you." The king snatched the ale from George and took a long pull.

Ulch gulped, looking up at the king, stammering some incoherent blather that finally formed into words: "Sire, that amulet is for protection. I originally meant it for George, who gave it to you because it wasn't the one he'd picked out. It indeed was not the one he'd chosen, but it still has protective powers. Have you escaped any mishaps since you took possession of it?"

"Oh..." The king frowned, heaved a weary sigh, and looked away, rubbing his temples. "A beam in my bedchamber collapsed, destroying all but the jewelry box, with the blasted thing in it."

"A-ha!" Ulch expelled in relief. "And had it been adorning your Grace's person, and were your Grace standing in the chamber, your Grace would have been spared. So you see? 'Tis working!"

So mayhap the puttock was speaking the truth. Ned decided to open his mind and suspend his disbelief. "Exactly what was this amulet given the power to do?"

"I endowed it with true protective properties, sire. 'Twas originally for George, to protect him from a malevolent spell cast upon him by a wench's overbearing mother. But, as I know George and his propensity for, eh—mischief, I generously bestowed upon it a general protection from all and every harm. 'Tisn't simply a piece of polished rock. It contains a chip of a true relic, King Arthur's little toe bone."

"Well, now that we know Richard's little toe is protected, can you tell us where he is?" Ned didn't bother sitting; he simply stood over Ulch, towering over the wizard. Ned wouldn't trust him until Richard appeared before him, unharmed. "He's gone nigh on two days now, and even his mastiffs are frantic. You'll cook up a spell to bring him back here, or you'll be trying to magic your way out of a pair of leg irons!"

Ulch nodded, sweat beading along his hairline. He wiped his palms across his robe. "Aye, sire, I shall, sire," he managed to croak, polishing a crystal mound, staring into it.

Ned realized it was shaped like a woman's breast.

"I thought wizards had crystal balls," George commented, approaching them, trying to nudge Ned aside in order to leer more closely.

"If you had to do this all your life, you'd rather look at breasts than balls, believe me." Ulch began caressing the crystal object. His eyes widened, and he leaned over till his nose touched the erect nipple at the top.

"What in blazes do you see?" Ned implored,

peering into the glass but seeing nothing but Ulch's hands firmly clamped round it.

"Richard. I can see him now. He's seated at a strange-looking box, reading some words that are in it, his hand over some instrument, sliding it around."

"Is he all right?" Ned's tone approached begging. In desperation for his brother's safety, he forced himself to believe what the lout was saying.

"He appears well and fit. I can't make out exactly where he is, but I've sent folk into the future, and I've seen them sitting at these contraptions."

"The future?" Ned straightened to his full height and looked down at the wizard hunched over the crystal. Now Ned could see the crystal letting off a green glow. He forced any doubt from his mind, his spirit caught up in this bizarreness. It didn't seem such rubbish now. Or was his mind playing tricks, denying the possibility that any harm had come to Richard?

"God's truth, I can see in there, too!" George leaned over. "I see Richard!"

Ned began to worry again. "Well, I don't see bullocks," he hissed. Mayhap 'twas a good thing he didn't see what these two did.

"Aye, he's there; just like I've seen so many others," Ulch murmured, his voice a low monotone, his words slow and deliberate. "By God, he's five hundred years into the future."

"How did he get there, and how do you get him back?" Ned, ever composed and good natured, clenched his fists, only wishing they were fast around this flap-dragon's neck.

"The time continuum is infinite," Ulch replied, still slowly and softly, as in a trance. "'Tis possible to travel on its path. The amulet could have exercised its powers; he must have been in danger and the amulet swept him out of it, into a different part of the time continuum."

"Will he ever come back to us?" George piped up, and Ned had never heard him sound so concerned. As his eyes met those of his younger brother, his heart went out to George as never before. Now they stood united in concern for their baby brother.

"I don't want to commit myself to an answer on that. If 'tis my amulet that sent him forward to escape some kind of harm, I can't bring him back. Once I send someone forward in time, I can't bring them back. But if he went forward some other way, or by the power of some other wizard—then there's no telling how it worked."

"Then send us to him!" Ned commanded, and George let out an audible gasp.

"Ned, you don't want to go—wherever that is. You heard him; you'll never come back. The Lancastrians will decimate the kingdom in a pillaging orgy of savagery, the French will plunder and divvy England up into morsels. God only knows what will become of the realm!" George clutched at Ned's sleeve, looking like a scared little boy.

"Sod the realm; this is my baby brother, and I'm going after him!"

"Then—then can I be king, Ned?" George asked in a meek little voice, clasping his hands.

"Surely you can be king, George," Ned replied ever so kindly, and as George's eyes widened in unabashed covetousness, he continued, "of my privy closet! Now, how do you get me there?" he demanded of Ulch.

The wizard straightened, still staring into the crystal breast. "I can see him yet. He's pounding on the desk, and if he begins cursing, I'll have a good idea exactly what time he's in." After a second, he nodded. "Yup. Windows Seven."

"What the feak is Windows Seven?" Ned once more bent over the object, straining desperately to catch but a glimpse of this elusive other world.

"I'm not so sure myself, but 'tis something to do with that contraption. But from what I've seen before, I can tell you he's in the twenty-first century."

"God's truth, the twenty-first, that defies comprehension."

George peered in and shook his head. "I've lost him."

"He's fading," Ulch informed them. "But that's where he is."

"You will send me there if you can't get him back," Ned ordered once again.

"Are you certain you want to do this, sire?"

"I shall get my affairs in order, name my heir..." He glanced over at a silently pleading George, "and will be ready to go in ten days' time."

"Ned—are you certain—"

"Not another word, George." Ned turned to leave, George at his heels. He just wanted to walk through the fields—alone, no entourage, no servers, not even a wench to unleash his uncontrollable mélange of emotions on. And most of all, no George.

As the king exited the cottage, George turned and faced Ulch. "I must go too," he said.

"Be you certain? With King Edward gone, you're our next king!"

"I know. But these are my brothers, Ulch," George sighed, gazing once more into the crystal, now cloudy and translucent. "Mayhap I'll be king someday if by some miracle I come back. But for now, I have to be with them."

"Are you not afraid to make such a journey? Those are dangerous, treacherous times. They have weapons and wars on a scale that can only be imagined, and in the imagination of a madman, at that."

"Aye, but I'm more prepared to go there than I am to remain here."

****

"More tea, Richard?" Julianna held the teapot over his empty cup as they sat in her small but functional kitchen, a fire ablaze in the hearth. The uneven flagstones under his feet felt somewhat familiar.

"Aye, this beverage is fine indeed. Tea. It soothes, comforts one. Much better than that bitter—what was it?"

"Coffee."

"Aye. That pongs." He took a sip and savored the sweet perfumy aroma. "That is something we would have fed the Lancastrians had we known of it. Would've blown their mushy heads off."

"Caffeine'll do that to you," she replied, and as Richard looked up, he caught her staring.

"Sorry." She shook her head, forcing her eyes down. "I'm just so amazed you're here. You look so—solid, like a real person."

He dabbed at his mouth with the linen napkin. "I wish you would believe me when I tell you I am as real as you are. As for this summoning of my spirit, I remember naught of visiting here last year or any other year. Do you not think I would have remembered something like this?" He waved a hand at the strange appliances, that man-sized box that kept the air frigid inside, the cooker with its orange glowing rings, the contraption that popped toasted bread.

When he'd awakened this morn in the big four-poster bed and beheld the sunlight streaming through the leaded paned window, he thought he was back in his own bed. Yawning with contentment, he re-ran the reverie through his mind. But when he heard a strange whirring noise, then a roar overhead like a wild beast, and could see that shiny water closet and its handle in the next room, he knew he hadn't awakened or returned home.

He was still dreaming. But how can one wake and still be asleep? He'd studied dreaming in the new science texts whilst visiting Oxford. It was possible to be aware of one's dreamlike state. But these folk seemed to think he was something else—a spirit. How daft. He felt as mortal as ever, especially when a dizzy spell overtook him upon rising, making him bump his head on the poster and bear a throbbing lump, very mortal indeed.

"Well, maybe your spirit was on a different plane then and just doesn't remember. But you definitely came back—we had the most talented medium in the country here, Lady Dorothy Warburton. She contacts spirits with incredible results. They're willing to materialize for her, more than for anyone else. She even brought back William the Conqueror. But she was nowhere near here last night, and you—came walking up to us, just as I summoned you," Julianna said.

"I remember no summons, no medium calling upon

my spirit. But mayhap—" He cut himself off as his thoughts began to wander again. Had he died at the hands of those robbers and come back to this? "I believe dying is a mystical experience; when the spirit departs the corpse, it needs to go somewhere. But why do I not appear as a ghost? I cannot see through my hand." He held it up and focused on the stone in his ring, which she'd finally let him keep, and wear on his very solid finger.

"I don't know all that much about spirits, but why do they all have to be translucent, ghostly images?" Julianna brushed a lock of her straight dark hair behind her ear. "I believe they can manifest themselves in all different forms. I mean, why can't you come back as a fly?"

"I suppose it's possible one can, under scientific principles. I wouldn't care to, though. 'Twould be rather unappetizing, would it not, considering their choice of cuisine?"

She laughed, although he hadn't intended any levity. He glanced at her over the rim of his teacup. She watched him as if waiting for him to sprout wings or horns or perform some marvelous feat. Waking up in his own bed would be enough of a miracle to him.

He adjusted the uncomfortable waistband of the stiff trousers she'd given him last eve—jeans, she'd called them. He'd never seen anything quite like the contraption that held the flies together, a zip. In an uneasy moment of embarrassed fumbling, she helped him close it. It stuck with his thumb in it, and she tried to lighten the awkwardness by commenting that she'd never helped a bloke *on* with his clothes before. The shirt she'd given him was far more comfortable, a T-shirt, with a little reptile embroidered on the front. He much preferred his White Boar to this "alligator", too small to be significant. But she'd explained it wasn't a personal emblem; it showed that the garment was of an upscale nature, as were the jeans whose label boasted some Italian name he'd never heard of.

"Why display other people's names and emblems on your raiment?" he'd asked last eve, as she stood him before a looking glass, spread a foamy white concoction on his hair and combed it through.

"Just like in your time, people are into status symbols. You wear a designer shirt or designer jeans, it means you can afford things like that. Sort of like the king being the only one allowed to wear purple or the nobility allowed to wear beards."

"So pettiness hasn't diminished in five centuries," he commented as she handed him what looked like a pair of mittens, so he slipped them onto his hands, but she told him they were socks, to go over his feet.

"Some things never change, Richard, and human nature is one of them. We're as greedy, territorial, and apathetic now as our ancestors were five hundred, and five thousand years ago. Probably more so now. You'll see when you get out there." As she tossed her head in the direction of the world outside the window, lights still shone and an occasional passing roar made him jump.

Now this morn he devoured the extraordinarily generous meal of eggs, bacon, and endless rounds of toast with jam, and fought the urge to open that top button of his trousers. "After what you told me last eve, I'm not so sure I want to see what has become of this world." He sipped the last of his tea.

"Well, as long as you might be staying a while, I think you should." She took the dishes to another contraption that opened downward, and deposited them on a rack within.

"I know not how long I shall stay, or whether I can simply will myself back. I may just awaken one day back in my own realm, knowing as much about how I got back as how I got here. I should begin praying. No longer trusting of science, which could very well have brought me here, I now must rely on my Maker to secure my fate."

"I hope you do stay a while, Richard. Please don't will yourself back yet." Her voice rang so sincere, guilt overcame the possibility of his departing. She was genuinely fascinated with him, more than anyone he'd ever known, even Anne. He loved Anne as he loved his sisters. But this woman's interest bordered on the romantic, the way she assured his comfort, dressing him, fixing his hair, cooking his breakfast, like a doting peasant wife.

"We want you to see what we've done in honor of your memory. We've all worked so hard to exonerate you—uh, well, never mind that."

"Exonerate me from what?" His voice dripped with indignation. "What have I done?"

She shook her head and motioned for him to follow her back into the large solar, with the strange contraptions bearing letters, numbers, and pictures that moved. He would rather have walked through a garden or among tombstones and simply savored a warm breeze, but apparently folk didn't do things like that here. She'd explained they spent most of their time hunched over these computing things. Did that not make the mind go stale? he wondered. Did the twenty-first century allow for any outdoor recreation, or was it just toil at these machines all the time? And she'd said computers had made life easier?

"I'm going to show you some history books and other things so you can see what happened. Even if you're going to be here a short time, you need to know."

She pulled a book off a shelf, and he blanched when he saw the cover. Richard the Third, the title boasted in large lettering, with a sketch of a man that vaguely resembled him.

"Richard the Third—is that supposed to be my likeness?" He shook his head in stunned amazement. "This is fiction, I take it." She handed him the book and he flipped through the pages.

"No, it's not fiction, Richard. It's history." She guided him over to her long cushioned seat. "You'd better sit down," she warned, and as he sat, he needed to make another adjustment. The 'jeans' she wore were identical, but seemed to fit her much more comfortably. God's foot, this garment was tight; it hugged and pinched him in the worst places.

But it was nothing compared to how he felt when he finished reading that book.

Chapter Six

King Edward, before his Lords spiritual and temporal and all of Parliament, did something no English monarch had ever done—he abdicated. He named his nephew John de la Pole his heir and Parliament gave Pole an oath of fealty.

But if by chance Richard was able to come back alone—and Edward knew anything was possible now—he made John swear, under oath and on parchment, that he'd step aside for Richard to take the throne.

Edward ignored the open-mouthed stares and mumblings, held his throbbing head, and swept out of the chamber, two guards flanking him.

George followed at his heels.

"Oh, Ned..." George plucked his sleeve. "I just remembered something."

"What could I possibly have forgotten?" He turned to George, rubbing his temples. "Yes, I packed clean underdrawers." He waved his guards away. The retinue disbanded, leaving the brothers alone in the corridor.

"No, not that. But Ned, I'm able to think of naught else. Every time I think of traveling to a distant future, mayhap never to return, I halt in my tracks, struck numb with fear. He glanced around wistfully. "All our familiar surroundings..." he choked on a sob. "They'll soon be a fading memory."

Edward wrapped his arm round George's shoulders

and gave him a brotherly hug. "I understand, lad. I know how hard this is. But we'll get through it together, I promise. And I never let you down before. Now what did you just remember?"

"Dame Elizabeth Woodville has been requesting an audience with you. She's badgered your groom of the chamber, your seneschal, your gentleman usher, your groom of the stool, your jester and your eunuch. Duly rebuffed, she pestered me, on her knees, mind you, praising my pultchritude." He buffed his nails on his surcoat. "How could I resist such an entreaty? I assured her I'd relay her message."

Edward rubbed his eyes with thumb and forefinger. "Dame who?"

"Woodville. Earl Rivers's daughter. She said she must speak to you about a matter most urgent."

Edward stood back and shook his head. "Deliver my condolences, but I have more pressing tasks to conduct before our departure. She'll have to wait—a long time, mayhap."

George clapped a hand on Edward's shoulder as the brothers exited the chambers and strode down the corridor. "Ah, Ned, this was not the course I'd expected my life to take. Is it not more practical to tell one of our trusted courtiers that we're going fishing off the coast of Cornwall so they'll think we've been drowned when we don't return?"

Edward shook his head. "We cannot purposely stage our death, for we may just return someday. After all the other craziness that's happened, I'm not leaving aught up to chance anymore. Should I decide to return, I shall reclaim my throne and pick up where I left off. Should only Richard return, de la Pole will step aside.

Should you decide to return alone, you're second in line for my throne, as you well know. I didn't need mention that to the Lords. If I don't reappear here and you do, the throne is naturally yours."

George let out a longing sigh, remembering how he once coveted that throne. But to come back without his beloved brother—no kingship was worth that. "I will never come back here without you, Ned. Not on my life. I only hope warring factions don't rise up. You know how greed overcomes uncertainty."

"I've no choice, George. I cannot be everywhere. I'm a mere king, not a god. My powers are limited to what I can do whilst here. Once I depart, the kingdom's fate is out of my hands."

"Once we get..." George jerked his thumb in a vague direction..."There, I mean then, I mean...to that place, you'll no longer be a king. The fates will control us instead of the other way round. How do you feel about that?"

"Nay, I'll no longer be a king." They took the stairs to the ground floor. "Only a brother. And better a loving brother than an impotent king, I reckon."

George departed the king's company and returned to his apartments. He gazed out the window and sighed. Four more days and they'd be on their way. He hoped they'd improved the methods of brewing ale in five hundred years.

****

Lisbet hired a coach to take her from the inn on the Thames to Ulch's cottage, but rain delayed the journey two days—two agonizing days during which she could do nothing but watch the rain pelt the window and wonder what had gone wrong with the love spell. Now she returned to the coach, huddled against the blast of wind that rendered her cold, angry, and lovesick. She'd requested another audience with his Highness, but he'd rebuffed her. He cared not even to see her! It could have been a dire emergency, he cared not. A warm tear mingled with an icy raindrop. Shivering as the rain slapped her exposed cheek, she hugged her King Edward love doll to her breast. She wasn't going to take any codswallop from that spleeny soothsayer; her mother had paid good money for a spell that was plain rubbish. The Grand Wizbar certainly had some explaining to do. The clouds hung as gray as overwashed linen, threatening to soak the earth once more.

As she alighted, she noticed several mounts draped with royal colors and guards brandishing the royal standard. God's truth, the king was here! She instructed the footman to take the coach round back.

How could it be? Why on earth was he at this silly wizard's dwelling, except mayhap to arrest him? Her heart lurched at the thought of coming face to face with his Highness, her beloved Edward, right here. God, whatever would she say?

She pulled her cloak over her head. Bent over, she dashed round to the back of the cottage as the coach headed for the woods beyond. God forbid if King Edward saw her. All she knew was that she had to see him. Just one glimpse of that majestic blond head, those flashing blue eyes, a sweep over that fabulous physique, those muscular arms tapering down to the large, warm hands that held hers so gently. She thrilled at the memory of his touch. What magic those hands could do to her inviting body.

She almost forgot the biting cold as she straightened and peeked into the back window. The shutters were open to the first notch of the lever, and she could hear voices, but couldn't distinguish words. Peering in the narrow opening, she could see three figures, the tallest of which was the king himself, towering over the other two. The figure in the long robe was Ulch, only because the third person had to be George. No one else wore a black and red checkerboard cloak with a matching hat in the presence of the king. No one else sat in his Highness's presence either, not even his mother. However, only his Highness and George were within; the servers and guards all waited out front. Mayhap the king didn't want any of his subjects to know he was engaging the services of this questionable alchemist. Her heart melted at the sound of his voice.

The sound of fluttering of wings caught her off guard. She stumbled and slid to the muddy ground. As the mud sucked her shoes into its murky depths, a bat swooped down over her, grazed the top of her head, and circled her. It perched on the window sill, staring at her, head cocked. She took a ragged breath; he'd literally knocked the wind out of her. Struggling to her feet, she clenched her teeth to keep them from chattering. Oh, to hear what they were saying in there! But she was happy enough to get but a glimpse of his Highness from a crack in a window. Just standing this close to him made the bone-shivering cold worthwhile. Mayhap the spell would work now. She willed it to take effect, although her logical side knew he must lay eyes on her first. But she couldn't let him see her now, even if he did fall into unconditional—whatever ma mère had paid for.

They continued their conference, George taking a swig from a horn, the king folding his arms across his chest as Ulch explained something away. The king's eyes darted about. He paced to and fro. Was Ulch trying to cast them a spell for a political reason? Were they in danger of another attack from the Lancastrians? She hoped not; she didn't want her king away at war again. The bat watched them as if trying to discern their words.

"Oh, do speak louder," she whispered, and the bat turned to her as if she'd addressed him.

"Going to the future, the twenty-first century, where Dickon was sent, amulet, twenty-first century, Middleham, we're ready to go, have to be with Dickon, send us, we're ready!" the bat chirped.

She pushed her fist into her mouth to keep her gasp from echoing through the entire shire. God's truth! A talking bat. Well, this was the home of a wizard after all, and she'd heard of talking animals in fables, so she didn't think it so extraordinary. 'Twas what he'd said that really stunned her. Traveling to the twenty-first century! That little coxcomb is capable of doing such a thing? Why, he must be, if Richard was already there. Some amulet had sent him? A jumble of questions raced through her mind, each running into the other. She knew royals were a superstitious lot, but this! The king himself coming here? Traveling to the future? Would he come back?

She grew frightened, nervous, anxious, and the cold did nothing to numb it. She turned to the bat, silently urging him to reveal more. But he simply perched at the window. He wasn't even looking in anymore.

"Hey," she whispered, nudging him with a gloved finger. "Tell me what else they're doing. Why are they going to the twenty-first century and are they coming back? This is the king, you know. He can't just leave the kingdom like that; it must be for a reason. Is he bringing back some knowledge or does he plan to change history? Tell me, please. I must know, for he is my future husband."

It didn't occur to her until she realized how much she'd babbled, that she'd been spilling her heart to a bat. But naught about this entire day made sense, since she first picked up her Edward love doll and the codpiece fell off. Was that some kind of sign? she wondered. Now she was spying on the King of England at a daffy soothsayer's window, begging a bat to make her privy to the king's private business. But somehow, in the realm of the truly insane, it all made sense to her. The bat could hear better than she could, and he could talk. So why not ask him?

"Depart on the morrow," he rambled..."safe journey, Godspeed, will send you to where Richard is, you'll get there, cannot bring you back, that'll be twenty pounds, please." The bat flapped his wings and cleared his throat.

"Dear God..." She turned and leaned against the cottage wall, sliding to the muddy ground, too shaken to stand. A cold drizzle fell, and she licked the icy drops off her lips. The chill moisture revived her somewhat. She stood dizzily, hanging on to the wall for support, and stumbled back to her coach in the woods. Spatters of mud covered her as the coachman approached.

"My Lady Woodville, why did you not call on me

to fetch you? Mud doesn't become your pretty countenance."

"Neither does worry, but I shall have to do my best. Take me back to the inn. I've some serious thinking to do." Whether to tell anyone was not what she agonized over. Her decision was whether to follow her beloved king to the future. Having learnt he would never return, she couldn't bear living here in the fifteenth century while he sojourned forever in the twenty-first. So they headed to the wizard's cottage, but only after the royal retinue departed.

****

"I reckon that's it, George. We're on our own now. Anytime we want to depart this world, we can. Come on, let's go for one more ride and say goodbye to the land as we know it." Tears choked Ned. He swept at his eyes with his sleeve.

"As long as I'm with you, everything is going to be fine, my brother." George opened his arms and the brothers embraced.

Ned halted his mount at the top of a hill and George reined in next to him. The king gazed wistfully over the land he ruled over, the land he'd fought for, the land his father died for. But it was still simply a land. He wasn't so arrogant to think it couldn't survive without him. He had a displaced baby brother who needed him more.

George signaled the royal retinue to hold back. "Mayhap we can return by sheer force of will."

Ned turned to his brother and smiled. "Mayhap we'll adapt to the many comforts of the—which century was it?"

"Twenty-one, I believe."

"Aye—just imagine what's over there. There may well be flying machines and medicines to keep us from aging—fancy that—eternal youth!"

"I don't want to be young forever, or to live forever," George retorted. "Come now, Ned, you'll tire of it sometime."

"Depends on the quality of life, of course," Ned countered, his eyes sweeping over the lush green hills and pastures of his homeland. He wiped away tears.

"I think it depends on what you're accustomed to." George inhaled deeply of the realm he so loved.

"How can one not grow accustomed to having every comfort imaginable?" Ned argued back. But it mystified George. Ned already had every comfort imaginable; he was the king! What more could he want?

"I'm not thinking of the future in terms of comforts; I'm thinking in terms of scientific advances," George said. "Should we tire of life in the twenty-first century, we may be able to travel back here through the advances of science. There may be folk here from the future right now and we don't know it. From even farther into the future, mayhap the thirtieth century, even the fortieth."

Ned took a swig of wine from his flask. "Cease, George, you're making my brain ache. Save the fanciful meanderings for your poetry and your love sonnets. I can't think the way you do. My mind can only stretch so far. And far as I can see, right here is as far as I want to see at this moment. Do you realize we're in our final moments here?" Ned took another mouthful and rolled the sweet liquid round his tongue.

"Whatever do they drink in the twenty-first

century, if they need to drink at all? I may never taste this again." He emptied the flask, wiping his lips. "Make a note to bring as much Malmsey as we can carry, George."

"I already have. And should we perish during this journey, we'll perish together, you and me, Ned." He reached over and clasped his brother's hand. Ned clasped back, the first time the brothers had touched since childhood. "Just, when we're on our way, don't dare let go of me." George let out a brittle laugh. "You think Ulch can rustle me up an extra pair of balls, Ned?"

"You'll not need balls, George. You'll need faith." Ned waved his retinue on, and they proceeded back to the palace.

Chapter Seven

Richard closed the book and placed it on the table next to a silver tray holding a teapot, cups, and a plate of scones. But he wished neither to eat nor to drink. He could think of naught but the horrible ending to his life story. Oh, if only it were fiction, if only this were all a dream, if only he had died, this was God's kingdom, and he was simply waiting for his loved ones to join him.

But the pain had been too real. His heart beating through the thin shirt made him all too aware that he was still living, breathing, and hurting.

He glanced up at Julianna, and she looked as if she wanted to cry in sympathy. "I won't even show you Shakespeare," she mumbled. "Not to mention my own books."

"Who is Shake-a-spear?"

"Never mind, just—look, you can go back and change history, if you can go back. I don't know how any of this works either. By now I'm convinced you're real, but the others out there, the rest of the lot who saw you, well, maybe it's better they continue to think you're a ghost. You don't want the public to get wind of this, and if they do, it'll turn into a circus. Cameras everywhere, reporters shoving microphones in your face—" She stopped herself and connected with his unbelieving stare. "Oh, I'm sorry, you don't even know what I'm talking about. It's the media. That's the press, you know, those who publish the banns and the broadsheets—well, they've grown a bit in five hundred years. It's not just in print anymore, it's in pictures on screens like that." She pointed to another flat square with a shiny dark face, many times the size of the 'computer' thing. "Pictures are beamed all over the world in seconds from devices called satellites way up high orbiting the earth." She paused and caught her breath. "Do you want me to continue?"

"Not about objects in the sky and light beams and pictures round the earth. I just want to know why they made me out to be such a dragon. And had me killed in battle. By the treasonous Stanleys, of all people. Damn it all, I told Ned not to trust that old harpy, Margaret Beaufort. 'Twas her husband who did me in, was it not? Someone should have killed her off before she had a chance to whelp that Taffy son of hers and push him toward the throne. Preposterous." He struck his legs with his fists. "Who ever heard of a Welshman taking the English crown?"

Just then, they heard a crash in the kitchen.

Julianna popped up to investigate. Her ceramic Richard III mug lay shattered in a million pieces. But she didn't have to wonder how it could've walked off the shelf all by itself. It had help. That pesky poltergeist she'd dubbed Galahad. He played silly games, moving cups as she was about to pour, rearranging her furniture, switching lights on and off, pulling her bedcovers off in the middle of the night. But this time he'd gone too far. "Galahad, you stop that at once. That was a good mug, you berk."

With her brush and dustpan, she swept the pieces

up and dumped them in the bin. When she returned, Richard stood staring straight ahead, fiddling with his ring, brows knitted.

He raised his head, hands pressed together, as if praying. He saw her and lowered his hands. "Did you find out what the crash was?"

"Yes, just a little accident. No harm done." She didn't want to tell him about Galahad. Things were complicated enough as it was.

"'Tis—like a bad joke, this entire story." Richard smacked the book with his open palm. "Whoever wrote it should be executed. Not for treason, but for bad writing, because that's what it is, plain and simple. How can anyone malign me like this and profit from it? If I am destined to meet a tragic end, so be it. I'm prepared to die in battle. But I know not why they must drag my name through the gates of hell and disgrace me so." He swept his hair from his eyes. "I wanted to slam the book to the floor and stomp on it till it was ground into the dirt where it belongs. But what good would that do?" He shrugged. "There are thousands more copies in the hands of gullible readers. I considered calling for a mass burning of every copy, but then checked myself in time—I'm no longer Duke of Gloucester, or in any position to wield authority." He glanced down at his body and clasped his forearms. "I don't even exist in the true sense."

"That's the way it happened, Richard. A dreadful tragedy, but they betrayed you and changed the course of history. Yet you can change it back." She took a step closer. "You can even prevent George's drowning and Edward's death if you do some really fast talking. But don't worry about what people are saying about you.

Talk is cheap."

"'Tis even cheaper when 'tis not even true. I would never do half these things. And what's this about a withered arm? Do either of them look withered to you?" He stood to his full height and held out his arms, handing her back the hateful tome, and she slid it back onto the shelf.

"No, of course not. But as I told you, some things haven't changed. They just wanted to sell books."

"I just need to burn off some energy and let my emotions work through me." He took steady strides round the room. "I'm not afraid, not of those cowards who would betray me and proclaim that Taffy pretender king. I can't even begin to mourn George. Oh, no, George, who would push the good-natured Ned to the end of his rope and sign his own death warrant." He let out a loud sigh. "And if Ned weren't so hard and fast on wenching and living like the sultan instead of the king, his life wouldn't screech to a halt at forty, from who knew what, but I could bloody well guess." He halted, turned to face her. "All the lies, the—the distortion, the twisting of facts to suit them. Spin, you called it? These modern terms are strange, but they hit the mark at times. How do I change things within my power to change, if the world thinketh I'm a ghost? That's if I'm here at all." He patted himself up and down once more, turned his back and cupped his manhood. Aye, it was there all right, yet smothered in these blasted trousers. Now he knew what thumbscrews felt like. He faced her again. "Aye, I still feel like I'm here. Am I not? Can you still see me?"

"Yes, I can see you, hear you, touch you—" She gently clasped his arm. He cringed, then relaxed as he realized she wasn't going to dig those long red talons of hers into his flesh, as long as he had flesh. "You're not a ghost, Richard. Somehow you got here alive, and you're standing firmly in the twenty-first century. You can do wonderful things here, but as far as changing anything about your reputation—well, the Society's been trying to do that for decades."

"And have they met with much success in refuting this—that rubbish?" He gestured toward the bookshelf.

"To a point. Look." She showed him a pile of booklets with *The Ricardian Bulletin* and his emblem, the White Boar, printed on their covers. "This is the booklet we put out every month. It's got articles about Ri—about you, and others that lived during your time." She flipped through the pages until she came to a section headed New Members. "See? We sign up several new members every month, all over the world. We've got over four thousand members now."

He thought a moment and nodded. This relieved his ire somewhat. He relaxed his tense muscles. "'Tis not an inconsequential number."

"Well, when you consider there are nearly seven billion people on the planet, it seems we have a ways to go."

"How many?" He held up a hand. "Er, never mind. I can only take in so much." He paced round the room a few more times, stopping to stare at strange objects, which she explained. The timepiece was now called a clock, but it made not a sound. The writing implement was called a Bic Biro, which ink flowed through. Slippery reading matter was called a magazine. He didn't even want to look through it yet. Something told him not to—it displayed a woman with big heavers on the cover. He placed it back on the table.

Julianna stared, unable to take her eyes off him, struck dumb with wonder. And to think—here he was in her own home! She wanted to keep him all to herself, yet she wanted to proclaim her discovery to the entire world at the same time. "Richard, I think it's about time you saw the world—outside. You want to go out for a while?" She opened a door to a storeroom and retrieved two hooded outer garments. "This jacket should fit you. Just bring it, in case it gets chilly."

He put the remote control down after tentatively jabbing at a few buttons, took a look out the window and sighed. "I suppose I must. For curiosity's sake if naught else. But—must we go in that four-wheeled contraption you showed me last eve?"

"My car? No, of course not." She gathered her purse and keys. "Let's just go to the village."

"Mayhap we can fetch a few victuals for our midday meal," Richard suggested. "Where can we procure some lampreys and pigs' trotters?"

"I'll join you in trotters, but I have to draw the line at eels."

They headed out the door. She stopped to watch Richard take a deep breath of air—and screw up his face in a grimace. "Cor, do they not empty the privies round here? The very air pongs, 'tis even worse than my time."

She smelled petrol from the tractors on the adjacent farm. "That's another new word I haven't told you, Richard. Pollution. Pollution is all the harmful or poisonous chemicals in the air and the water caused by waste material that businesses dump into the oceans and rivers. We breathe it when the filth gets belched up by smokestacks. You'll see a lot of those when we travel the country." It scared her, thinking of how immune to pollution she really was.

****

George studied Ned's calendar. Three more days to go. He let his eyes slip down to the end of the month, and wondered where he would be then. After Thursday, time would be irrelevant. If he had forty-eight hours left on earth, he was going to make the most of it.

Quaffing Malmsey all the way, he rode to the Highgate brothel he and Ned had frequented in their youths. This romp with the sauciest wench in the house would be one to remember. Poor Ned. He couldn't indulge his carnal desires. He was too busy tying up loose ends, making sure he left the kingdom in capable hands. He'd probably be too tired tonight, but George planned on bringing home a doxy to await his Highness in his bed. He was partial to buxom blondes, so mayhap Ned could stay up an extra few minutes tonight.

****

"Let's head for the market first," Julianna suggested as they walked down the country lane toward the high street. "Don't be scared if you see some big noisy machines. They're only vehicles, like mine. They have engines that have taken the place of horses."

Richard nodded, lips drawn tight. He walked with his head down, looking as if he wanted to communicate with the earth, not everything man had done to it in the last five hundred years. "How much has England really changed?" His eyes warily followed a tractor riding over the field.

"In the broad sense or specifically?" She tried to narrow down his question, so she could narrow down her response. The paradox was that in some ways it was a different world to his. In others, he could easily adapt to life here. She hoped.

"I mean politically, economically—and who is king at present?"

"Uh—we have a queen," she informed him.

His brows shot up in surprise and he sucked in some air. "A queen, ay? Is she an effective leader? How many times has she ridden into battle?"

Julianna stifled a laugh. "Oh, monarchs don't fight their own battles anymore. Actually, she's just a figurehead. We've got Parliament and the Prime Minister running things. Hey—how would you like to go to London and visit Buckingham Palace? You might get a glimpse of her. Would you like to see your successor?"

He shook his head. "Not especially. Not if I cannot have a private audience with her Majesty."

"Frankly, that surprises me, Richard." She'd have thought he'd want to take the first train to London as soon as he discovered what trains were, to observe Parliament and take diligent notes to bring back with him.

"There are too many other things I want to do whilst I'm here. I deal with politics all the time; I want a rest from it. I want to explore science and nature and the humanities. I want to read more and look at art and listen to music. After all, we don't know how long I will be here. It may be only moments."

Once again, that dark curtain of sadness closed around her. She had to face it—she just didn't want him to go. And it wasn't because of the fascination that came with summoning a long-dead monarch's spirit, but having him materialize before her eyes, alive. It went much deeper than that.

"Don't talk like that, Richard. I want you to stay long enough to experience everything," she blurted out.

"Even if I decide I hate it?" He gave her a wry smile. In the numerous books attempting to characterize him, she'd read about his dry sense of humor, his understated wit. Oh, yes, it was just as they'd described it. So many authors would be chuffed to see the product of their imaginations come to life so accurately!

"Well, I don't guarantee you'll like everything about our world." She didn't know whether he'd been serious or just displaying that quirky sense of humor. But how could she expect him to be as open-minded as a modern man? He was very much a product of his times; she had to keep that firmly in mind. So she assumed he hadn't been joking. "I don't even like everything about it. But I suppose the conveniences and technological strides we've made all make up for that."

"For all the progress you've made, it looks as if some things haven't changed at all," he remarked as they approached a bend in the road. A horse and cart loaded with hay headed their way. The chap at the reins tipped his hat as he clattered past. Julianna smiled in greeting.

"You're right, some things haven't. Now, that's one thing that hasn't. Some farmers actually prefer horses and carts. It's still quite simple out here. But wait till you see what's happened to York—and London. I reckon I have a love/hate relationship with our world." She took a deep breath of the earthy air as they carried on. "I prefer it out here where the air is fresh—well, relatively fresh—where I can breathe in the aroma of newly turned earth, have a pint at a charming old pub, and grow my own veggies. But on occasion I crave the bustle of the city, the bright lights, the blaring of horns, the crowds. I suppose it comes down to which pace you prefer."

"When shall we visit York and London?" he asked as they approached the first market stalls.

Again he'd taken her by surprise. She didn't think he'd care to see a big city so soon. "Well—whenever you want."

From the medieval market cross, she led him to a fruit stand. He plucked an apple from the pile, polished it on his shirt, and began chomping on it. She gave the startled vendor a pound coin, mumbling, "He's got a hearty appetite."

She led Richard back to the center aisle. He said, "If we embark this eve, we should reach York by mid morn, if you don't mind traveling all night."

He stopped at the next stand, lifted a bunch of bananas and twirled it round, his eyes crossed in puzzlement.

"You're not in the fourteen hundreds anymore, Richard. We can take my car and be there in less than an hour." She kept a close eye on him, knowing she'd have to take those bananas away from him, the way he was contemplating how to eat them.

"Uh—why, of course. I keep forgetting where I am—and when," he said distractedly as he held the bunch by one banana, turned it sideways and took a healthy bite.

"Richard, you don't eat them like that!" She paid the vendor a few pounds, retrieved the bunch and broke one off. He spat out the mouthful, uttering a string of

Anglo Saxon expletives. "You peel them—like this, and eat them from the top down."

"Cor—that's amazing!" He spat on the ground. "What is that fruit called?"

"A banana. It tastes much better without the skin. Here, take a bite."

He took the proffered fruit and inspected the peelings, closed it up and opened it again, held it upside down, held it to his eye like a telescope, and took a tentative bite. "Strange taste. Chewy but not too sweet. They would go well with strawberries, I reckon."

"Oh, we've got the biggest, juiciest strawberries in Britain here, but first we've got to pay for this lot."

"How rude of me. I shall remit the proper..." He patted himself up and down. She realized he was searching for money.

"I keep forgetting I've not got my own raiment on. I keep forgetting so many things. I had brought a few groats in case I encountered any beggars, but I left them in my doublet." He let out an embarrassed chuckle. "I hope you don't think I'm accustomed to freeloading; I'm just a trifle disoriented here at the moment."

One thing that hadn't changed was classic British understatement. "No need to worry, somehow I don't think they'd have taken your groats. I'll pay." She paid for the bananas and the apple as Richard wandered off to the next stall, displaying more produce—tomatoes, cauliflower, squash, all the usual fare to her, but he looked as if he'd just discovered land. He picked up an ear of corn and began beating it against the edge of the stall. "How do you get it out?"

"Just like the banana." She peeled back the husk to reveal the cob. She handed it to him, and he held it like the banana. He lowered his head and bit down.

"No! Not like that. You eat it across, but it should be cooked first."

"Across and cooked? Now, whose idea was it to eat the nabana or whatever it was—"

"Banana."

"Eat the banana—from top to bottom, and this piece of fruit sideways?"

"Actually, it's a vegetable. And you can't eat it like a banana. It's got a hard core. This came from the New World, as did the bananas. We have a lot of exotic foods we've imported over the centuries. Just wait till you taste my homemade pizza."

His eyes widened and he blinked. "Piece of what?"

"Pizza. A marvelous invention. It's made with these." She placed a tomato in his palm. He squeezed it a bit too tight and it squished, spurting juice into his face and over his hand.

Julianna gasped. "Richard, you're not supposed to squeeze them!"

"Now she tells me."

She fished some tissues out of her purse and wiped the drippy mess from his face. He took the tissue from her, playing it through his fingers. "It's so soft." He swept it over his cheeks and lips. "Even softer than the rolled up parchment in your loo."

"Oh, yes." She nodded. "They make tissues really soft these days, to make it easy on your nose when you blow it."

"You blow your noses into this?"

"Sure, what did you—oh, never mind." She didn't want to know. From what she'd heard of fifteenth-century nose-blowing, it didn't involve anything more than a hand, if that.

"What is this squishy item called?" He wiped his hand on his shirt. "Crikey, it looks like I crushed an enemy's heart in my hand."

Rather a graphic way to put it, but then he would make a comparison like that. "A tomato. Also brought from the New World. They were originally called love apples."

"I choose not to know why. And how does one consume this? We can rule out sideways or from the top, as it seems to be mush. Dare I dive in and lap it up with my tongue?"

"You can eat it like an apple, or cut it up. We cook with them, and make sauces. That's what you top the pizza with. Pizza's only bread with tomato and melted cheese, but in recent times we've gotten quite creative with toppings. You can top it with most anything."

"And how does one eat this piece of pie?"

"Piz-za pie." She grinned. "Sideways."

"Ah. Is there a book of rules as to how these different foods must be eaten?" They carried on through the market.

"No, you just pick it up as you go along. Just like anything else. It's basic etiquette."

"I wish not to make a spectacle of myself." He glanced round the market; no one gave him a second look. With his jeans, T-shirt and trainers, he looked like any other villager or tourist. The hair was a bit long, but she'd tell him in due time how much she was dying to take a scissor to those locks. Layers, maybe, just ending at the collar.

While lying awake last night, marveling at the miracle in the next room, she'd made a mental list of how she could modernize his appearance. He would look cute in a Beatle haircut, but she decided a dark auburn henna would bring out the hazel flecks in his eyes and give some color to his complexion.

"Don't worry, Richard. When you start doing something that might attract attention, I'll signal you." She considered giving him the drawn finger across the throat, but decided against that one. "A jab in the ribs maybe?"

"A subtle clearing of the throat should suffice. Or, if you're close enough, a discreet squeeze."

She didn't ask where.

She made sure she was out of anyone's earshot before saying "Your wish is my command, your Highness."

As they approached the next stall piled with nuts, she heard "Julianna! Yoo-hoo!" She turned round, face to face with Lady Dorothy Warburton, the exalted medium. Spirits willingly abandoned their netherworldly havens to appear, before her, vivid and audible.

"Dorothy! I, uh—" Oh, God, she didn't want her to see Richard here, not even jeans and a hoodie could hide his true essence from an eye as sharp as this psychic's.

She shifted over to block Richard, now inspecting a handful of peanuts. "No, don't! Not that way!" She yanked one from his mouth as he chomped down on it, shell and all. "You don't eat the shell!" She kept her voice barely above a whisper, but Dorothy peered over her shoulder at the bloke obviously unacquainted with peanuts. Julianna knew what was coming next.

"And who's your companion, Julianna?" She

studied Richard's features, swept up and down his body in less than a second, then focused once more on his face, as if trying to place him.

Julianna held her breath.

"Don't pursue that, dear," she addressed Richard. "Try pit spitting. Much easier on the oral cavity."

Julianna blew out a relieved whistle, but she knew she wasn't off the hook yet. "He's uh"—think fast!— "My cousin, from The Isle of Wight. Ri—er, Rick." Not another name came to her mind, human, animal, or vegetable. She hated lying to the most loyal and dedicated Richard III Society member, but she couldn't reveal who he was. Not here in the open market, with all these people around, most being devoted Ricardians. If Dorothy slipped, unable to conceal her surprise, the peaceful Wensleydale landscape would become a mob scene.

"Hello, Rick." Dorothy held out her hand for a handshake, but Richard clasped it and kissed it in the manner of royalty.

"Charmed, my lady." The gesture would've looked phony on anyone else Julianna knew, but Richard made it look purely natural. And it worked: Dorothy nearly swooned at his laced-up trainers. She hadn't even done that with Napoleon when she brought him back, and it wasn't her hand that he'd kissed.

"And where have you been hiding, my handsome prince?" Dorothy flashed a delighted grin.

"Not a prince, my lady, I'm a duke—er, I mean— was." It was out before he realized he'd slipped back five centuries, but thankfully, Dorothy started tittering.

"Uh, he loves to joke around, he's just a plethora of shenanigans, so look out, Dorothy, or you'll find yourself at the business end of one of his practical jokes," Julianna butted in, clearing her throat in a clear signal, shooting glares at Richard.

"I'm sorry I couldn't attend the séance last night," Dorothy said as Richard went back to playing with his newly found nuts. "Bess calved and I wanted to make sure she was well."

"Bess?" Richard tossed the nuts back onto the pile and took a step forward, toying with his Wensleydale Ring.

Heaven above, please don't let Dorothy notice that! Julianna stepped in front of his hand to block it.

"My cow."

"Fancy that, another cow named Bess. My brother—er, on second thought, I'd best shut my gob." He nodded, turned, and busied himself sweeping pistachios into a bag. "Now, these look like a challenge," he remarked over his shoulder.

"Sure, Ri—Rick. Get as many as you want," Julianna urged.

He then started plucking strawberries.

"Is he one of those health nuts? Because he's taking the organically grown ones, they're frightfully expensive." Dorothy's eyes stayed fixed on Richard. Julianna hoped the strawberries didn't provoke any sparks of recognition; all Ricardians knew how fond Richard was of strawberries.

"Uh—that's all right, he's never been known to overindulge in anything, good or bad," she explained away.

"Did he attend the séance?" Dorothy's eyes followed Richard, filling another bag with plums.

"Yes, he did, actually." At least that wasn't a lie.

"What did he think? You know, many folk find us, well, a bit—odd. Especially southerners. They just don't have that Yorkshire devotion to Richard as we do. How did he take it?" Dorothy asked.

"Oh—" Julianna nodded, shrugged, glanced over her shoulder, made sure he didn't wander off, and turned back to Dorothy. "He found it a bit scary, I suppose, but after a while, he rather got used to the idea. One thing about Rick, he's open-minded, no possibility is too farfetched to him."

"Anyone who eats unshelled peanuts has to be open to all possibilities. Might he be adept at computer hacking?" Dorothy raised a quizzical brow.

"Not at all. He's just plucky. But I've been trying to mellow him out in his old age. Sometimes he's too dauntless for his own good."

"Would he care to join the Society?" Dorothy looked him up and down again, obviously interested, although Richard was a tad younger. She never figured Dorothy as a cougar. "He looks as if he'd enjoy our more adventurous activities."

Julianna knew Dorothy well enough to know she wouldn't hint around like this if she suspected something weird was going on. If she had any inkling that this was the genuine Richard III, she'd have bowed at his feet and kissed his ring—at least twice.

"Oh, he probably will, eventually. He's just started getting interested in history. I, uh—I loaned him a few of my books, and he's taken more than a passing interest in the events that culminated in Richard's fall. It quite captured his fancy, just like it did the rest of us. He's becoming quite the Richard sympathizer."

"That's grand." Dorothy nodded. "Because we can

always use more southern members. Even things out, as it were."

"Southern?" fell out of Julianna's mouth.

Dorothy gave her a raised brow. "You did say he was from the Isle of Wight?"

"Oh, yes, yes, he is...but he, uh...doesn't live there all the time, he lives in, uh, Warwick...I'll ask him. I'm sure he'd be interested in maintaining Richard's good reputation. Funny, I never thought to ask him about joining before."

"Splendid. Would you and your cousin like to join me for tea?"

Julianna threw another glance over her shoulder. "Actually, we've got—" She dug into her purse for some money and handed Richard a few pound coins. He turned them over and over in his hand, picked one up and scrutinized the queen's profile, screwing up his face.

No, don't bite it! She held her breath until he paid and took the change, which he inspected without biting.

Dorothy announced, "It's nearly teatime. I'll treat you and your cousin to a ploughman's and a pint. I'm meeting with an American filmmaker at the White Rose. We're producing my screenplay. I'm the executive producer," she added with an air of pride.

Dorothy's screenplay, Home of Thy Heart, was set in Richard's time, and she'd portrayed him very sympathetically, so his death in battle was especially tragic.

"Why, that's fabulous news indeed!" Julianna clasped her hands in happiness for her friend. "I loved the story. I hope it wins an Academy Award!"

"I'm so glad you were able to help me with it. Of

course you'll get your due credit. It's not exactly Hollywood, but I do believe it'll make a splendid film. Well worth the investment." She lowered her voice to a near-whisper. "I took out a lien on the farm."

"Oh, Dorothy!" Julianna invested in aggressive growth funds, but that's as daring as she was. She never spent money she didn't have. "That's so risky, even if it is your creation."

"But I happen to know it's going to be a winner." Dorothy punctuated the sentence with a wink.

"Did your Tarot cards tell you that?" Julianna asked.

"No, an old—and I mean old—friend. Came to me in the night. Told me not to wait any longer. I was going to meet a filmmaker and to forge ahead with the project, no matter what it took, even if I had to make major changes." Dorothy's voice shrilled with excitement. "Spoke of many changes, profound changes, changes for the better. Sure enough, I met Jonathan Garrett at the York Film Festival the next day and we began discussing the project."

"So who came to you in the night this time? If it's Mozart, don't listen to him. You know how he handled his finances." She gave Dorothy a wry smile.

"No, none other than the Bard himself, our own William Shakespeare. Said he couldn't do a better job himself were he living and writing for the silver screen."

She never argued with Dorothy when it came to her encounters with the other side. Simply because she was right so bloomin' much. But not often enough for Julianna to put much stock in her predictions. Even if it was Shakespeare. He'd made his share of gaffes.

"Did he tell you what these changes should be? Or did he mean your life in general was going to change for the better?"

"I didn't question him," Dorothy replied. "The answers always seem to come to me in due course. It's impossible to read between the lines with him. Unfortunately there aren't any Cliff Notes accompanying his predictions. But in the end I always realize what he meant. And he comes through every time. So I'm meeting Mr. Garrett and his associate at four in the pub and would be mighty chuffed if you and Rick would join us. We still haven't done the casting, you know," she nearly sang, brandishing another wink.

Julianna knew not to get her hopes up about an acting career. "Oh, I'm sure they'll want to audition professional actors."

"Well, you never know. Besides, we'll need extras. Your cousin looks like he'd be smashing on the silver screen. I'm sure Jonathan would love to try him out. Does Rick have any inclinations that way?" She cast a glance at Richard as he thumped a squash with his knuckles.

"What way?" Julianna asked.

"Toward the performing arts. He's got that—it's hard to explain." Dorothy's gaze fixed on Richard, then wandered up and down. "That dramatic look about him."

"As opposed to comedic?"

"No, dear, I mean he's got a star quality I can't pinpoint. He just seems to exude presence. Even dressed so casually, standing there munching nuts. Just imagine him in a rolled brim hat, velvet doublet and chausses, dripping in jewels."

"Oh, he has presence, all right," Julianna agreed. "But you were talking about extras. I thought that meant the rabble. You've practically cast him in the leading role."

"One never knows, dear. Stars get discovered in the strangest ways." She moved a step closer to Richard. "Do join us, will you?"

Julianna did want to meet a filmmaker. She never passed up a chance to network. After all, she had her own books to promote.

She signaled Richard over. "Care to go for tea?"

"Tea?" His features puzzled. His eyes darted about. "Ah, yes, tea. Lovely beverage."

"And a ploughman's lunch. Dorothy's treating us at the pub." Julianna gestured at her friend.

"Ploughman's? But we've engaged in no labor."

"Everyone eats them, whether you've worked or not. Don't worry, the servings aren't that generous. Not the way they were in"—she stopped herself. Her hand shot to her lips. She had to be more careful!—"in times gone by." She turned to Dorothy. "Very well, then, we'll join you."

They left the market behind and headed up the high street to the Hare 'n Hounds, built in early 1500, so it was Richard's first visit.'

Chapter Eight

"Ready for your rendezvous with destiny, little brother?" Ned gave George's earlobe a tug. He hadn't done that in twenty-five years. Mayhap he was feeling a mite nostalgic as well, leaving their home for what might be forever. Ned wasn't too tough to shed a few tears, even in full view of his subjects. But today he was especially stoic.

George wanted to tell his beloved older brother it was all right to weep, to tremble, to feel blue. George had a good wail the eve before, whilst deep in his cups, and the doxy he'd tried to jumm had snuck out and left him to it. He'd been too snockered to perform, and what a fine bird she had been. Any other time, he'd have still been raking her as the bells pealed for morning Mass.

"Of course I'm not ready, Ned. I shall never be. But if Richard could make the journey, I shan't be yellow enough to stay behind." Truth be told, he was yellower than the sun at high noon and Ned knew it. Too yellow to stay behind, alone, with the kingdom on shaky ground. But Ned had named their nephew John de la Pole Protector of the Realm in his absence. He left word that they were traveling to the continent on a diplomatic mission and would be abroad indefinitely. The methodical Ned left his legacy firmly in place for the ages to marvel upon, as if he never expected to return. But George knew he was just being his thorough self.

Alone now, dressed in plain raiment and upon white palfreys, no retinue, grooms, or escorts crowding them, they left the palace for the last time.

"That wizard pillock was supposed to meet us at the five mile marker," Ned griped, looking round for the less-than-punctual Grand Wizbar. They reined their mounts in on either side of the sign that marked five miles to London. The earth provided only sounds: cawing crows, wind rustling leaves, their horses' gentle breathing. George felt like making a few earthly sounds of his own, but controlled his outlets.

"Ned, I feel like I'm about to face the block. Now I know how all those traitors feel in their final moments." He clutched his middle. "Oh, help me, I am ill."

"Here, take this." Ned handed him a flask, which George refused, for the first time in his memory.

"Nay, I can't. My very soul is in knots."

"You'll be just fine," Ned assured him. "Ah, here he comes now."

The Grand Wizbar reined in next to them, dressed like an ordinary country squire. He dismounted and bowed to the king, sweeping off his hat.

George's heart took another lunge. His stomach cramped more severely. "Oh, I'm so deathly afraid." he muttered to his maker.

"At least you look like a common slob this time," Ned commented as the wizard slid off his mount.

"I only dress in my regalia for official functions, your grace, and when I'm on my own territory. I don't travel in ceremonial regalia. Would draw too much unsolicited attention. I've got all the business I can handle at the moment. So, shall we commence with the first part of the journey?"

"First part?" Ned brushed himself off, a habit of his before entering the great hall or the council chamber. But did he need to spruce up for this journey? George wondered. They'd be covered in filth straight away if the air in the future was as bad as Ulch had described it.

"As I chant the spell, close your eyes and concentrate, then a wall of smoke will arise between us. It will swirl round your bodies, then you'll feel a tingling sensation. You'll be swept off your feet, but fear not, you won't fall. It's the time continuum sweeping you along. Don't struggle to regain your balance. For the second part of the journey, you'll hit the ground with a thump, not enough to hurt, but 'twill be a jolt. When you open your eyes, you will be there."

"Very well, carry on, we haven't got all day. George, dismount, will you? We're not taking the horses."

"Why not, Ned? It's not a bad idea. What will we use for transport?"

"We'll be in that future place with all those contraptions. What do they call it, an auto—some such?" Ned turned to Ulch. "You will land us in proximity to Richard, will you not?" When he used this tone, no one dared refuse.

"Why, of course, your Grace. I'm reuniting the lot of you. You shall land in his immediate vicinity, if not right there in the house where he sits, mucking about with that long rat-tailed thing."

George slid off his mount and took one last look round. "This is it, Ned."

"I already bade my farewells, George. Had my last sweeping gaze from the Tower ramparts. I'm ready in every way." The king nodded to Ulch. "So carry on, start chanting or whatever you must do."

George slowly inched over to Ned and clutched his sleeve. His knees wobbled, his heart slammed against his doublet. He prayed.

Ulch pressed his hands together and began to chant in an eerily sounding tongue.

"Wait!" George cut the spell short, leaping forth, knocking Ulch's hands apart.

They turned and gaped at him. "What is it?"

"Uh—Ned—couldn't we just take one last visit to the brothel? 'Twill calm my nerves ever so greatly."

"Nay, we cannot!" Ned thundered. "You had time aplenty to sow your oats, now 'tis time to go!" He turned to Ulch, thrust his chest out, and shook George's hand from his sleeve. "So get on with it."

"Please let me hang on, Ned," George begged, sounding more like a little boy than he cared to, but what did it matter now?

Ulch resumed chanting.

George gasped. "Wait!"

"Now what?" Ned's gaze pierced George like daggers.

"Ulch, I'm letting loose here. Can you dispense a remedy?"

"There's no time, George. I've got to complete this spell before the stroke of four. But worry not. Once you're there, you'll have medicine aplenty for every ailment imaginable—diarrhea, constipation, crotch rot, male limpness. And that's just for the men. Wait till you see what ails wenches. Whew! You'll never want to tail one again."

"Carry onnnnn!" Ned's voice approached a plea.

George clutched at his brother's sleeve once again. This time Ned didn't pull away but grasped George's arm and squeezed reassuringly. The gesture reduced George to a sobbing emotional wreck. Tears flowed when he looked up at Ned and saw his brother's eyes glistening.

Ulch chanted, on and on. Ned's eyes were shut, his brow furrowed. George couldn't bear to close his eyes. He stared at his brother. Again he prayed.

"We're still here," Ned finally said, wearily.

"I—oh, so sorry. I'm supposed to be facing east."

Ulch got out a compass, faced east, and resumed chanting. Ned's eyes closed. George stared, trembling.

As the sun began its dip below the treetops, Ned let out a puff of air. "What is amiss this time?" he rasped.

Ulch yanked a spell book out of his pouch and flipped to the middle. "Oh, sorry, I thought I knew this one by heart. I was chanting the wrong spell."

"Dare I ask which one?" Ned asked evenly.

"'Tis supposed to make you irresistible to women. I do it so often it just stuck in me head."

"Well, I won't need that in the twenty-first century any more than I need it now, will I?" Ned raised his chin and patted the underside. "But—finish it anyway. One can never be too sure."

"Aye, sire."

George nearly knocked Ned over trying to embrace him.

"What are you doing, George?" Ned stumbled.

"I just want to make sure some of it gets on me, too."

"'Twill cover the both of you." Ulch chanted a bit more, then took a deep breath. "All right; this is it. The spell to sweep you through the ages."

This time he read from the book.

This time George closed his eyes. He staggered, dizzy and lightheaded, as on mornings after too many quaffs. The world spun. He stood stuck to its surface, paralyzed. Now he was floating, but felt strangely balanced. He had no fear of falling. "Ned? You still there?"

"I'm right next to you, George," came his brother's reassuring voice. Nothing could go wrong with Ned at his side. He reached out and Ned was there, his big warm hand enfolding his own.

A jolt jerked George's body forward. "Ned!"

"Hang on, George, just a while longer," Ned's soothing voice sounded from afar.

"Tell that to my stomach."

Ulch was true to his word. They landed with a thump, all right. On hard ground. But it wasn't earth. The surface was some black surface that felt like hardened gravel.

"Crikey!" George patted his head and body for injuries but felt no pain. "Ned!"

"I'm right here." Ned's voice sounded strangely calm and filled with wonder. He was already up and walking around. "Hm. I smell horses."

"No, that's cows, Ned." George could see a few bovine shapes in the distance.

"Figures you could tell the difference."

"I see some over there." He pointed at the creatures, and heard a faint mooing. "Ah—so the future is just as cowy as it was back home. That's a good thing. I do like my fresh milk."

"For what, to wash down the Malmsey?" Ned held out his hand to help George up. "Come, let us find

Richard."

"Richard can wait. Let's find my pecker first." George felt around inside his trousers. "Whew! Just where I left it."

"Well, where the hell did you think it was going to go?"

"If I've learnt but one thing about this strange universe, Ned, 'tis that anything is possible. Anything!"

Chapter Nine

The pub was filling with the teatime crowd when Dorothy led Julianna and Richard to a table by the fruit machine.

"Want to win a few quid?" Dorothy asked as Richard stepped up to the machine and began pushing the buttons. "You've got to put the money in first, luv," she said, throwing a puzzled glance at Julianna. "Don't they have these on the Isle of Wight? The poor bloke."

"Rick doesn't go to pubs very often. He's a teetotaler."

"Ah. Here, luv. Try this. Push these," Dorothy instructed.

In a matter of minutes, Richard had won over eight pounds.

Margaret motioned Julianna outside, so she left Richard to play with the fruit machine. "Don't leave this spot for one second," she whispered as yet another parade of pound coins tumbled out with a clanging of bells.

Once outside, Margaret turned to Julianna and smiled knowingly. Too knowingly. She knew that grin. *Here it comes.* She held her breath once more. This time she squeezed her eyes shut as well.

"Why didn't you tell me, Julianna?"

She opened her eyes to a beaming Dorothy, showing not one bit of anger or resentment that

Julianna had given her this convoluted tale.

"I—didn't want to create a scene there in the market, Dorothy. But I was going to tell you, I swear. I didn't want the others to beat me to it. Honest. I wanted to be the one to tell you. I was just waiting for the right time."

Dorothy nodded her understanding as Julianna expelled her breath. "So when did you figure out who he was?"

"When he lifted his hand to play the fruit machine and I saw your Wensleydale Ring. I knew you wouldn't let any mere mortal wear that. He couldn't be some bloke from The Isle of Wight. As backward as they are there, even they know enough to shell peanuts."

Julianna gave her an uneasy smile. "I'm so sorry, Dorothy. I didn't want to lie to you. But I wanted the best time to tell you. The others think we conjured up his ghost. And I thought just the same, until I watched him eat and drink and belch and get his thumb caught in the zip of his trousers. Then he told me how he got here, and dying had nothing to do with it. He hasn't even become king yet! He just got transported here somehow. But he's definitely not dead."

"All right, this is what we'll do," Dorothy stage-whispered. "We'll keep it to ourselves. Let the others continue to think he's a ghost. I have some ideas of my own." She gave Julianna's arm a reassuring squeeze and motioned her back in. "We'd better get back in there before he takes the pub for skint winning at that machine and we all get thrown out."

Richard was at the table studying the menu when the women returned. Dorothy approached him as a loyal, obedient subject, sweeping in a low curtsey. "Let me pay homage to you, King Richard. Your Highness. My great and noble king." She rose, kissed the Wensleydale Ring and curtseyed again.

Julianna hoped they wouldn't have to carry her home in a permanent curtsey.

"No need for the formality. I'm not king yet." He kissed her hand once more in that gallant manner. This time Julianna was so sure Dorothy was going to swoon, she dragged a chair up to the backs of the fawning woman's knees.

"You may address me as Richard, if you please."

"Richard? Oh, goodness, no, never, oh, no, I couldn't," Dorothy babbled.

"Maybe you'd better, Dorothy," Julianna warned. "We don't want any slipups in public, you know."

"Oh, right." Dorothy's voice shook. She finally sat, but regarded Richard with a renewed awe.

Richard gestured at the pound coins he'd won, piled neatly before him. "'Tis quite amusing, those fruit machines, but I don't condone gambling," he remarked after they ordered a round of pints. "Gambling can make folk lose their nether stocks."

"Gambling does," Julianna replied, still wondering if this film was going to be worth Dorothy's risk. She'd hate to see the sweet lady lose her farm, even if Shakespeare had come to her in the night. After all, he was a ghost—what did he have to lose?

Dorothy waved and yoo-hoo'd as two well-dressed gentlemen entered the pub. Jonathan Garrett was an independent filmmaker from New York, physically fit, with sharp intelligent eyes. His associate, David Collins, was of Indian heritage, tall and well built, sporting a white turban. They all shook hands and neither producer noticed Richard's resemblance to—Richard.

They must not be serious Ricardians, Julianna figured.

She kept one eye on Richard as they ordered their meals. Neither of them slipped and forgot where Richard was as the men and Dorothy discussed the film's budget, shooting schedule, and finally, the casting. She thought at least one of them would notice Richard's 'star quality' as Dorothy had. The more they discussed the prospect, the more it intrigued Julianna. Historicals were enormously popular now, and Dorothy's story was just so compelling. Her agent had marketed the property everywhere. Unfortunately, the major studios passed. They didn't believe the masses would sit through the drama, with its large cast and complicated, twisting storyline fraught with political intrigue and tempestuous romance.

Julianna and Richard exchanged glances when Garrett gushed about his fascination with late medieval politics and how he could make this film appeal to a wide audience.

"Plenty of indie films become blockbusters," he assured them all. "*Killings*, my last film, made millions more than it cost, filmed in France with French actors. I was in on that one," he boasted, sporting a smug grin.

"How did you do on that?" asked Dorothy.

"Let me take you for a spin in my Ferrari," he gloated, then got back to the business at hand. "We'll be filming around England and Wales, and the interior shots will be done at a studio outside London."

Then came the moment Julianna half-dreading, half-anticipated.

"Richard, are you interested in a role?" Garrett asked him.

Julianna held in her gasp when he said yes. She couldn't even imagine what he was going through emotionally, without having film offers thrust upon him. What was he thinking?

"I may prove to be rather difficult," he said modestly, displaying that fine smile. "Let's say I prefer to give orders rather than take them."

Julianna grinned. Spoken like a true future king.

"But I'm sure you wouldn't clash if he had a simple walk-on," she assured Garrett.

"I was thinking more along the lines of a major role," Garrett said.

"Which one?"

"I was thinking he'd make a great Henry Tudor," Garrett replied, innocently enough.

Richard choked on his lager.

Garrett went on, "He's got the right attitude, the right kind of expression. Rick, can you say 'I could have vivisected Gloucester with my bare hands!' in a low and menacing tone? I want to see what kind of king you'd make."

Richard sat up straight and gained his composure more quickly than she could have imagined, but his clenched fist looked ready to draw a sword and run the Yank through if he'd had one. "If you want to see me as a king, why not cast me in the role of Gloucester?" he asked, ever so persuasively. "Tudor was a—what was that term you used earlier, Julianna? A wussy."

"But he's the one who won the crown," Garrett argued.

"Aye, and from whom? And how? Not by any

courageous or noble act of his, as anyone with a kernel of knowledge of English heritage knows."

Garrett toyed with the cherry tomato on his plate, unable to get it onto his fork, and replied, "The script's pretty close to the way it happened, isn't it, Dorothy?"

"It's factually accurate, but I didn't go into much detail about how Richard's own army turned on him. It's told in flashback. But Tudor emerges the victor, and Richard is killed at the end. Why would you want a role where you die, Rick?"

"Mayhap I don't." He leaned forward, folding his hands on the table. The producers as well as Dorothy mimicked his body language as he drew them in. "How much dramatic license would you be willing to take with this supposedly accurate chronicle of events?"

"Well, you can't rewrite history," Garrett argued, still struggling with the elusive tomato.

"No?" Richard's blue eyes turned stormy. "Is this not fiction?"

"Well, sure, but—"

"Then if it's fiction, let's consider a different outcome. With Gloucester as the victor. Why is that so difficult to conceive? 'Tis quite plausible, actually. I— he would have won had he not been betrayed by those wicked, degenerate traitors. That's what it was, by God. Treason!" His voice trembled. Julianna placed a hand on his arm to calm him down.

He went on, "Treason by a trusted general and his faithful army, whom Richard forgave time and time again, and that was the final insult, inflicting tragedy not only on Richard but on the whole future of England! Treason, I say, 'twas naught less than seditious, subversive treason!" His voice boomed through the pub. People turned to look.

Just then, Garrett's tomato rolled off the plate and onto the table. Richard's fist came smashing down on the tomato, sending juice and pips flying in all directions. Garrett and Collins both got it in the face.

Julianna handed Richard a napkin.

"My, he is passionate!" Garrett proclaimed, and the others nodded in certain agreement. He began to clap. Collins followed.

Dorothy stood and applauded him as if he'd just recited the Hamlet soliloquy. "Bravo, bravo!" she sang. If she had roses, she'd no doubt have hurled them at his feet. "Superb performance, young man, dramatic enough without being melodramatic, just the right touch. You sure you never studied method acting?" Dorothy gushed.

"Certainly not," Richard replied, his voice back to its usual calmness. "This is merely my mode of self-expression."

"Then the role of King Richard is yours if you want it. We can draw up a contract tomorrow, can't we, Jonathan?"

Garrett nodded in Dorothy's direction, obviously taken in with this untapped well of talent sitting across from him. "I'll entertain any ideas you have about changing the storyline. I've always been fiercely devoted to Richard, and a strong sympathizer. He was an effective, kind king, tragically betrayed at the end. I would love to see a story where he emerges the victor—quite deservedly. So we may have to take license, but—I have a knack for taking chances that pay off—big time."

Dorothy signaled for another whiskey. Richard,

calm once again, broke off a piece of cheese.

Garrett carried on, "So, please, your hi—uh, Rick—make any changes you want to the script. I believe our hearts are in the same place. I trust your ability as a dramatic and highly creative artist." He sat back in his chair and patted his tummy. "That was the easiest audition I ever gave. Looks like we've got a built-in script consultant in the bargain. Now please don't tell me you want to direct."

Richard cast him a thoughtful glance. "Mayhap on the sequel."

Garrett looked at him questioningly, as if trying to figure out if he was joking or not. Julianna thought not, knowing how Richard joked. But Dorothy kept beaming at her new discovery, as if the universe's every riddle had been solved. Julianna couldn't help thinking it wasn't a bad start.

"This Wensleydale cheese is as tasty as it ever was, but pongs a bit more than usual," Richard said, spreading Branston pickle on a slice of bread. "I must speak to the larders about this. Nothing with my—er, his name attached should reek so."

"It makes great pizza," Julianna commented, bursting to talk to him alone about his artistic endeavor.

"We shall discuss this further on the morrow, here, as we sup," Richard addressed the producers, waving his hand in dismissal. Force of habit, Julianna figured.

"Now we've got to cast the hero and heroine," Dorothy said as she signaled the waitress over. "Another round—for King Richard."

"I'll never get used to that," Richard murmured to Julianna.

By the time they parted, Julianna was the newest

investor in Dorothy's film. This was her way of willing him to stay for a while. She'd already decided it was worth redeeming her Blue Chip fund.

****

That evening he watched her spread tomato sauce and grated cheese on the circle of dough. "Richard, you know what a big step we both made today," she warned. "Does this mean you've completely abandoned the possibility of going back?"

"I'm a realistic man, my dear. At this point, I don't expect I am ever going back. How can I possibly get back there? We know I'm not a spirit. I'm as alive as you. Who is going to summon me back there?"

"Well, you did mention that wizard character. Maybe he'll cast a spell to bring you back. By now they realize you've gone missing."

"'Tis a long shot, a near impossibility, I fear," he said, and she could tell he was struggling to keep his voice even. She'd have put her arms around him if she weren't covered in sauce and flour.

"I want to make your time here as easy as possible for you, Richard," she tried to reassure him, as he busied himself making tea. "But at least you're in your beloved Middleham and not in some foreign country where they don't even speak the language. I mean, Yorkshire hasn't really changed that much. You saw that. I know you miss your loved ones, but—just let me make it as pleasant as possible for you. I'll be your best friend, if that's what you want. Anything you want."

She knew she was leaving herself wide open. She was apprehensive, but thrilled at the same time. Could she handle it if he expressed romantic interest? The thought had crossed her mind a few times since he appeared—and still did, at shorter intervals now. She was already emotionally attached to him. Romance naturally followed—but she'd have to keep her emotions in check. This just wasn't your average Middleham sheep shearer.

"Thank you for your kindness." He nodded and their eyes met. "That is why I need to keep busy, and making this—film, as you call it, will keep my mind occupied, and help me sort things out. I shall revise that entire script until the outcome suits me. Then mayhap life will follow art, as it is said it does."

"After this episode," she mused as she slid the pizza into the oven. "I'm convinced anything is possible. Anything!"

Chapter Ten

The former King of England and the former Duke of Clarence walked side by side down the narrow country lane. Twilight fell upon them. George refused to let go of Ned's sleeve.

"Ned, it feels so strange. This path beneath us, and—by God, the moon is gone! They've gone and demolished the moon!"

"Cease, George, you are in a state. 'Tis merely a new moon phase. If you'll remember, there was no moon when we departed either."

"'Tis awfully dark, except for those lights up above. Cor, 'tis a cottage, lit up like a blaze. Should we stop there?"

Ned squinted at the lights in the distance. "We shall stop there, whether we should or not."

"This hard path is murder on my piggies." George rubbed his feet. "You sure this is the twenty-first century, Ned? Our surroundings are no different than what we left, except for this strange roadway."

"Not everything changes in five centuries, but we'll soon find out, lad," Ned assured him as he stopped at the roadside to rest and take a swig from his flask.

"I hope they have some Malmsey in there," George expressed his deepest wish of the moment. "I can but drown in a cask of one."

"I'm sure they'll extend some hospitality. They've always been kind to me in Yorkshire, and they adore Richard. Mayhap that's the house he's gone to."

"'Twould be too perfect. I'd be just as happy to see a tankard of plonck as to see Richard."

"We can only hope that gobshite wizard didn't make a balls-up of this," Ned scowled. "I wouldn't have trusted him to scrape rat droppings from my floor, much less steer my very life, if Richard weren't in such peril."

"Mayhap he's not in peril at all, Ned. Mayhap he's having a grand old time here. Can you imagine what twenty-first-century wenches must be like?"

"No different from ours," Ned said. "Why should they be?"

"Ulch said he'd heard they shaved their body hair."

Ned blinked. "Whatever for?"

George thought for a moment, his usually wild imagination now strangely tame. "To keep the bugs at bay, I reckon."

"Mayhap it makes for better friction," Ned guessed. "Or to help find things better."

George's eyes lit up; he wished he'd thought of that. No matter how much he tried to emulate the earthy Ned, he always fell short. Mayhap by the time he was his age...

Ned stood and brushed himself off. "Make haste, I'm counting on the threshold of that cottage marking the end of our journey—for now."

****

"Are you sure I'm to eat this sideways? It looks easier if I just hold it over my mouth and let it drip in." The pizza flopped around in Richard's hands like a live fish.

"When it cools, of course." She tucked a napkin into his collar and handed him a knife and fork. "You've got to eat the bread part, too. Some people cut it up and eat it like a steak but it's much more fun with your hands." She demonstrated by pulling apart a slice of her own and taking a generous bite. "Needs anchovies. But I'll do that next time."

She was still very much counting on him being here long enough to indulge in many more pizza dinners. He nibbled, but nodded when she offered him some more soda. He guzzled the stuff; nearly half the two-litre bottle was gone. She was glad he enjoyed modern beverages but didn't want to make him a caffeine addict.

"I know not how I can even possess an appetite after what transpired in the last few days. I go from being a gentleman duke to a player in a film about to embark upon an endeavor to change history. And now I'm eating—what's it called again?"

"Pizza. And remember, no matter how famous a film star you become, you can always come back here for my homemade pizza." They shared a smile.

"You mean famous as opposed to infamous, which is what I currently seem to be."

"Only to those who don't know any better," Juliana said. "Eat up. I'm glad you've got an appetite. We've got so many different dishes I want you to try. Besides, I do think you can stand a bit of plumping up. Look around, you'll notice people have grown over the centuries, and not just vertically."

"I did notice." He took a bite and chewed. "Especially the wenches. Eh, present company excepted, of course. But nonetheless, I should keep my observations under my hat."

"I struggle to keep my weight down," she admitted. "I imagine in your time, it wasn't much of a struggle, as you didn't have the temptations we have today, like what I have planned for dessert."

"A simple handful of strawberries always tops off a perfect meal for me." He took another sip of soda.

"Well, you're in for a treat. It's called ice cream, and I guarantee, one spoonful melting in your mouth and you'll be hooked on the stuff."

"Hooked?" His eyes widened. "Must we eat it with a hook?"

She laughed. "No, hooked means when you can't get enough of something. You'll love it! Would you like Vanilla Almond Fudge Swirl or Heavenly Hash?"

"Surprise me."

And sure enough, he did love it. She combined the flavors, and they polished off an entire pint of Heavenly Vanilla Almond Fudge Swirl Hash. After tea they sat in her garden, watching the stars appear one by one. They shone especially brilliant in the moonless sky.

"When I was a lad I could name all the constellations," Richard mused, his tone wistful. "Then more important matters occupied my time, and I had to abandon such fanciful frolic."

"Don't you have any free time?" She knew he was an excellent dancer, and quite well read. But nowhere near as well read as he'd be after a few more visits to her library.

He shook his head. "Precious little. But mayhap that's a good thing. That's less time to dwell on the evil that stalks us, the temptations that test our strength of character."

Oh, yes, he'll make a great actor. She pictured him on the stage, grasping the gold statuette..."I'd like to thank the Academy..."

Without preamble he took her hand and held it to his cheek. It wasn't a romantic gesture, only the need of one human being for closeness to another. "I don't want to have time to miss them all," he said. "They must think me dead by now, and are all in mourning. 'Tis them I worry about, not myself."

"I wish we could get a message to them somehow." She sighed, clasping his hand. She felt the Wensleydale Ring, snug on his third finger. All the times she'd slipped it on, she'd felt a powerful link with the past. Now it seemed the five hundred years between them were but a second. "We willed you here, I know it, and I feel so terrible about it. But I want you to stay long enough to see everything, and I feel even worse about that." The jumble of emotions she'd kept at bay now threatened to burst forth in a torrent of tears.

He looked up and saw her trying to keep her lip stiff. "Don't punish yourself over it. Mayhap 'tis God who willed me here. He does have the final say in our destinies."

"You can be right. It's just common human arrogance to assume a bunch of mortal history nuts could bring someone here from the distant past. Conjuring up spirits is one thing, but you're not a spirit. It could have been divine intervention."

"Then 'tis up to Him whether I go back or not."

"If you could go back this minute, would you, Richard?" she dared ask, afraid to hear the answer, but she had to prepare herself.

"Well, mayhap not this very minute." His eyes sought hers and they shared a smile in the darkness. "I've never thought of my fate in terms of what I want. I never believed we have that kind of power. Mayhap here in your time, you feel you're more in control of your fate, as you well are, with your ability to manipulate genetics and prolong life. But in our day, our fates are sealed. Whether it be what we're having for dinner or becoming king, 'tisn't up to us."

"But we have free will," she said.

"To a degree." He gave a small nod.

"So you still have that free will, whether you're here or there."

"And I shall make the most of it, for I was put here for what I'm sure is a profound reason. God has better things to do than play tiddlywinks with English dukes." A wedge of a smile creased his cheek.

"There's still so much about the universe we don't understand," she whispered over a sigh, gazing up at the Big Dipper, looking low enough for her to pluck like tiny diamonds.

"And 'tis futile to try. Shall we cease wondering how I got here and begin planning how to exploit this situation to the fullest?" His voice took on an anxious tone. "For one thing, I would obtain a journal. Oh, if I could have brought one item with me, 'twould have been that."

"Sure, I'll get you one. You want a Compudate?"

"What is this now?" His brows shot up.

"An electronic diary. Keeps your whole life in order. I swear by it."

"Mayhap I should continue keeping my life in order with pen and parchment," he replied a bit uneasily.

"Whatever makes you most comfortable." She smiled, her mood lightening, as she thought of him caught up in modern life, with everything from a blow dryer to an e-mail address.

They sat quietly for a few more moments. She wanted to bring his head down to her shoulder, but didn't want to seem too forward. *No, let's not go anywhere near there,* her sensible quarter reprimanded her impetuous three-quarters. She wasn't in halves, like most people.

She saw two figures approaching, one tall and well built, the other shorter and slighter of build.

"Are you expecting callers?" Richard's voice resumed its velvety quality.

"No. Unless it's some of the Society members coming back to see if you're still here." She'd meant to e-mail them for an update, but she'd been too caught up with Richard.

He gasped, dropped her hand and sprang to his feet. "Sweet Jesus. It can't be," he said, as calmly as ever, but his words injected trepidation into her.

"What?"

He waved and the tall figure waved back. Richard leapt down the stone steps with the grace of Nureyev and ran toward them. Then all three met in the shadowy darkness at the end of her garden path and embraced. She heard laughter and sobs.

She approached them, but kept her distance. Richard finally broke away and turned to her. "Julianna—these are my brothers. Ned and George, this is Julianna, the woman who—who found me." His voice cracked with emotion.

For a long moment, they all stood and stared, stunned. Then Ned took a step forward and brought her hand to his lips with a large calloused paw. "My lady, thank you for being ever so kind to our Richard. How can I ever thank you?"

"Don't thank me. I don't deserve to be thanked. I've always wanted to meet Richard, but thought I'd have to wait till my next life to do it. Please—come in."

Julianna led them to the house. Ned and George stood at the threshold, just as Richard had, peering in. "It's okay," she assured them. "I don't have any wild animals in here."

"'Tisn't animals I was warned about." Ned went ahead of George and entered her living room. "All the machines I'd heard about—they do outlandish things, like run folk over and cut off their limbs."

"Well, there's nothing like that in here," she assured him as the newcomers ventured in, gaping at everything in sight. "I reckon the Hoover can get a bit unwieldy if you don't know how to use it, but I won't make you do any Hoovering."

"What is a Hoover?" Ned turned to her. George still hadn't said a word, but was already examining the contents of her liquor cabinet.

"Never mind—I'll introduce you to all our modern marvels in due course. Just sit down, make yourselves at home, and please explain how you got here, your Highness." She gestured at the sofa.

"The first order of business is that I command you to call me Ned." An air of authority overshadowed his playfulness. He gave her a wink and a smile that lit up the whole room. She now knew why the ladies swooned at his feet and let him sweep them up to his chambers.

Half of them probably faked it just to *get* to his chambers.

She offered them refreshments, and they were equally taken with the soda. She considered putting a splash of rum in their drinks, but on second thought, didn't want a tipsy medieval king in her living room. Not to mention what she knew about George...

Ned explained about the Grand Wizbar's spell to reunite them with Richard and how the amulet Richard wore whisked him through time as protection from harm.

"Aha!" Richard gave Julianna a reassuring nod. He took the pendant from round his neck and slipped it over Ned's head. "Now it's yours again. Wear it in good health."

"So that's how you got here!" Julianna heaved a relieved sigh.

"He can't bring us back, but I trust we'll return someday, somehow," George finally spoke up, stirring the soda with his finger. "We mustn't restrict ourselves to scientific principles, must we? Though we can't see it, there's magic all round us, but we're too mundane to give it any credence."

George struck her as intelligent and ever so eloquent. She immediately began wondering what part he could play in the film.

"I agree with you, George." She nodded, rising to pour them refills. "We're even worse in our day and age. Everything's science nowadays, and we're sorely lacking in spirituality."

"Whether it be science or magic or God that got us here, we're all together again, and 'tis all that matters. Whether we get back is a moot point," Ned said. "I couldn't live out the rest of my days knowing Richard was here all alone."

Richard scowled at his big brother. "I am hardly all alone. I am in quite warm and welcoming company. And I wish you'd stop treating me like a defenseless pup, Ned." His eyes blazed. "Can you not trust me to do anything for myself?"

"In our world, mayhap. In this new and frightening realm, in a word, nay. There must be some end to your arrogance, Dickon."

"I am not half as arrogant as your smallest appendage!" he shot back.

Then George pitched in: "We've been reunited through a miracle over five centuries and you two joitheads are blathering already! Can you not shut your gobs just on this one occasion?"

The three of them went silent and gave Julianna contrite looks.

After declining the offer of a meal, they asked her if she could simply show them round the house and explain what things were. She began with her books and ended with her computer.

By midnight, Ned and George were as informed about history and their outcomes as Richard was, and it affected them each quite differently.

It didn't faze Ned in the least that he'd died at 40; he knew he'd soon perish, the way he was living.

"But now you can prevent it," Richard urged, his finger in the page of the biography where Ned takes ill. "You needn't eat and drink to excess and grow corpulent. Look what it did to you."

"Calm down, Dickon, forty is a ripe enough age to attain. I wouldn't want to live much longer. Who wants to be a feeble old bunghole?"

"Never mind him popping his clogs at forty; I don't make it past twenty-nine." George's voice trembled more than his hands as he sat in her reading chair, shocked by the horrifying revelation. "Ned, how could you do that to me? Execute your own brother!"

"You must've yanked my crank once too often." Ned now browsed her novels. "You no doubt deserved it, sunbeam. At least Dickon waited till I was dead before he snatched the throne."

"What mean you, snatched it? You named me Protector of the Realm and Parliament declared me king!" Richard made a fist and slammed it on the sofa arm.

Good thing there are no tomatoes around this time, Julianna thought.

"Oh, what are we rowing about?" Ned turned to face the others, a romance novel in his hands. "Julianna, my lady, this is all conjecture, is it not? No chronicle ever holds complete accuracy. Must at least some of these authors have taken license, especially those paid Tudor biographers? Hell, they were naught better than whores, drumming up all that defamatory rot to satisfy a ravenous rabble. I know not who is worse, the public for demanding that drivel, or them for providing it."

"It's even worse these days," Julianna remarked. "But you're right, Ned. We don't know for sure what really happened. I mean, look at how they've made Richard out to be."

George started thumbing through a book from her 'Richard shelf' and let out a guffaw as he read: "...severely deformed, hump-backed, with a withered arm, one shoulder higher than the other and a severe limp, Richard was a monster born with teeth, whom some believed was the spawn of the devil. In later years he was known as Dick the Shit." He looked up at his brother. "Come to think of it, Dickon, you did begin teething rather early, in the birthing chamber, if I do recall."

"Oh, shut up," Richard spat. "Go soak your dome in a butt of Malmsey so you'll be accustomed to it by the time of your final dunking."

"At least I went with a smile on my face, King-Blood-and-Guts."

"Hm. And by the looks of things, so did I," Ned mused, a dreamy expression softening his features. "I hope I was jumming one of my doxies when my ticker petered out. Or more than one."

"More likely the latter. According to the story, not even marriage vows prevented you from sowing your wild oats, Ned," Richard commented. "And married to one while pre-contracted to another. Why not just one woman? You've only one pud."

He nodded. "Aye. Good to know old age didn't hinder me any."

"And they've got you married to that Woodville lass, the one who wanted an audience with you the other day," George added. "Mayhap she knew something."

"She doesn't know much now," Ned replied. "The only way I can woo her now is if she comes and gets me."

"Some things never change," Richard mumbled.

At three a.m. they were all punchy with fatigue, but no one wanted the night to end. She'd shown them every modern appliance and convenience she owned, as well as pictures of the ones she didn't own. They'd talked about everything, including the film, and how Richard was going to amend the script. Finally George fell asleep in the chair and started snoring.

"Turn him round and smack him on the arse, will you, Dickon?" Ned stood and stretched his massive body. Powerful sinew rippled underneath his hose; she could see his muscles straining under his linen shirt. He'd already taken off his doublet at her invitation.

"Let him sleep." Julianna stood to lay the afghan over George. "He can stay there. I'll get you some clothes." But what to give Ned? He was huge. At least Richard fit her size ten jeans. The biggest clothes she had were some gray sweats and a pair of briefs left by a well-built ex, so she gave them to Ned and pointed him in the direction of her spare bed and bathroom.

"So," Ned spoke before heading down the hall, "How do we inform the public of our appearance here? Contact the—what was it called, a profusion of letters—BB—NN or some such."

"For hell's sakes, Ned, we can't tell anyone who we are!" Richard chided his brother. "'Tis risky enough those few devotees of mine saw me at the séance. We tell anyone our story, they'll declare us certifiably daft and lock us up for certes."

"Why not? I'm the King of England!" Ned threw his shoulders back.

"Tell that to the Queen of England."

"Oh." Ned nodded, drumming his chin. "Rather a hard habit to break, is it not? But we still must tell the public who we are. A former king then. And the Dukes of Clarence and Gloucester, fresh from the fifteenth century. Why, our feat is even more remarkable than that alien abduction phenomena Julianna spoke of. They're quick enough to terrorize poor folk and perform hideous experiments on them, but don't have the stones to tell the world who they are and from whence they come, the slitty-eyed sneaks."

"I have an idea." Julianna rubbed her tired eyes. "Ned, why don't you and George go with Richard to his meeting tomorrow. Just keep the story straight. You're my cousins as well. But use different names than your own. I couldn't think fast enough on my feet and said his name was Rick. So you can go out into the world, but it's not a good idea to let on who you are—maybe not yet. I'm not sure the world is ready for this—even in our advanced age."

"Aye, there may even be roles for you in my—er, the film," Richard added, turning away to make a slight adjustment in his crotch area.

"Very well, for now. Sometimes I do slip a bit ahead of my time." Ned bade them goodnight and headed down the hall.

"We'll get you some modern clothes tomorrow, Richard," Julianna offered.

"And you say not all trousers are made of this rough sail cloth?"

"Not at all," she assured him. "We'll get you some comfy trousers—a business suit, some shirts and neckties—but you might not like neckties. They kind of squeeze your collar."

"Better a necktie squeezing my collar than these trousers squeezing my—aye, even before I attempt to change history, a visit to the tailor is in order."

Chapter Eleven

Lisbet scooped up a handful of gold coins and swept them into her pouch. No matter how much it cost, no matter where he was, she was going to be with her beloved Edward.

Today ma mère was visiting her tenants and ma père was in London on business—a perfect time to get away without cooking up an explanation. What a relief! They'd trailed her to many a tryst before she was wed. Ma père broke one paramour's nose and nearly ran another through with his sword. So ended those dalliances. 'Twas fortunate she'd never trysted with King Edward—yet.

On the day-long journey to the Grand Wizbar's cottage, she traveled with one groom. "Stay at the inn whilst I complete the trip alone," she ordered him.

Ulch's jaw dropped when he opened his door. "You are...are you not..."

"Yes, yes, Jacquetta's Woodville's daughter." She invited herself in.

He sat her in an overstuffed chair, the very same that King Edward had used. She hoped to breathe in his lingering essence, but alas, she smelled only bat guano.

"Your lovely mother has come to me for many a remedy," he gushed, tugging his robe, kicking the table leg, his left eye twitching.

Well, why shouldn't he be overwrought? If she'd

committed his cock-ups, she'd be a quaking mess, too.

"I know all about the love spell gone awry." Her coins jangled as she crossed her legs. "Now I need you to pretend you're competent and make it right."

"B—but—milady—'twasn't my fault, you see..." His hands fluttered. "...the king was meant to fall under Complete Unequivocal Surrender at First Sight and Unconditional Tender Devotion with the first Elizabeth he laid eyes on, and through no fault of mine, the first Elizabeth was that Devon lass. 'Twas a case of bad timing." He gulped and wiped sweat from his forehead.

"Rather sloppy phrasing, I would prefer to say," she countered, swinging her foot. "The realm is chock full of Elizabeths. He could have fallen in love with a barnyard hog named Elizabeth if he'd seen her first. Why did you concoct a spell with such a low probability of success?"

He gulped. "I heed your admonition, and I do apologize, my lady. Were there a way to make it up to you, I would. However, the king is abroad, as we know, and not expected to return any time soon—"

"Cease the codswallop." She cut the air with her hand. "I know exactly where the king is. He went to join his brother Richard, and is not on the continent. In fact, I know they're still here in England. Rather, still there in England." She swept her hand left to right. "Suffice it to say I know where and when they are and 'tis because you sent them."

"How—how did you come to know this?" He twisted his belt, his eyes darting about like wayward hailstones.

"Never you mind how I found out. Mayhap I have magical powers. 'Tisn't important. I need to be there with him and I you must send me there."

"To the twenty-first century?" His eyes bugged out. "My lady, do you know what you are asking me?"

"Aye, I am asking you to take this." She extracted the pouch, tossing it onto his table. It landed with a loud clank. "And in return, send me there."

He shuffled his feet and scratched his chin, as if deciding whether to jump from a burning building or simply burn. "My lady, the king, George and Richard are seasoned military men and can fend for themselves should harm come their way, but you—"

"Cease the big brother charade," she cut him off. "I can well take care of myself."

His eyes focused on the bulging pouch, as if trying to calculate how much coin filled it.

"That pouch holds enough to keep you comfortable into your old age, believe me," she answered his unspoken question. "My husband left me quite well off, and I've nothing here. My sons are away being educated, and the love of my life is five centuries away. So send me there, I beseech you." She stood and slid the pouch toward him. He backed away, as if it would bite him.

He nodded. "Very well. I shall grant your wish, as you so desire it. However, you must wait at least a fortnight. Sending his Highness and the duke there depleted nearly all my energy and I need to replenish it."

She planted a fist on her hip. "Why was your energy not depleted when you sent Richard?"

He spread his fingers. "I didn't send him, my lady. He was wearing the amulet meant for George to ward off harm. When he was confronted with harm, the amulet transported him through time."

"Then I shall return in a fortnight." She grabbed her pouch and nestled it back in her chemise. "Meanwhile, please show me if they fare well." She glanced at his crystal breast. It stood uncovered. Mayhap he'd been using it. She didn't want to know what for.

"Aye; I checked on them the morn after I sent them," he assured her, nodding. And nodding and nodding.

"Then do they fare well?" she prodded.

His head didn't cease nodding. "Ah, yes, George sprawled in a chair and King Edward was in the privy, donning raiment uncomfortably small for his figure, as was Richard. I shan't describe to a lady what I saw Richard doing to his tight trousers to keep from pinching him, but suffice it to say if he doesn't procure some loose-fitting garb, he'll be singing soprano."

"I care not what the king is doing or what he is wearing. I just want to see him." Her voice took on a half pleading, half whining tone.

He placed his hands on the crystal, and it began to glow. An image began to form within its depths. She fixed her eyes on the orb as a human figure came into focus. "'Tis him!" she squealed, staggering backward. "Oh, King Edward, oh, blessed!" There was her beloved Edward, preening before a full-length looking glass, tossing his head about, flexing his muscles, strutting to and fro. Only a tight piece of cloth concealed his manly bulges. So her codpiece wasn't an exaggeration after all. "God's truth, he's exquisite," she breathed, bending over and peering into the crystal until her nose touched its surface. "What is he wearing? 'Tis hose with no legs!"

"'Tis the undergarments they wear in the future. Rather revealing, eh? You should see what the wenches wear. I took a peek into the twenty-first century after Richard landed there, and I beheld a sandy coastline where they all lolled about. Why they bother wearing aught at all, I know not."

She couldn't tear her gaze from the sight of her king, especially from the waist down. He was the most gorgeous specimen she had ever seen. Finally, her back about to break, she straightened up. "Aye, that is where I want to be, with him. He looks so miserable and lonely."

Ulch peeked into the crystal and cocked his head. "Does he? Seems like he's enjoying himself enough to me."

"Oh, what do you know?" She looked down her nose at him, her tone berating. "You cannot fathom what a woman sees. I can see straight through to his heart!"

"Didn't look to me like it was his *heart* you were trying to see through to," he quipped back.

"Spare me the ribald remarks. Just send me there," she demanded.

He bowed before her. "So I shall my lady, as soon as I wizardly can."

"And this time you'll cast a love spell on him that's going to work," she warned.

"Your wish is my command." He straightened and bowed again. "I intend to reword that spell soon as I get round to it. By the time you return, it'll be well revised and ready to cast upon your fancy man—and you shall be the only Elizabeth with whom he falls under

Complete Unequivocal Surrender at First Sight and Unconditional Tender Devotion."

She turned and headed for the door. "I shall stay at the inn down the road and check on my Edward daily. You will be here, I trust?" she called over her shoulder.

"Why, aye, but I'm sure he'll be all right. He looks quite content with—well, with himself if not his surroundings."

"Nonetheless, I cannot bear to wait an entire fortnight without knowing how he fares every day." She stopped at the threshold. "I shall send a message to ma mère and père that I've embarked on a journey and shall stay at the Rose and Crown until you regain your energy. I need to see my king every day, no matter where he is or what he's doing."

"Then 'tis a bloomin' good thing he can't see you," he muttered.

She swept out of the cottage and climbed atop her mount.

Chapter Twelve

The next morning Julianna brought her visitors to York. She left them alone at Micklegate Bar to gaze up at the spot where their father's head had rotted on a spike after losing his final battle.

Each brother took it in his own way. Ned knelt and said a prayer. Richard paced beneath the city gate, lost in thought. George merely commented, "I observe the lack of heads gracing the gate today. From what I've read about modern times, criminals commit crimes far worse than treason, and nobody displays their heads on city gates."

"We do not display heads and hold public executions since we've become civilized," she explained to him. "If you call us civilized."

After the somber moment passed, they headed to magnificent York Minster and wandered the Gothic church's ancient aisles and transepts. George pointed out his initials carved in a stone near the high altar.

"How could you deface something so sacred?" Ned thundered. "When did you do that, you prat?"

"About eight years ago." Which meant about five-hundred-eight years ago. And there they still stood, as if time had stood still. Julianna began to wonder what time really was.

But time flew as she fished out her Barclaycard and they hit the stores. Ned promised to repay her with the gold he'd brought through time. After lunch at Crumbles, the medieval tea room, which Ned remembered from his childhood, they strolled the winding medieval streets laden with shopping bags, looking like any other group of overspent tourists.

They attended their pub luncheon, the men dressed in modern trousers, shirts and blazers, leaving the ties for more formal meetings. Even George looked handsome and businesslike, although he didn't say much, just tried one variety of lager after another with no outward effects.

"Pubs make great meeting places," Julianna said as they sat at a scarred wooden table before a crackling fire. "I wish all meetings could be held in pubs. It's so much nicer than a stuffy windowless office with fluorescent lights that turn my skin the shade of tub margarine."

Jonathan Garrett handed Richard a copy of the script, and the newest indie screen star hurtled through each page. His gaze swept back and forth like a floor waxer. But when he flipped to the end, his brow furrowed. Julianna could tell he was trying to hold his emotions in check. He flinched and wiped his eyes. Peering at the page, she saw the post-battle scene where they paraded his slain naked body through the streets.

"Jesus," he mumbled.

Her eyes filled with tears. That horrid scene always broke her heart. She turned away and wiped her eyes. *But,* she assured herself, *he's sitting right here next to me.* So it hadn't happened that way—yet. She shook her head clear and took another sip of her wine. The last few days' events were a bit too much to take in.

Richard opened his newly purchased leather folder

with attached legal pad, whipped out his new pen, which he'd opted for instead of more clothes, and wrote faster than Garrett could turn the pages of his copy to keep up.

"Now this lot can come out, and this bit"—Richard crossed out entire passages and jotted notes in the margins—"will have much more impact if we change it." He looked up. "May I take this with me and revise the other bits I feel need improvement?"

If the British were masters of understatement, he was the grand master of them all. She just knew he was going to rip it to shreds.

Garrett nodded. "Why, of course, we can't expect to rewrite an entire script sitting in a pub."

"I have a few turns of events in mind that can change the outcome—for the better, of course." Richard fixed his eyes on Garrett, as if daring him to disagree.

"Uh, well, that's feasible, I suppose." The producer nodded into his pint and gulped. "Dorothy's willing to make whatever changes you suggest. She sure thinks the world of your creative talent."

"Feasible? Creative? There's no other way it could have happened. Or rather, should have happened." Richard glanced round the table. "In the new version, of course."

Garrett gestured to the waitress for another round.

"What say you consider my brothers for roles as well?" Richard boldly pressed on. "Cuthbert would make a striking King Edward—"

"Oh, he's already dead by the time this opens," Garrett said.

Julianna watched Ned's jaw drop and bounce back up again.

"Not if he lives another decade or so, owing to discretion and moderation regarding indulgence in activities of the salacious sort." The brothers' gaze stared daggers at each other. Yet Ned kept quiet.

"But then he wouldn't be King Edward," Garrett argued. "That's who he was. An oversexed lecher who literally got banged to death."

Ned blanched. "Hm. Should I be flattered or insulted?" he muttered.

"The way it is now, he's not even in the story," Richard countered. "Set it a few years back and give him a longer lifespan. I have a delightful way for him to meet his demise." His eyes twinkled. The half-smile crept up his cheek.

"Do I have any say in this, Rick, old bean?" Ned finally spoke up.

"Nay, Cuthbert. Do you want a part or do you not?" Richard shot him a glare.

"Let Bert audition, Jonathan," Julianna offered. "He's got a gift for memorizing lines and public speaking."

"He's got a gift for lines, all right," Richard mumbled, then turned to George. "And you, Wilberforce, you can be the bloke who kidnaps the heroine. What's his name?"

"Galfrid Blome," Julianna injected. She knew every character in that script as if she'd written it herself. She'd been through it enough times.

"Ah, yes." Richard flipped the pages backwards. "A right rogue, and a slimy bugger as well. The perfect role for you." he nodded at a beaming George.

"Instead of playing King Edward, I think Cuthbert should play the hero, Rick." Julianna envisioned Ned as a romantic hero the moment he touched his lips to her hand. "Starting it earlier and bringing in King Edward would add unnecessary weight to the story. But he's definitely hero material." She gave Ned an approving smile, and he returned it with that ice-melting wink.

"You believe he'd be better for the hero's part than King Edward's?" Richard spoke deliberately, as only Julianna and her visitors knew the double meaning of his words.

"Why, yes; for the purpose of the story," Julianna said.

Richard made a notation. "I'll let it fester."

"Can I see my part?" George piped up after draining his pint. "How many lines do I have?"

"Oh, you'll love your part, Wilberforce," Richard assured him. "You get to ravish your lover in the most extraordinary places, in a tree, in the Thames—"

"What's so extraordinary about that? Just last week I—"

"We digress, Wilberforce," Ned broke in. "The hero sounds like a most fitting role for me. Now—I hope the heroine is a looker."

****

After a dinner of takeout Thai, which Julianna delighted in bestowing upon her visitors, George and Ned went to explore the Internet further while she and Richard worked on the script. He'd covered the kitchen table and floor with pages, to see entire sections at once. With his new pen he made more slashes in the text and notes in the margins, as well as on his legal pad.

"This writing implement glides so smoothly—it makes the words come out faster than I can think them," he commented, marking up a page.

"You should try composing at the keyboard," she said. "That's what you'll be doing when you start sending e-mail."

"Let us leave that to Ned." He jotted more notes. "He's the progressive one among us. I've had my fill of modern miracles for the time being."

As she made tea, he called to Ned in the next room: "Ned, which of these situations do you prefer? You name me your heir and you're killed in battle; you name your son your heir and you're killed in battle, but he flees to Tibet to become a monk and I take over the throne, or you abdicate and run off with one of your doxies and I take over the throne?"

Ned appeared in the doorway, a half-eaten protein bar in his hand, his fifth or sixth that evening. "I don't like any of them."

"Well, aught's better than the way it really happened!" Richard glared at him from the far end of the kitchen, where he'd cornered himself with pages. "You had to go and marry that chit in secret whilst pre-contracted to Eleanor Butler—"

"All right, all right!" Ned waved the bar through the air. "I have no fear of dying suddenly. 'Twas my fate and I accept it. As long as I'm playing the hero, we can achieve dramatic effect that way. But scrap the perishing in battle. I go the way I want to go." His wink told Julianna exactly how he wanted to go.

Richard sighed. "Very well, in a bedchamber crawling with slappers. And no issue."

"You're clearing the path to the throne quite easily for yourself, Dickon, are you not?" Ned grinned.

Richard *tsk*'d. "Very well, I'll set up a bit of

conflict: I'll place a few enemies here and there."

George, now in the doorway next to Ned, snickered. "A few here and there? I thought you were only changing history, not public opinion."

"Shut your gob, mush-brain," Ned snapped.

"What about me?" George implored. "Where am I when you swagger up to the dais and plop your tichy bum on the throne?"

"Sorry, George, but you're already dead," Richard informed him.

"I thought you were going to change things round!"

"Aye, for the better." Richard gave George a haughty huff.

"Bosh!" George, fists on hips, turned to his older brother. "Ned, you can't just kill me!"

"Don't look at me." Ned stepped back, hands held up in surrender. "Argue with Good King Vlad."

"Very well, you're alive," Richard gave in, tiptoeing over several pages to get to a later scene. "But you're under house arrest."

"I'll show you and your bleedin' poxy story, White Bore," George stuck out his tongue. "I'll escape."

Still facing George, Richard cast Julianna a sideways glance. "Julianna, can we procure some leg irons as props? A key won't be necessary."

"Very well, I shan't escape," George called over his shoulder, following Ned back into the lounge. "Just as long as you give me a pretty cellmate or two."

"That's in then," Richard mumbled as he scribbled. "George under house arrest. Cellmates—Bruce and Percy Muttondagger."

As George and Ned returned to their Internet

exploring, she and Richard tossed ideas around.

"I'm going to meet Tudor in person," he spoke as he wrote, flipping over another page. "We'll have a duel when he first sets foot on English soil. I won't kill him, just run him through enough times to render him crippled—in some rather essential places." His thin smile widened. "Then I put him under house arrest. With George."

"Tudor stays under house arrest for the rest of the story?" Julianna asked. "It would be better if he were exiled. Turf him out of the kingdom and banish him to France or some other horrible place."

"Not just yet." Richard shook his head. "I have plans for His Pretendership." His eyes narrowed as he stood and searched the floor for another scene.

"He's going to rot in prison?" Julianna guessed.

"Much too easy." A sly smile spread Richard's lips. "I'm going to make the rest of his wretched days a living hell. The ratsbane." His fists clenched and his eyes darkened. "I'll show the world what that lily-livered foot-licker really deserved!" But his voice remained strangely calm. She wondered if he ever raised his voice. "And his mangled old meddling mother."

Just then a draft blew through the kitchen. Pages swirled in all directions.

"Oh, damnation!" Richard spat, scrambling to recover them. She looked round. No windows or doors were open. Neither of them had moved enough to create the slightest breeze. "Galahad, cease this instant!" she hissed under her breath. Richard looked up, trying to straighten the stack of papers in his hands. "Beg your pardon?"

"Nothing—oh, Richard—" She let out an exasperated breath and slid to the floor to help him with the mess. "I might as well tell you. I have a poltergeist here I call Galahad. He's ever so mischievous—plays silly pranks on me nearly every day. But sometimes he can be a right prat."

"He? What makes you think it's a he? Might it be a wench, who's jealous of you?" His smile disappeared behind the array of papers he was straightening.

"I never really thought of it." She shrugged. "I just assumed it was a man."

"Till the other night I never believed in any of it, any of the hocus pocus brewed up by wizards and alchemists or any human claiming to have unearthly powers." He sat on the floor and crossed his legs, tossing the pile of papers aside. "Aside from what Jesus did in the Bible, I only believed what I could perceive with my five senses. But we now know there's much more to it, don't we?"

"Of course there's more. It would be ignorant to believe otherwise." She sat next to him. "You're living proof of that."

He nodded, lost in thought.

"Sometimes we can't fight our fate, we have to take it as it comes." She moved closer. "That's why, even though you should never give up the wish to go back, I want you to enjoy being here to the fullest. There's a lot to enjoy about modern times, you know. Pizza—and everything else."

That brightened his eyes.

"Let's enjoy revising this script, too. Remember, it is only an art form."

"I know." He rubbed his eyes. "I admit I'm taking

this fictional device too seriously. But it's the only way I can change things. As long as we're here, we must live our lives out as Rick, Cuthbert and Wilberforce. The main thing is, my brothers are here with me. And"—he pinned her with his gaze—"you." He clasped her hand and kissed it.

Her cheeks burned from the unabashed flattery. Her heart bubbled over. Unlike any man she'd ever known, Richard was above flirting. "We'd better get back to the script. Good thing the pages are numbered." She busied herself gathering the strewn pages.

"Invite your ghost into the next room," he suggested. "My artful brothers will give him a run for his money. Especially if it is a her."

****

The computer was off, tea was served, and with Brahms playing softly in the background, the four of them sat, occasionally speaking, but more often, just thinking.

Finally Ned stood and paced the room, hands clasped behind his back. "I've been probing that Internet of yours, and I'm just astonished at how manipulative this media has become, how they persuade the masses. Just how did they get that way?"

"Having satellites that broadcast sound bites round the world in a fraction of a second has helped," Julianna offered.

"But still—it isn't always straight news. They do put their spin on things."

"Aye, spin." He halted before her globe and spun it, peering at the southern hemisphere when it stopped. "Australia. By God, who would want to live down there?"

"It's a beautiful place," she answered. "Actually used to be a colony of ours."

He gave it another half-turn. "This is what the United States of America looks like? Cor, I had no idea it was so immense."

"Another former possession of ours," she explained. "When it was only thirteen colonies, they declared war on us and won their independence."

"Cheeky buggers. I reckon some things will never change and know not if that's good or bad. But the media—" He raised his head, gazing at a faraway thought. His eyes, the same deep blue as Richard's, sparkled. "We can manipulate them as they manipulate the masses. All we needs do is tell them who we are. Why pretend? I hate pretending, living under an assumed name, hiding, wearing disguises. Acting in the film is one thing, but I don't want to live the role of a fictional character. I'm who I am, and the hell with the world if they don't like it."

"We died five hundred years ago, Ned, so technically we don't exist," George argued. "The world at large wouldn't believe you. You'd be seen as one of those hoaxters, ridiculed, laughed at."

"So let them call me names and ridicule me." Ned's voice rose. "The joke is on them, is it not? Because 'tis true! This is the twenty-first century. Surely they wouldn't debunk time travel. Aren't they sophisticated enough to realize it's possible?"

"Unfortunately, no," Julianna said. "We tend to debunk what we don't understand. As far as we've come, we still know our limitations. The more we know, the more we realize we don't know. You'd have zero credibility, Ned. Anything to do with the supernatural—alien abductees or astrology or ghosts, is good enough for entertainment on tabloid shows and in the movies, but it's just not accepted into the mainstream."

"No one in the so-called mainstream would believe me—the way you do?" Ned sat on the hassock directly in front of her and captured her gaze with his. "Surely you're not the only person in the world who would believe who we are and how we got here."

That she couldn't argue with. "Sure, there's plenty of believers." Starting with the devoted Ricardians who brought their beloved slain king's spirit back every year, and now his live, solid person. "A few would believe. But not enough for you to go on the Internet or on television and claim you're King Edward the Fourth who traveled through a time warp. You just wouldn't—" She shook her head, wishing the world wasn't so lacking in blind faith. "You just wouldn't be taken seriously."

Ned said, "You realize debunking is just a form of fear, the way prejudice comes out of fear. That's why I thought the media, as powerful and persuasive as they are, could convince the masses."

"But first you'd have to convince them."

"Then would you present these few to us? The believers? And see where it goes from there?" Ned implored her with those gorgeous eyes. The light glinting off his blond head made him look like a Greek god rather than an English king.

She met his gaze. "Naturally such a powerful presence as you does have a burning need to be recognized. But what kind of situation would that create? I always ask myself, if something otherworldly happened to me, abduction by aliens, or possession by the devil, would I take my story to the media?" She raised her hands in a questioning gesture. "The answer is a firm no—only for fear of ridicule and loss of credibility, and that would affect my career."

"Is that a rather selfish reason not to share something so extraordinary with the world?" Ned asked.

"All right, Ned. I hope I'm not doing something I'll later regret. I'll invite the séance people over here. But let's not tell them who you are—just yet. Let's feel them out first, dance round the subject and not say a word till we're absolutely sure we feel comfortable telling them. They believe Richard's ghost appeared and went home with me. We can stick with that story. But you and George—just be my cousins Cuthbert and Wilberforce for the time being. I know I can't completely deprive you of human contact. That wouldn't be fair. But bear with me, just for a while. Let's not jump into anything."

"Well put and convincing." Ned nodded his golden head. "We shall take it slow. I want to enlighten folk, not shock them."

"I'll have to tell Dorothy the truth, though," she thought aloud. "I can't go on deceiving her about you guys."

"She won't go blithering?" Richard asked.

"No, not Dorothy. She's the one who made up that loyalty oath for the Society, that includes your 'Loyalte me lie' motto. She'd never tell a soul." Julianna's heart raced and her palms grew sweaty. This was getting scary. "I've known her a long time, I trust her, and she's bound to find out about Ned and George sooner or later."

"We can tell her we're merely ghosts if it would be easier to swallow," Ned offered with an amused grin. "They seem to really go for that ghost codswallop round here."

She rolled her eyes. "Don't even think about it! Things are weird enough without time travelers pretending to be ghosts."

So she invited the loyal séance attendees. Then she took all three brothers for haircuts, but she couldn't convince Richard to get that henna. Her guests arrived the next evening, bottles of wine, lager, and crisps in tow. They bowed to Richard, kissed his ring, called him 'your Highness.' Ned looked on with slitty eyed jealousy, sitting apart from the group and scowling into his pint. George sampled the lagers, recited his original poetry, and held up his end of the conversation quite well. They were Cuthbert and Wilberforce Hammond, her charming, albeit peculiar, cousins.

The small talk eventually evolved into deep discussions about the events of Ricardian times. Now they no longer had to rely on theory or conjecture. They had it all first-hand. Richard delighted in recounting the battle maneuvers he'd led as a general in the Battles of Barnet and Tewkesbury, and his lesser skirmishes on the Scottish border as Constable of England. The drinks and snacks remained untouched. Everyone was too captivated by their exalted monarch's presence to dip into a bowl or pour from a bottle.

Ned's jealousy of his attention-capturing brother finally went by the wayside the first time he noticed Pippa gazing at him with unconcealed ardor. He picked up on her signal with one of his knee-wobbling winks, and five minutes later, they were huddled in the corner deep in mutual adoration. As the group chatted on, with Richard as the topic of conversation as well as the center of attention, they eventually discussed the film and Richard's artistic contribution.

"He'll be playing himself, but to the public he's Rick Hammond, another cousin from the Isle of Wight," Julianna explained to the delighted and enthusiastic group. "We can never let on who he really is." She glanced over at the poker-faced Richard, already starring in his first acting role—as his own ghost. They'd already taken the oath of loyalty: "Loyalte me lie," they chanted, hands clasped. This ritual made even Richard screw up his face in puzzlement. And of course they all wanted parts in the film.

Toward the end of the evening, Pippa entered the kitchen where Julianna was brewing coffee. Julianna feared the girl would melt all over her flagstones. "Oh, Julianna, Cuthbert's turned my heart inside out; he's so smart, and funny, and gorgeous!"

"Yes, he's got quite a commanding presence, Bert, my old cuz. Seems to just run in the family," she couldn't resist adding, dipping into an untouched snack bowl. Now she was getting hungry.

"Julianna, don't think me too forward here, but I've invited him home." Julianna's jaw nearly dropped into the party mix. "W—w—what? Home? For when? Where? How long?"

"Just for the night. I'll bring him back tomorrow. Actually, he asked me." She raised her chin in triumph.

"Er—I don't think that's a good idea, Pippa. He's, uh—" She searched her brain for a reason she could talk about.

"I'm a big girl, I can handle it, Julianna." She placed a fist on her hip. "I know what I'm doing—and boy, he sure looks like he does!"

Julianna knew she couldn't stand in the way of raging hormones, but what if Ned got into trouble— went for a late walk and got lost, or slipped and said something? Maybe if he had a responsibility other than finding his trousers in the morning... "Would you mind taking Wilberforce home with you, too?" Julianna talked fast. "He'd love to see your lovely home and your gardens and your horses—he loves horses, he's an expert horseman—and then maybe tomorrow, the three of you can—"

"Hey, that's a great idea! He can meet Maureen. My sister is just as vivacious—and adventurous. She thrives on blind dates."

"You think she'd like to meet him?" *Please say yes*, she silently pleaded.

"You must be joking." Pippa laughed. "The Joan of Arc of the singles hotlines? But would Wilberforce mind? Mind you, he's never laid eyes on her."

Now Julianna had to laugh. "Him pass up a tryst? It wouldn't be his eyes he'd want to lay on her anyway. Willy would be delighted if you brought him home to meet Maureen. I'm sure you'll all have a lovely time. Just ring me tomorrow and let me know you and the boys and everything's all right."

"Oh, I shall, they shall, it shall!" She floated out of Julianna's kitchen.

After the company departed, Julianna and Richard were alone for the first time since Ned and George arrived. They looked at each other and breathed a collective sigh of relief, but apprehension still weighed her spirit down.

"What if Ned or George slip and tell Pippa or her sister who they are, in the heat of passion? Maybe I should have just forbade Ned to go, or threatened to take away his bathroom privileges—"

"Julianna, it was fated the moment she walked through the door." Richard settled on the sofa. "By the time he got over being cheesed off at me and fastened his eyes on her upper anatomy, it was sealed. Naught, not even the force that brought me here, could keep those two apart tonight. Worry not. Ned always keeps his senses intact. Even at—" He lowered his eyes and cleared his throat. "Those moments."

"What about George?" she asked.

"I would fear George prattling before Ned, but he has such a way of pribbling, no one would ever believe him. He'd be branded a hoaxter for certes."

She nodded. "Guess I'll just have to trust them to keep their lips sealed." She connected her iPod to the stereo and searched for Silver Thunder, one of her favorite bands.

"They will. They can be good actors, too. Just like me." He gave a toss of his newly cut head.

"Oh, Ned's a natural for the hero part in the film." She poured them each another glass of wine and sat next to him—a respectable distance away. Somewhat respectable. "But for the heroine, I'd love to get a better-known actress. If only we can find one who'd work for charity."

"What about you?"

She quickly picked up her wineglass to conceal her delight and disbelief. "Me? Oh, God, I'm no actress.

Especially in a romantic lead like that. I wouldn't want to ruin Dorothy's chance for success, not to mention our investment. We need a professional who knows what she's doing."

"Don't belittle yourself like that. I myself would love to play the part of a romantic hero, but I'm just not the romantic type." He shrugged. "'Tis just as well. I'll be too busy saving my kingdom and the lives of my loved ones to dally. I'm not quite the ogre I was in every other role I'm portrayed in, but I'm not the romantic hero either."

"Well, you're certainly a hero," Julianna lavished well-deserved praise on him. "You're kind, sensitive, brave, warm, and very good looking. Everything a hero should be. But why don't you think you're romantic?"

Richard shook his head. "I never brought a lady flowers, I don't pour honeyed flattery over them like Ned, I don't recite poetry like George, I don't cook gourmet cuisine. All I can do is spread bananas on pizza."

She smiled and sipped at her wine. "It's romantic if your intentions are sincere. I enjoyed your banana pizza more than any gourmet meal I could get at LaGrenouille."

"Sincere?" He buffed the Wensleydale Ring on his shirt. "Mayhap. I don't put forth any false fronts. Nay, there's naught false about my front." He took a quick glance downward. Her eyes couldn't help but follow.

"That's my idea of romantic," she assured him. "Not flowers or poetry or flattery. Just sincerity. That other stuff is just veneer, and it wears quite thin after a while."

His gaze pinned her and she took another sip to

ease the tension. "Simply speak your heart. Share your heart. That's what romance is all about—to me," she said softly.

He reached over, took the glass from her hand and placed it on the table in one swift, graceful movement. "Then may we share some tonight?"

The hearth glowed, seductive music floated through the lounge—the perfect ambiance. But now that the moment was here, the reality of it nudged her in a stern warning:

Don't.

"Come here, Julianna." The way he opened his arms to her, she couldn't refuse. *One warm embrace can't hurt.* But once she was in that embrace, and his lips sought hers, it felt as natural as breathing. He kissed her lovingly, gently and thoroughly. Stopping him would be as wrong as telling the sun not to shine.

Her heart beat the same primitive tattoo as the music surrounding them.

When his hand slid to her breast, she knew she had to take charge or nature would. "Richard—" She hadn't meant sound so whispery, but her voice was nowhere to be found. She cleared her throat. "We can't get involved. It'll be too much heartache if something happens and you get sent back." She wondered how convincing she really sounded, with her fingers still wound through his hair and her body half pressed up against his.

"I'm not going back, Julianna. I'm resigned to my fate. I'm not like Ned, I don't rake every wench that crosses my path. I keep my desire firmly in check. But right now my desire is about to burn a hole in these thin trousers so I'll have to go back to wearing that torturous denim castrati garment."

She let out a deep sigh and tried to calm her breathing. There'd been some pretty heavy breathing till now. "Richard, I've been fighting my feelings all along and doing a pretty good job of it so far. Don't let me weaken. Don't let me fall in love with you. There's enough weird stuff going on here already. We've got enough to do."

"I've grown very fond of you, Julianna." He stroked her cheek. "And I'm still growing." He relaxed his embrace and brushed her lips with his before sitting back. "However, you must lead and I follow, as this is your domain. I'm also a gentleman. If this were Ned sitting here, you'd have been ravished thrice already, in six different ways, and on your way to fetch him a beer."

"Doesn't he take no for an answer?" Her hand still played through his hair.

"He doesn't even ask."

"Looks like he doesn't mind never going back to his own time. After tonight, George might not, either."

"Well, Ned covered his arse quite well. He informed me he left the kingdom in good hands with no detail unattended to, and George will go anywhere there's wenches and booze, even if it's back to the Stone Age."

"I wonder if you can go back by sheer force of will. Our minds are so much more powerful than we think." A jumble of thoughts entered her head and vanished. This wasn't the time to ponder telekinesis, as he tickled her earlobe and ran his thumb over her bottom lip. All she could do was close her eyes and let the exquisite sensations take over. She instinctively moved closer. Their bodies touched, his skin against hers. *One more kiss, just one more of those delicious warm kisses, and I'll call it a night*, she convinced herself. Their lips met.

The door knocker pounded.

****

Lisbet's farewell note to her parents explained that she'd gone abroad to join a nunnery. She propped the note up on her mother's trestle table and slipped out the door. Her lady-in-waiting and one groom accompanied her to the Rose and Crown, where they'd stay until her journey to the future, then the servers would return home. Without a look back, they clattered away. Once they reached the Rose and Crown, she couldn't wait till morn, so she made the short trip to the Grand Wizbar's cottage alone.

"How is my Ned?" were her only words when he opened the door, the bat perched on his shoulder. She could have sworn it winked at her.

"I haven't looked in on his Highness since you were last here." He stepped aside as she headed for the crystal breast.

"May I?" Her hands already covered it, her gaze boring into its depths.

"If you have powers, you may. If not, I'll have to get it started." He approached her.

She stepped aside and let him do his work. It turned milky, then cleared as an image formed.

"King Edward, I presume." He stepped back and let her take a look. She leaned over it, squinting to see within. "Ned. Why, he's in bed with a wench already. He certainly doesn't waste any time!" Only his back showed, but it was unmistakably her beloved king.

"The rogue!"

"Tut tut, my lady." He wagged his finger. "He's got every right. Has he not? He's not married, he's no longer king, just a bloke." He took another glance at the energetic lover, a streak of envy clouding his gaze. "A bloody lucky bloke, but just a bloke nonetheless. At least you know he fares well, and the journey through time hasn't had any adverse affect on his energy reserve."

"I've seen enough." She took a step back. "I need more than ever to get there now. Before Edward asks that doxy for her hand in marriage. What about your energy reserve then?"

"Why, I'm no King Edward, but I've been known to go for thirty seconds, give or take a thrust." He buffed his nails on the front of his robe.

"Not that, you puttock, your magical energy. Is it returning? I'm ever so anxious to go!"

"Oh. Well, I do tests every day, and it seems to be returning. Shouldn't be long now, I promise you, then you'll be on your way."

"By all that's holy, 'long' could mean anything, if you think thirty seconds is aught to brag about."

Without another glance at the crystal, she saw herself out.

Chapter Thirteen

"Are you expecting callers?" Richard whispered. He and Julianna pulled apart as if caught doing something wrong.

"No, unless somebody forgot something. But I do have a doorbell."

She got up and, out of force of habit, opened the door without asking who it was. A microphone flew in her face, followed by a camcorder with *The Royal Issue* splashed across its side. A blinding light shone into her eyes, stunning her.

"Miss Hammond!"

"Uh—" She nodded dumbly.

"I'm Brooke Hill from BBC One's *The Royal Issue*. We heard you summoned the ghost of King Richard the Third, and he's living with you. Can we have a comment from you? Where is he? Harry, get a shot of the living room. Zoom in on the Richard the Third Society plaque there."

"No! You heard wrong!" Julianna covered the camera lens with her palm.

"But Miss Hammond—"

"What's all the commotion here?" The stern yet calm voice from the sofa commanded attention. Both reporter and cameraman halted in their tracks, stared and blinked. Richard stood there, shoulders squared, head erect, a challenging smile touching his eyes.

Still staring, Brooke dug into her satchel and yanked out the now-world famous photo of Richard's facial reconstruction. Black lashes rimmed the expressive eyes, dark hair fell to the shoulders, a ruddy flush colored the cheeks, an amused smile played upon the lips.

With two strides, Brooke stood beside him and thrust the photo next to his face. "See? The resemblance is undeniable. It's him!" She then backed away, as if the revelation scared her.

Richard stepped forward, now invading her space. "How daft." He plucked the photo from her hand and perused it with a tilted head and cocked brow. "I do not resemble this image in the least. I'm much better looking than this apple-john." With a quick wink at Julianna, he thrust it back at Brooke. "I am insulted. What a personal affront. I demand an apology at once."

"Not Richard? But—but—" She turned to Julianna in desperation, but she wasn't about to help her.

"It's plain to see, my cousin Rick is actually quite a babe." Julianna beamed at her 'cousin'. "And Richard's brother King Edward isn't—uh, wasn't too hard on the eyes either. But Richard was the hottie in the family." She smoothed a lock of his hair.

"You're not entirely wrong, my lady," Richard spoke, his tone accommodating. "Yes, I do resemble Richard the Third. In strength of character, loyalty and integrity. I forgive my enemies as he forgave his, and I treat my fellow subjects fairly and equitably. He was a kind and just king, a splendid example of what a monarch should be, and I have naught but the utmost respect and admiration for him. I strive to emulate his evenhanded and exculpating nature in all my endeavors." He tossed a glance at the photo. "As Julianna says—I am far more handsome. Any Ricardian experts will agree. Not that I am known to be a braggart, but..." He hadn't raised his voice one iota, but somehow he managed to project.

The cameraman stood there with his mouth hanging open, looking like he'd have applauded if his hands were free.

"You are a board member of the Richard the Third Society, are you not?" Brooke thrust the mike back at Julianna, not missing a beat.

"Yes, I am, but how does that make my cousin from the Isle of Wight Richard's ghost?"

"Your cousin from the Isle of Wight?" She spoke as if that were the unbelievable explanation, not that a ghost was living with her.

"Does he look like a ghost?" Julianna held Richard's hand up to the light. "Does he feel like a ghost?" She squeezed his raised hand and he responded reassuringly. "See? He's as solid as you are. Maybe even more so in the head area," she couldn't resist adding.

Brooke dropped her satchel and mike on the sofa. She approached Richard, more curiously this time. She didn't look quite convinced yet. Richard stood still while she eyed him up and down, pinched his cheeks, and pressed her hand to his chest to feel for a beating heart. She tugged his hair, kneaded his arm, and peered into his eyes. She circled him like an art critic scrutinizing a marble sculpture as he waited patiently, tapping his foot. When she finally backed off, Julianna gave her a little shove. She fell into him, then jumped away as if he were electrified.

"Now, you would have fallen right through a ghost, wouldn't you?" Julianna asked as Brooke straightened her collar, shook out her bangle bracelets and smoothed down her frosted hair. "As you can now plainly see and feel, my cousin possesses the same physical properties as any other human male."

"Perhaps bigger at times," Richard added.

Brooke shook her head, obviously not convinced. The cameraman shrugged, as if to say 'I only work here.'

"I've been on the beat for a long time, Miss Hammond. I've investigated haunted houses, castles, prisons and graveyards, seen anomalies and heard EVP's, witnessed exorcisms, and experienced every unearthly phenomenon a paranormal researcher can encounter. I've seen ghosts of all degrees of translucency—I've seen them as no more than a shapeless mass of ectoplasm. I've seen images with some human form, and I've also seen ghosts who—" She pointed to Richard as she spoke, "—appear just like him, solid flesh and—" Eyeing him up and down, she concluded, "bone."

"I won't deny that ghosts can perform divers feats which the living human mind perceives as unexplainable, including their forms of manifestation," Richard debated. "However, that doesn't naturally follow that I'm a ghost. According to your logic, Miss Hammond here could be a ghost, or even—you!"

"Me? I'm as alive as life itself!" She swept a manicured hand over her tweed suit. "You can't accuse me of being a ghost!"

"Then how can you accuse me?" Richard cocked his head.

"I was informed of your presence!" she shot back.

"And where did you get that misinformation?" Julianna demanded.

"I can't divulge my sources." She raised her chin. "That would be unethical."

"Unethical?" Julianna couldn't help screeching. "But it's ethical to barge into a private home with a mike and a camcorder and accuse a man of being a ghost. Even if he were—it's nobody's business."

That was the wrong thing to say, because Brooke's eyes lit up like two "On The Air" signs.

"It certainly is our business! If the ghost of one of the most infamous and wicked Kings of England is haunting an innocent subject, the British public has a right to know!"

"There's the infamous and wicked bit again," Richard mumbled, making a note in his leather diary. "I must correct that in the opening scene."

"Haunting? Does he look like he's haunting me?" Julianna turned to him and he clasped his hands behind his back, his lips curved in the sweetest of smiles.

"You can deny it all you want, Miss Hammond, but I know he's a ghost. I can feel it in my bones. I do have some psychic ability, you know. I'm not giving up on this. I'm a believer. I believe in spirits returning to earth if they've not attained a peaceful conclusion and come to terms with their demise, and we all know the violent and traumatic death Richard suffered. It's no wonder his spirit is restless and unsettled, and wishes to make amends with his fate before retreating to the great beyond for the rest of eternity."

Richard, now lounging in her recliner, challenged, "Do I look restless and unsettled to you?" He crossed one leg over the other and swung it casually.

"Don't sway me otherwise, either of you." Brooke pointed at each of them in turn. "I believe, I believe!"

"Look." Julianna heaved a sigh and threw her hands up. "You can see with your own blue-contact-lensed eyes that he's obviously not a ghost, so whoever tipped you off gave you a bum steer. Now if you want to chase royal ghosts, go to Hampton Court and wait for Catherine Howard's headless body to show up, because you'll find none here."

"Chasing Catherine Howard's headless body through Hampton Court—oh, that is *so* Vincent Price. This is real—this is believable—" Brooke gathered up her materials and signaled the cameraman to leave. "I'm not giving up, Miss Hammond. Remember, I believe, I've seen the light! Let's go, Harry."

"Nice digs you got 'ere," Harry called over his free shoulder as he lumbered out.

"Britain needs enlightening, and together we can do it!" The reporter's last words rang out as Julianna shut and bolted the door.

"Sounds like she's on our side," Richard commented as Julianna went round pulling all the drapes shut. "A bit dotty, but on our side."

Trembling, she took a few calming breaths.

Richard came up to her and clasped her hands, steadying them. "Don't be frightened. They're just doing their job. That hasn't changed in five centuries, I assure you. You know how the tongue-waggers had me betrothed to my niece and I had to publicly deny it, according to certain sources."

"I know. But to come barging in here—" She allowed herself a violent shudder, which he calmed by taking her into his arms. "And her of all people. She never gives up. She'll keep badgering and badgering, camping out in the garden, peeking into windows, invading our privacy, she'll never leave us alone. She stalked Windsor Castle to scoop Prince Philip's piles, for God's sakes."

"I thought reporters didn't buy into ghosts and such." He guided her to the sofa and they sat.

"Oh, if it's about royalty, she's on the trail. Let me tell you a little about Brooke Hill. For one thing, she's a groundbreaker. In her career she's covered subjects that have caught the attention of the government and have caused legislature to change, like smoking laws and sexual harassment laws and labor laws." She poured herself another glass, emptying the wine bottle. "Now, her favorite subject matter, to the point of obsession, is the royals. She's got her own television show, *The Royal Issue*, and it centers on the royals. She started by tailing them incessantly; every ribbon cutting, every hospital opening, every dedication, she was there. Then she graduated to invading their private lives, and she now manages to expose who they're socializing with or romancing or sleeping with, married or not. The public devours these stories." She took a sip of wine—then another. "The royal family's sex lives became a real-life soap opera—a never-ending story of scandal and disgrace and shame. She was the first to scoop the Fergie story in the Eighties."

"What is a Fergie story?" He got up, went to the fridge and got out another wine bottle.

"Oh, she was the Duchess of York."

"Why, that's my mother!" Richard came back in with a corkscrew.

169

"Not any more, I'm afraid. She's yielded her title to someone who's very definitely a product of our times. The girl couldn't indulge in any horseplay without a telephoto lens trained on her, and Brooke Hill was right there behind the scenes, ready to beam the images round the world. She's turned the royals into tabloid fodder. And you think you didn't have any privacy in your time."

"Why has she not been imprisoned?" He sat back down, stuck the corkscrew into the cork and twisted.

Julianna shook her head. "She's done nothing illegal. They get away with infinitely more today than they did in your time. Believe it or not, she's a respected journalist. Won numerous awards. She's also been in a few halfway decent movies. So she can act—in case you haven't noticed."

"But you seem to think her ethics are dubious."

"Let's put it this way." She took another sip. "You'll never see a reporter for *The Times* or *The Wall Street Journal* badgering royals, ghosts or not."

"Well, she's encountered the supernatural first hand. 'Tis hard to be skeptical once you've witnessed an unearthly phenomenon." The cork popped, and he poured himself a refill. He held it out to her, but she shook her head.

"But I couldn't convince her she's just plain bloody wrong about this. So all right, ghosts do exist; I believe that myself, but you aren't one of them." Her blood began to pound again.

"'Tis all right. That's why I didn't go out of my way to deny her allegation." He leaned in a bit toward her.

"What's all right? She's a hard-nosed reporter,

Richard, I've seen her in action. She's reduced royalty to tears with her incessant prodding." She made another attempt at a calming breath.

"We shall play along with them." He moved closer and stroked her hair.

"To our advantage. So 'tis win-win."

"What do you mean?" Their eyes met. She still trembled, but for a different reason. She enjoyed it now.

"When you want publicity, what do you do? You try to attract their attention, with press releases and such. But they've done that for us. They came to us. We've got their attention. So now that we've got it, we can use them to our advantage. This will lead to great publicity for the film." His hand dropped to her shoulder and stroked her arm.

"But—to tell the public you're Richard's ghost? It's bad enough we've got to use that story with our séance members. Like I told Ned, the rest of the world should just think you're my hick cousin who's a little odd and eats unshelled peanuts—until we decide otherwise, anyway." His touch made her tingle. She was seconds away from jumping him.

"She's firm in her belief and naught can change her mind. So if she continues to insist I'm Ri—my ghost, who am I to argue?" His hand moved down her arm and clasped her free hand.

She gasped. "But—what we talked about the other night. They'll think you're daft!"

"That's if we go to them like Ned wants to do and try to convince them we came from five hundred years in the past. That would be rather hard to swallow."

She laced her fingers through his.

"But they already think I'm a royal ghost, and it

seems they're challenging me to prove I'm not. It might be to our advantage if I not deny it. They're sold on us already. So consider it a blessing they came forth tonight. They're dying for a good royal story. We want to promote our film. I want the world to know King Richard wasn't a mangled ogre who killed innocent children. We each have what the other wants. You heard her—she's a believer. We just may need a believer in the not too distant future." He clasped her hand.

"All right, we'll invite them to the set, we'll let them do a story on us, we'll even let them interview you. But—you sure you want to go public with this— ghost story?"

She shrugged. "They're already convinced, so there's no credibility problem. Let us just play along with them, follow their lead, as it were."

"I'd just like to know who started all this. Who could have leaked it to the media? Surely not Ned, not this soon."

"Nay, he just wouldn't. If he's leaking anything right now, it's not a story. Mayhap one of your mates from the séance." He rested his head on the sofa back.

"It couldn't be. We're too bound by trust and honor. In all the years we've been summoning your spirit, we always kept it confidential. All the media knows about was the anniversary of Richard's death, because the Society always runs an obituary in the *London Times* and *New York Times*. We're sworn to secrecy, even disclosing any information about our archaeological excavations is grounds for expulsion from the Society. No member has ever betrayed us that way."

"Hmmm." He drew her to him and draped his arm around her shoulders. "Then it was a non-member. I'm aware of my betrayers. Did it ever occur to you it may not be someone alive?"

She pulled away from him and studied his face. His eyes intensely focused on her. "You mean it might be a ghost who blabbed about your being here to the press?"

"Face it, my dear, there are more dead people who want to create trouble for me than live ones."

She nodded slowly, unable to wait another second. It was time for that ravishing. She brought her lips to his. Their arms wound around each other.

Chapter Fourteen

Lisbet fidgeted, on the verge of madness. This sitting and waiting was torture. After morning Mass at the village church, she left her servers and returned to the Grand Wizbar's cottage, this time on foot.

She found him on his knees planting herbs in his garden. "I'm back."

"God's truth, you look terrible." He squinted up at her, shielding his eyes from the sun. "You're positively gray."

"I'm bored, restless, fraught with anxiety, in love with a man who's not aware I exist, about to follow him through five centuries, never to return. Would a vibrant shade of puce be more comely?"

He stood and shook dirt from his sleeves. "'Tis a major decision and huge risk you wish to take."

"He's worth it," she insisted.

"He may be, but you may have to pry him off that bed once you get there." He cocked a brow.

"Well, you did say you'd revise that love spell, didn't you?" She urged, turning to face the cottage.

"Of course." He nodded, fetched a watering can and tipped it under the rose bushes. "I'll even throw in another spell for free, a BOGO."

"What is a BOGO?"

"Buy one get one, of course." He sprinkled his herbs.

She pondered, strolling over to his rose bushes and plucking a white one from the vine. Holding the white rose, the Yorkist symbol, to her heart brought her closer to Edward. "Another spell, hmm? What else could Edward possibly need? He is simply perfect."

"Mayhap a dose of fidelity would be in order. To me, it would be worth it, with a bloke like him. You don't want to get there and find out he can only squeeze you in twixt ten and ten fifteen every other Thursday."

"As long as I'm the one he truly loves, I don't mind if he—strays. I'll look the other way." She twirled the rose by the stem and inhaled its sweet fragrance. 'Tis a wife's duty to please her husband, to honor and obey."

His mouth turned down in a disapproving frown. "You don't know much about the twenty-first century, do you?"

She shook her head, twirling the rose. "I know naught about it. But it matters not. Just as long as I'm with him."

"Well, I'm rather well versed on the subject. I'll share a little secret," he whispered although they were alone. Not even that pesky bat hovered round. "I've been there."

Her eyes widened. "And you've come back? Why didn't you stay there? It's so much cleaner."

"Not really." He placed the watering can on the ground. "Some things are dirtier, like politics."

"But why did you come back?" She rubbed a petal twixt her thumb and forefinger.

"It wasn't my idea. I was sent back here as a punishment. I did a naughty deed and this is my sentence. To live the next hundred years in the fifteenth century, helping folk with my love spells, health spells, giving them protective amulets, whatever they wish, doing good deeds."

"So—when you've served your sentence, you can go wherever you want?" She waved her hand toward the heavens, "Whenever?"

"To whichever time I wish. I might try the eighteenth century when I get out of here. I like décolletage." He grinned. "At least it leaves something to the imagination."

Her curiosity never piqued this way before. Ladies didn't pursue anything beyond child rearing, domestic duties and growing lilies. "Why can't all folk go through time?"

"It's called magic for a reason." He wiped his brow with a cloth. "If there was a rational explanation and available to the masses, it wouldn't be magic."

She closed her eyes, unable to fathom it all.

He cupped her chin in his palm. "I know what you're going through, Lisbet. I'm in love, too, with someone in another century I can't be with. I felt it only right to share my secret with you. Even eight millennia in the future, love is still considered a form of magic." He waved his ringed hand and the colored stones glittered. "By magic I don't mean pithy spells and pongy potions. I mean, it's our most powerful emotion and it defies logic. My love spells—" He shrugged. "They're not entirely in my power, because we know not how love works. I can't force someone to love another."

"So that love spell you cooked up for me—'tisn't a true spell?" She slid the rose over her cheek.

"You can call it a spell. Only because no one quite

knows how love works. If you love strongly enough, you can even create your own spells. I only cast them because folk don't believe in themselves enough. They think they need someone like me to manipulate love. So I bestow my positive energy on the spellee, who believes I cast magic upon him. 'Tis naught more than positive energy. There's no hocus pocus about it. Someday we'll figure out what love is and why it drives us to act in such imprudent, senseless, foolish ways."

"Sometimes I think love does more harm than good. But I'll feel differently when I'm back with Ned." She expelled a longing sigh.

"'Tis a magical and elusive emotion, love is." He nodded. "Defies all principles of science and logic. Everyone I've sent through time has gone because of love, because they wanted to save a loved one, like his Highness did with Richard, or to be reunited with a deceased lover, or go back and undo damage or hurt they've done to a lover. But love has to be the reason, Lisbet. That's why I want to make sure you truly love him, because if you don't, no magic will enable me to send you anywhere."

"Of course I love him," she declared, her voice sure and steady. "I loved him from the moment I saw him."

"Then I shall send you—but take some more time to think about it."

"More time than your required fortnight?" she asked.

"You should, for both our sakes. Performing such a feat exhausts my mental resources. I want to be sure I'm completely replenished so nothing goes awry." He pointed both index fingers at her. "But you should take more time to think about your decision. It's not like choosing which color lip stain to wear."

A sharp pang stabbed at her middle. "Waiting to be with Edward feels like hunger. Oh, but you're right. I must admit, over these past few days, I must have changed my mind a thousand times about going. But not about my feelings. I'm so in love with him." Tears welled up in her eyes and spilled over.

He squeezed her arm. "I'll be here when you're ready to depart. If you still want to."

"May I take another glance at him?" She peeked over his shoulder into the house. A brocade cloth covered the crystal breast.

He led her in, took a swig of ale, and shucked the cloth off the crystal.

It clouded over, then cleared as her beloved Edward appeared before her eyes. "Oh, Ned." Her heart thumped against the crystal as she leaned into it. All by himself, he held a strange food item to his mouth and let it drip in. He held a brown bottle in his other hand.

"What on earth is he eating?"

Ulch stepped forward to take a look. "God's truth, he really ought to learn how to eat that stuff. 'Tis called pizza. Pizza and beer for breakfast? Cor, he must've had a busy night!"

Chapter Fifteen

After that ordeal, a passionate encounter was the last thing on Julianna's mind. "If anything can spoil a romantic mood, it's a reporter and a cameraman," she moaned as she and Richard sat that respectable distance apart again. "I wonder how far Brooke Hill will go with her story—will she tell the world that the ghost of Richard the Third and I are simply roommates, or concoct another royal sex scandal?"

"Would it make you feel better to ring Dorothy and unburden yourself once and for all?" Richard suggested.

"After another drink, definitely." She nodded. "Before Ned and George come back and Brooke shows up again, repeating the whole dreadful scene." She let out a sigh of frustration. "It's late, but this is too important to wait. The show airs at seven tomorrow night, and I have a feeling 'Blabbing Brooke' as they call her is really going to unleash a gusher."

****

"Nay, I'm not going to change my mind." Lisbet stood her ground. "You'll know for sure that I love him when you chant your spell and I vanish into the mists of time. Now, please, for the last time, do it!" Lisbet clutched her bag of gold coins in one trembling hand. She clenched a sack of belongings in the other and breathed deeply to calm her pounding heart. "I want this over with, finally, so I may start my life anew."

"Very well, if you're sure." Ulch shrugged.

"I'm sure as I ever will be. Must you torment me so?" Her voice rose, quivering.

"A life you hate in a place you despise will torment you more," he warned. "Just making sure you're ready and you're sure about this. You don't want to take another glance at the king so you'll recognize the bed when you get there?"

"The only bed he'll have a desire for is mine," she declared, chin up.

"Let's just hope you're in it when he does."

"Mayhap you should send me directly to his bedchamber." Her voice breathy with excitement, she clenched her fists.

"Not unless you fancy threesomes. Nay." He shook his head. "That won't do. I'll land you in the immediate vicinity of the cottage he stays at. It belongs to Julianna Hammond, in Wensleydale, a stone's throw from Middleham Castle. Just rap on the door; she'll take you in as soon as you tell her who you are. And I'm sure she'll give you some modern raiment so you really don't need that lot." He gestured at her sack.

"I've not just raiment in here. I've some keepsakes I can't bear to part with." Her Edward love doll was among them. Just in case the unthinkable happened and she never found him, at least she had a symbol of him to hold close to her heart.

"Let's go outside and I'll send you forth. Come." He led her out his door into the garden. She stood rigidly, glancing round at the surroundings she knew she'd never see again. He got out a battered book and turned to a dogeared page. "This is it." He squeezed his eyes shut and bowed his head, as if in prayer.

"Wait!"

He looked up. "What is it?"

"What about the love spell? Or—whatever it really is."

"Oh, yeah, that. I'll be looking out for you." He flicked his hand. "Fret not; you'll live out your life as his lady love. I'll send my positive vibes your way."

"Over five centuries?" Her mouth gaped.

"Trust me. He'll go crackers over you." He gave her an indulgent smile.

She was too shaken up to argue. She simply nodded, licked her dry lips and let him carry on.

"God, no!" she screamed as she felt herself falling, falling, faster and faster, into a bottomless chasm, darkness all around her. Before fear could even invade her, she fell into a soft pile of hay. She opened her eyes to a velvety sky brilliant with stars. Still clutching her sack and gold, she lay her head back and breathed deeply of the air. She detected a strange aroma she'd never encountered before. A buzzing sound in the distance scared her. What on earth was that? Some kind of animal?

Thankfully it receded. She stood on shaky legs, brushed hay off her body and looked round. She was on a farm; cows and sheep grazed around her. Stumbling off the pile of hay, she made her way out into the road, black and hard against her slippered feet. She hoped the farmhouse across from the barn was the one he'd told her about. Bright lights blazed in the windows. In her frenzy she'd forgotten the woman's name. Hammond, was it? No matter; she hurried toward it, her heart knocking as if to burst. *Oh, please be here, King*

Edward, she begged. She gave the door a timid rap, but it seemed there was no one within.

Just as she was about to peer through a window, the front door opened. A plump round-faced woman peered out, caught Lisbet's eye and stepped outside.

"May I help you?" Her accent was Yorkshire, but much lighter than what Lisbet was used to. She hoped they'd be able to understand each other.

"I—I'm looking for the Hammond cottage. May you be Mistress Hammond?"

"No, she lives up the road." The woman spoke slowly, her eyes riveted on Lisbet's attire, roving up and down, puzzling. *Who is she to stare?* Lisbet wondered. Her garb was surely strange—her head was bare and her knees actually showed!

"Are you lost?" the woman asked. "I can drive you there so you don't have to walk alone in the dark."

"I trust I shall find it if 'tis just up the road," she replied. They approached other more closely as they spoke.

"Are you a friend of hers?" The woman held out her hand. "I'm Dorothy Warburton. And you are?"

"Elizabeth Woodville."

Dorothy stumbled back as if struck with a bag of feed. "You aren't. You couldn't be. But I believe you. Some credulous, steadfast, unfettered corner of my mind believes you!" She took Lisbet by the elbow and ushered her inside. "Come in, dear, please, do come in. Let me make you some tea. You must be exhausted. Would you like a repast? When was the last time you ate?"

"Well, I—" Lisbet gawked at everything all at once. So many unfamiliar items lay about. Some scared her—like that tall thing standing in the corner resembling a bagpipe with a long rope coiled about its body. The big shiny box facing her. The strange instrument on the writing desk covered with numbered and lettered buttons. The brilliant light blazing from the candles that never wavered.

"Come, sit down in the kitchen and I'll explain just what everything is." Dorothy led her through the warm cozy room.

The kitchen looked comforting enough, its hearth high enough to stand inside, copper pots hanging from hooks, cupboards piled with dishes. After fussing about, Lisbet heard the ding of a little bell. Dorothy placed a steaming plate of vegetables and a meat pie in front of her, along with a cup of a steaming beverage. "That's tea, my dear. Drink it, eat the hearty meal, and I'll tell you as much as you want to know."

Lisbet lifted the strange implement beside the plate and turned it upside down, observing the four pointy prongs.

"That's a fork, dear. You eat like this." She placed the knife and fork in Lisbet's hands and went through the motions of gathering food from the plate.

"This will take getting used to!"

Lisbet wished she could just stuff the meat pie into her mouth. If only she'd asked the wizard about basic table etiquette. She'd been so anxious to come here, she hadn't inquired about daily life. She had only one thing on her mind—being with Edward.

Dorothy stood. "Excuse me while I make a phone call."

Lisbet looked up, puzzled. "Beg your pardon?"

She smiled. "Never you mind. You just eat. I'll be

right back."

****

Julianna hung up the phone, stunned. "Seems I don't have to ring Dorothy after all," she said to Richard, shelling peanuts onto the Richard III biography cover.

"Ah, that was she?"

"Yes, but she's not alone. She's got company." She stared at the floor, unblinking, still reeling with shock.

"Oh, no, don't tell me Ned found his way over there!"

She shook her head. "Not Ned. But close enough."

"George?"

"Nope. Elizabeth Woodville." She met his puzzled eyes.

Then he held up his pointer finger. "Ah, I know her. Woodville—she's the daughter of Earl Rivers, is she not? She marries Ned when he's still pre-contracted to Eleanor Butler."

"Right. Then when Ned dies, his sons are declared bastards and—" She stopped herself; she didn't want to rehash that scenario. "She's at Dorothy's." She couldn't believe she'd just said that. But of course it had to be true.

"How did she get there?" Richard asked.

"Same way you did, I suppose." She headed for the sofa and plopped down. "Or the same way Ned and George did. Maybe that Wizbar chap sent her. I don't know. Dorothy said she showed up at the door. I invited them over so I can find out what's going on here."

Richard slid the peanut shells off the book into the bin and held the book over the bin as if he wanted to let it follow the shells. But he replaced it on the shelf, spine in, pages out. "God's truth, that's quite amazing indeed. Ned will be mighty chuffed."

"Why do you think Ned had anything to do with it?" She looked over at him, munching away.

"She's obviously smitten with him. As he was with her, as the story goes. Married her in secret just to enter wedded bliss with her. And if you believe what you read about her, she held out on him, and he was so crazed with desire for her, he married her. Shrewd lass. Don't know how she held Ned off."

"Well, everything's different now. They might not be able to stand each other."

"Ah, she's here for a reason, just as we are. And what other reason than Ned?" He gave her a wry smile.

"Can't argue with that one."

Dorothy and Lisbet arrived just as Julianna put the kettle on. After the customary round of introductions, Richard and Lisbet politely acknowledged each other. They exchanged some small talk, like "how do you like the twenty-first century, seems a bit warmer for this time of year," and Julianna told Dorothy the truth about her other two visitors.

Julianna made Lisbet as comfortable as possible, but the young woman kept riveting her eyes toward the door as if Ned would walk through it any minute, even after Julianna explained he was out visiting for the night.

Dorothy took Julianna into the kitchen and helped herself to a wedge of blackcurrant pie.

"I knew it, Julianna, I'd have sworn on my first edition Thomas More Ricardian biography—the autographed one—that those chaps were Edward and George, but I didn't want you to take me for a complete nutter, especially after my bold assumption about Richard being who he was. I'm so glad it's in the open now." Dorothy's smile was one of profound relief as she licked currant off her fingers. "As soon as Lisbet told me who she was, the penny dropped—or rather two tuppences dropped. Now we've got the four of them here. It's a miracle, nothing short of a miracle." She shook her head, eyes shut, a dreamy expression softening her features.

Julianna didn't even ask about her autographed Thomas More book—that was a story for another time—but did ask, "Dorothy, how did you manage to stay so calm when you'd realized you were face to face with your most adored historical figure?"

"The lads are just so easy to be with." Dorothy shrugged. "I took an immediate liking to all of them. And Lisbet is the sweetest thing. They're all such dears. After all, they're people, like you and me. They've made this amazing journey, and maybe someday by the grace of God we'll find out why. But for now, let's just enjoy having them here and make a blockbuster film!"

Dorothy put her dish into the sink and brushed her hands off. They headed back into the living room, where Richard was showing Lisbet the globe.

"But what are we going to do about Blabbing Brooke?" Julianna fussed around the room nervously straightening things and picking up Ned's used protein bar wrappers. He'd attacked the chocolates in her candy dish, too, she noticed, and arranged the little foils into a heart shape. He certainly was a romantic.

"Well, as his Highness—uh, Richard said, don't deny anything, but don't encourage her either," Dorothy said. "You know what happens when you deny something to the media. It's even more ammunition for them than if you admit it's true."

"But she's probably in the back of her limo editing the film as we speak. We'll be on her show tomorrow night, surely!" Julianna started dusting the room, an activity she engaged in only to work off nervous energy.

"Can't you arrest her now?" Richard turned to them, fiddling with the Wensleydale Ring. "Bring her to the constabulary and confiscate the film, which she procured quite illegally?"

"There's nothing illegal about it, unfortunately." Julianna emptied her incense burner and lit a new cone. "Sometimes I wish the laws hadn't gone so lax since your day. She'd be in the Tower by now, swapping ghost stories with sewer rats."

"Well, Richard is right, we do have her attention now," Dorothy said quietly, as if thinking out loud. "And we do have a film to promote, and who better to promote a film about the royals than the queen of the royal stalkers herself."

"You mean offer her a piece of it?"

"Better. Let's give Brooke the role of the heroine in exchange for her buttoned-up lip about who your star boarder is. She'll jump at that like Jaws on a dangling leg. After all, she would make a great heroine. She's a decent actress. Not only that, we're guaranteed instant publicity—what better publicity can you get than the star of your film having her own royals-hounding show?"

Julianna breathed the sweet fragrance of the vanilla incense and sneezed. "You think that'll make her keep her gob shut? I think the urge to blab is programmed into her damned DNA."

"She'll be thrilled to have that part," Dorothy said with a wide grin. "You know how she fancies herself a romance heroine. She has that silly contest every Christmas where she dresses up as one of Barbara Cartland's heroines and acts out the love scenes with the hunky winner. The mince pies might be on the table, but the ham is always on the telly."

"Yeah, I suppose she'd be good for the part, if she doesn't look too goofy." Julianna nodded, finally calm enough to sit. "But she'll have to ditch those red-framed glasses and hide the tattoo of that serpent with the foot-long tongue wrapped around her thigh."

"You think going without a manicure will kill her? They didn't wear bright red claws with gold tips and fake diamond chips in the fifteenth century, did they?"

"And if she can knock a few inches off—" Julianna remarked. "Women in those days weren't anywhere near as hippy."

"You sure you want this woman as the heroine and not the Court Fool?" Richard, shelling his peanuts, commented from the bar.

Julianna snickered. "Sorry. Just can't resist sticking it to her sometimes. The way she follows the royal family around and scrutinizes their every move."

"Now—how to get hold of her before she gets back to her studio and onto the air tomorrow. Dorothy, you're psychic—can you conjure up her cell phone number?"

"Unfortunately, I only conjure up spirits. Phone her studio and send her an e-mail," Dorothy replied. "If that fails, we'll get on a plane and fly to bloody London and wait for her outside her flat. I have her address somewhere."

They called her studio and left an urgent message on the machine there. A half hour later, as they watched an Oliver Cromwell biography DVD with Richard and Lisbet, Julianna's phone rang. Blabbing Brooke was calling from her plane to London.

"Name one thing you'd be willing to kill a story for," Julianna goaded, and from that moment on, she had her. Julianna hung up the phone and turned to her guests. "We've got ourselves a heroine—and a few feet of tape on the cutting room floor."

"Ah, yes, this calls for a celebration!" Richard headed for the kitchen.

"Richard, the bar's out here." Julianna called after him.

"Who said anything about the bar? I'm celebrating with a culinary feast."

They followed him into the kitchen where he proceeded to create a Richard specialty—leftover pizza topped with sliced bananas and caramel coated popcorn. Washed down with blackcurrant juice and lemon soda.

Lisbet nearly dropped after several hours of conversation. She didn't tell them she'd begged Ulch to send her here to be with Edward; she simply explained that one of his curing spells had gone awry and he'd sent her here by accident. She didn't want them to know she was daft over Edward. She didn't divulge Ulch's claim about being from the far future, either. She kept all that inside, not sure she believed it herself. She didn't want them to think she was totally crackers.

Finally, Julianna gave her some clothes and Dorothy took her back home. "She'd better stay with me for a while. You've got a full house," Dorothy said as Lisbet eyed the odd-looking raiment Julianna had given her. What was this—a pair of trousers!

"We'll check with you in the morning," Julianna said as she bade them good night.

Dorothy led Lisbet back into that strange contraption that made such noise, it petrified her—what was it called? A Geek?

"Jeep," she read when she slid into the seat. It was noisy as a flock of wild geese before the Feast of St. Paul—but the ride was as smooth as a Thames crossing on a calm day.

****

Julianna and Richard remained in the pew after the service ended the following morning at the ancient Saint Alkelda church. As the worshipers filed out, he quietly dropped to his knees, head bowed, fingers laced. She got up to walk around, leaving him alone. Running her hands over the ancient stone tombs as she loved to do, she let her mind wander. Religion and science did seem at odds at times. She found most things were easily explained away by faith. But sometimes that wasn't enough; she craved proof. Would she ever have proof how Richard and his brothers got here? She had to stop thinking about it; all it did was make her head hurt.

Richard came up next to her, holding a Bible. "May I take this with me?" he asked.

"I've got one at home you can have. Or better yet, I'll buy you your very own."

He put it down and gazed at the vaulted ceilings, the stained glass fitted into the ancient stone frames. "Little has changed here," he commented, then his eyes darkened and his brow furrowed as he pointed to something up above. "What an atrocity. Desecrating a house of God so."

She turned to see what he was pointing at. It was a television set, bolted to the wall between two stone columns. "That's the world we live in, Richard."

He shook his head, his eyes still troubled. "People really are addicted to that boob box, as you say." He picked up a hymnal and flipped through the pages. "'Tis truly bad if they must even watch it whilst at worship."

"They might use it at Easter and Christmas to watch the Pope in Rome," she said, ashamed she'd never been to this church on either holiday, or any church, in years. Maybe with Richard here, she'd become a more avid churchgoer.

"I'm surprised they don't have those computer contraptions set up at each pew," he said, studying a hymn. "My, how the service has changed. I'm not sure I quite agree with this Church of England dogma."

"It never would have happened if—" She didn't want to go through that here. He hadn't taken much interest in the Tudor dynasty and she didn't push it. "Do you want to stay here a while longer, Richard?"

"Nay, I've said my prayers and sought my answers. Now I'll just have to wait." He lit a candle for his father before they left the church.

It was nearly dinnertime when Pippa came back with Ned and George. Ned strolled in nonchalantly enough, but George strutted through the door like a bantam cock who'd just broken dawn. Pippa passed on Julianna's offer of dinner; she had to get back and work on the next issue of the Ricardian.

"Uh, Pippa, I don't have to tell you what to leave out of that issue, do I?" Julianna asked quietly when they were alone at the doorstep. "Specifically who appeared at the séance and decided to stay."

"Of course not, Julianna, how could you even ask such a thing? We're bound by loyalty, just like King Richard. Having his Highness here is an honor only we're privileged to have, and word of his presence can go no farther. Now, about your cousin—" She fanned her hand as if to cool herself down. "I think I'll send last night's diary entry to one of those hubba-hubba websites!"

"That good, huh?" Julianna tried to hide her smile. So, history books weren't all exaggeration and propaganda. "Is this the beginning of a regular thing?"

She shook her head casually. "He just thanked me for a lovely evening and that was that. But that's quite all right with me. I don't want any kind of commitment, either." She let out a whistle. "Oh, he's the greatest—and so thoroughly modern."

"Oh, yes, he's modern, all right. Way ahead of his time. How about your sister and Wilberforce?" Julianna got a tea towel from the cupboard.

"Oh, uh—" she snickered. "He fell asleep. Or she did. I don't know who went first. But they both were so snockered, we found them on the sofa this morning fully clothed, an empty Scotch bottle between them."

"Well, at least two of you had a good time."

"It was grand, Julianna. Keep me up to date on the film."

She didn't mention Blabbing Brooke's visit. The plot was thick enough as it was.

Chapter Sixteen

Today was the day Lisbet had waited for. Up since daybreak, she couldn't sit still, so she strolled round Dorothy's farm. "Finally, I get to see my darling Edward!" she sang to the sheep and cows clustered round her, some cocking their heads in curiosity. "I'll soon be his, his only love, his only lady love!" She chanted a song she'd known since childhood. A little dance accompanied her joyous singing. The animals provided an attentive audience, till they lost interest and one by one, wandered back to their grazing.

She had spent her first full twenty-first century day chatting with Dorothy about everything—history, how the world had changed, beauty potions. Then finally Lisbet could hold back no more. Feeling a need to confide in someone, she broke down and poured her heart out, telling Dorothy why she abandoned her entire world for Edward.

"I had that wizard send me here just so I could be with him. Oh, how I adore him, Dorothy, I've been in love with him from the moment I saw him. It was something I knew—I knew we were destined for each other. And he needs someone like me. I'd care for him in every way, meet his every need." Her voice wavered as tears stung her eyes.

Finally, he was within a mile! Hoping to run into him by chance, she strolled down the road toward

Julianna's cottage, knowing he was almost within reach. Just a glimpse of his golden head from behind a tree was enough. She didn't want to speak to him without being formally introduced.

"I had a feeling you just didn't drop here by accident. I knew love had to have something to do with it. All right, we'll go over there right after breakfast," Dorothy assured her, leading her into the kitchen.

"Breakfast! Nay, I just couldn't. The thought of food makes me ill." Lisbet stroked her Edward doll's blond head. It had made the journey in better shape than she had, not a scratch on its perfect features, the armor as shiny as the day she'd dressed him in it.

"You've got to eat something, Lisbet." She gestured to the lavish spread on the table. "Come now, some fresh eggs with bacon and sausage, homemade bread, fresh butter, everything from right here on the farm."

"I appreciate your hospitality, Lady Dorothy, but I cannot—" A shrill ringing made her jump practically into Dorothy's arms. "God's truth, what is that?"

"The telephone. Remember, I showed it to you last night? Nothing to be afraid of."

Dorothy lifted the strange instrument to her face and talked into it. Lisbet was even more fascinated with that thing than she had been with the huge box full of pictures and the machine connected to the lettered buttons which sent messages all over the world. But this—one could talk into it and be talked back to!

"That was Julianna, she said to come over any time we like."

"Will Edward be there?" Her heart leapt.

"Of course, dear. That's the whole idea—to

introduce the two of you. I mean—reintroduce you." Dorothy winked.

"Pray the love spell works this time," Lisbet whispered. She hadn't understood what the wizard had told her about transferring positive energy. It sounded like so much mumbo jumbo, an explanation centering round magic would have made more sense. But she had to trust him—she had no other choice. "Oh, I so dread Edward's not noticing me, as the last time. 'Twas such a disaster." She swept away tears.

"He'll notice you, all right. I saw some of the clothes Julianna gave you last night—that skinny ribbed sweater with those tight jeans will turn his head, or he's just not human."

Lisbet knew not what a skinny ribbed sweater or jeans were. All she knew was she hadn't liked any of the raiment the woman had packed into the large black bag. The shoes were even more hideous. She'd tried walking in them, and nearly fell on her face. The undergarments fit like instruments of torture. Yet if she was going to spend the rest of her life here, she was determined to get used to it. So she let Dorothy strap her into the brassiere or whatever she'd called it, and sat still while Dorothy slathered a foamy white substance on her hair and dried it with an instrument that emitted an ear-piercing shriek as it blew hot air.

She then showed Lisbet perfumes, creams, lotions, and gels for every part of the body, and strangest of all, the feminine apparatus. "You discard them after use?" Lisbet stared wide-eyed at the 'pads' of every conceivable shape and size, for 'light' and 'heavy' days, some with 'wings' on the sides. "It sticks to your undergarments?" she'd asked in disbelief as Dorothy peeled off a paper strip to reveal a sticky surface.

"Just make sure the sticky bit goes downward," Dorothy warned.

She actually looked forward to her next flux; 'twould be terribly convenient without the usual slippage and rinsing out of used ones to dry. Not to mention the array of medicines for bloating, cramps, irritability, headache and backache, before and during. "They thought of most everything, didn't they? Except mayhap how to stop it altogether."

Dorothy showed her the shower, how hot and cold water ran through the pipes, the soaps in solid, gel and liquid forms, the sponges, the cleansers for hair, face, body, and feet. What really amazed her were the woman's shaving implements. "Women shave their body hair?" She knew her mouth hung open in disbelief, but she couldn't help it.

Next came the oral hygiene apparatus, and she especially enjoyed squeezing the tube that made the long squiggly ribbon squirt forth—with blue stripes! "Cor—amazing!" She shrieked in disbelief when Dorothy showed her how to work a string called floss between her teeth, and warned her not to swallow the minty juice that she was to gargle with every day. "Every day?" She gasped. Who had time to carry out all this lot every day? Even once a month was excessive to perform all these rituals!

"You want Edward to find you desirable? This is what you must do," was her matter-of-fact answer. "You must be clean and smell clean."

Now she was showered, shampooed, conditioned, moussed, shaved, brushed, flossed, gargled, toned, moisturized, and bound in modern raiment. She didn't recognize herself in the looking glass. Dorothy stood back and admired Lisbet as if she were a portrait she'd just painted. "Gorgeous! He'll do handsprings."

But she couldn't bite a morsel, nor could she swallow a sip. Not even of that delicious beverage called tea that Dorothy showed her in every flavor she'd ever heard of, and then some.

They climbed into the Jeep, and Lisbet couldn't ever remember being this jittery. Even the last time she'd been presented to the king, she was calm compared to this. She could feel her pounding heart through the tight garment that enhanced the swell of her breasts. She was afraid he'd have her arrested for indecent exposure!

But Dorothy assured her, women these days wore much less.

The few moments it took Julianna to open the door were the most anguished of Lisbet's life. She'd rehearsed over and over what she'd say to Edward when presented to him—a deep curtsey, just as before, a polite greeting, some small talk about the weather. She wouldn't discuss the journey—not till he brought it up. She wouldn't dare tell him why she'd come this distance through time. She prayed the wizard's energy had reached her, and once Edward saw her, he'd fall madly in love.

Julianna greeted them and ushered them in. Lisbet peered round the room for the blond head, the flashing blue eyes, the dazzling smile. *Where is he?*

"Come through to the garden," Julianna offered. "They're out there."

Lisbet clutched Dorothy's arm and received a comforting pat in return. She saw him first, the blond head bowed over a chessboard, the blue eyes steely in concentration. Not daring to make another move, she let Julianna carry out her hostess role.

"Ned, George, this is Lisbet."

She didn't even see Richard or George. For all she knew, they could have been invisible. Her eyes remained riveted to Edward. The huge form unfolded, and he flexed his hard muscles as he stood to greet her. With each step closer, her breath quickened, her heart hammered, her knees quivered. Her hand shot out to meet his as she dipped in a flawless curtsey.

A spark of recognition lit up the eyes, followed by an accompanying smile. "Lisbet. Ah, yes. The Earl Rivers's daughter. No need to curtsey, my dear. I'm no longer king, but simply Ned Plantagenet. What brings you here?"

Did he mean here to Julianna's garden or here to the twenty-first century? It mattered not. She couldn't find her voice.

Dorothy saved the day. "She was hurled through time by an accident of nature no one can comprehend," she explained, helping Lisbet to her feet, for she found herself frozen to the ground after her deep curtsey. "Same as Richard, I expect, when he took that tumble from the horse and landed in modern Middleham."

"I just arrived here yesterday, your Grace." Enormously relieved she was able to talk, it almost calmed her.

"Now, now, 'tis Ned, and only Ned. I'm no one's Grace as long as I'm here." His smile outshone the sun glinting off his hair, turning it the color of spun gold.

She melted into his gaze. "N—Ned." She stood at a respectable distance, their fingers barely touching, when all she wanted to do was ravish him right there in the bed of roses, render him helpless under her caresses, thoroughly consume him. In due course, she assured herself. At least this time he was still looking at her. Mayhap the wizard's energy transference was time-released, like those medicines Dorothy had shown her.

"Say hello to Richard and George," came a voice from the distance which she barely heard.

Unable to tear her gaze from Ned, she felt a hand on her shoulder. She wanted to shake it off and scream "Leave us alone!" Instead she broke her gaze. It was physically painful, like pulling on a scab. In daylight, Richard looked more youthful and rested than he ever had. He kissed her hand as George swaggered to her side and gave an exaggerated bow. Handsome in their own right with their blue eyes gleaming, they still dulled next to Ned. The very sun dulled next to Ned. He was the sun, the moon, and every star in the heavens to her. So why was he turning away, to return to a chessboard?

"Shall we finish, Dickon? I do believe it was your move." In a second he was absorbed in his pawn formations. She may as well never have entered the garden. Why hadn't he given her some indication he found her attractive, one of the many signals of courtship ritual, the subtle squeeze of the hand, the nonchalant wink, the flicking tongue over the lips? He may as well have been presented to a fishwife. *It will happen*, she insisted. She believed. *It will happen!*

On wobbly legs, she walked to the picnic table and sat. She choked down a tart and a cup of tea, watching him out the corner of her eye.

"Checkmate!" he finally sang, slapped his knees

and roared in laughter.

With nerve from she knew not where, she stood and approached him. He swept a satisfactory eye over the chessboard, empty save for his two rooks and Richard's defeated king. "May I challenge you to a game of chess, Ned?"

He looked up, surprised she was still there. "Why, certainly."

Richard excused himself, mumbling something about writing more notes.

The game almost calmed her. She concentrated so hard, she'd nearly forgotten who her opponent was. She nearly had him, but he executed a crafty defense, sacrificing a rook in the process, causing her to eventually resign. But she'd put up a good battle.

They played another game, and another. The sun soared high, then began to sink below the trees in the distance. It grew chilly. She glanced round the garden; they'd all disappeared. Finally—she was alone with her beloved!

"Ned—" Her mouth was drier than parchment, but she knew not when they'd be alone like this again.

He looked up, smiled, and twirled a pawn between his fingers.

"Ned, I—" Her voice seemed to come from someone else. In a way, this relieved her. "I love you madly, Ned, I always have. You're the love of my life, and the only reason I exist. Please don't turn me away. I'll die without you. We belong together. I love you so much."

The smile vanished. His eyes registered surprise.

Time halted. She sobbed and trembled so hard, neither the tea nor the blanket nor the fire's warmth helped to comfort her. "No, never mind..." She pushed herself to her feet, turned and fled.

****

"All right, now start from the beginning and tell me exactly what happened." Dorothy pulled up a rocking chair and got busy knitting, yet kept an eye fixed on Lisbet.

"Oh, Dorothy, I made such a fool of myself. Such a silly lass. I wouldn't be surprised if he ran and kept running. But I could hold it in no longer. I told him just how I felt about him, how much I loved and adored and cherished him, how I lived and breathed for him, how I'd wither up and die without him."

"And what did he say?"

"He remained aloof and mumbled some kind of half-hearted attempt at graciousness. I ran out of there so fast, I fell and skinned my knees."

She *tsk-tsk'd*. "The fundamental mistake you made was coming on to him too strongly. Ned's sort like to do the chasing, it's all the excitement for them. Don't ask why; it's just the way their minds work."

"'Tis too late now, I've chased him, all right— chased him away!" A renewed wave of sadness overcame her and she sobbed freely into the soft cloths called tissues. Thank goodness these, too, were disposable.

"No, it's never too late, my dear. Just be more subtle; he'll come round." She gave Lisbet a reassuring pat on the arm.

"I know not how to be subtle." She attempted a sip at the tea, but now she had hiccups.

"The next few times you see him, don't even give him the time of day. Ignore him. But make him fully aware you're there. Make sure you're drop dead gorgeous. We'll get you some new clothes and a new hairstyle. Maybe put some blonde streaks in it." She lifted a section of Lisbet's hair and felt its texture. "We'll play with makeup, and we'll try out a thousand different kinds of perfume. That pheromone stuff is reckoned to attract the opposite sex without them even knowing about it. And you can do all this without even a word, all with the most raw instincts our distant ancestors were born with."

"Oh, that Grand Wizbar, I'd like to rip his face apart and feed it to that ratty bat of his! I was so sure he spoke the truth. I was so sure Ned would be incapable of refusing me."

"Don't take anything for granted, anyone's word. Don't rely on anyone but yourself. Your love life is controlled by you—with a little help from me, of course." The needles clicked rhythmically as Dorothy knitted. "Every young woman wants a fairy godmother. Well, now you've got one, and I'll try my best to get you your Prince Charming!"

Sufficiently calmed down by bedtime, she made sure Dorothy was abed before tiptoeing down the stairs and out the front door. This couldn't wait. Playing it cool, as Dorothy called it, wasn't her style. No, she had to face this head on.

She stepped out into the chilly evening air and headed for Julianna's cottage. The curtains were drawn across all the windows but one, a small one in back. The window was open to the third notch on the latch. This window didn't even have a curtain, just wavy leaded glass. As she peeked inside, she realized it was a privy. There was her beloved, shaving at the looking glass, naught but a scanty towel round his waist. He must've heard her gasp, for he turned and, wiping some white foam from his face, came to the window and pushed it wide open. She jumped back as not to get hit.

"Who's out there?"

She was too stunned even to run and hide.

"Lisbet? What are you doing out there?"

His presence alone paralyzed her; she felt like she were made of stone. Yet she melted as she focused on those dreamy blue eyes. Could stone melt? she wondered. "I—I was—j—just going for a stroll. I lost my way." He chuckled and shook his head.

Obviously he didn't believe a word of it, yet he grinned. "Well, I must say I'm amused, even flattered that you'd go to these lengths to get my attention."

Mayhap he did like to be chased after all, he just wasn't used to it. "I'll come round and walk you back. Just let me don some raiment." She turned away, her heart leaping in wonder and anticipation. Mayhap he would declare his love right here outside his privy! She prayed for strength to stay on her feet, naught else.

The night was dark as ink, but he glowed as he approached her, a white jacket fluttering behind him in the breeze. He cupped her elbow and led her round to the front. She clutched his arm with her other hand.

Now, talk now! she commanded herself. *You'll never have another chance like this!* By God, she wasn't going to spy through his window again! "Ned, about before—"

"Think naught of it, lass. The journey through time must have been harrowing. You must be disoriented and plain baffled. 'Twill pass, though, I promise. We've adapted well enough. Worry not, you'll make friends here."

But I don't want friends, I want you! she longed to scream as they walked down the road toward Dorothy's farm. She could see the buildings already. This was going to end too quickly.

"I—I meant everything I said, but I didn't mean for it to come out all at once, so abruptly. Please don't think any less of me."

"Of course I don't." He chuckled and gave her a brotherly pat on the arm. A man like Ned in a situation like this could lure her behind a tree or a hedge and ravish her till sunup, so why was he simply walking her back? Why wasn't he even trying to force himself upon her, alone and vulnerable in total darkness, out of anyone's earshot? She would have let him. That was what scared her.

"Ned—" She halted him and made an attempt to turn his hard, massive body toward hers. She leaned into him until their lips nearly touched. "Kiss me, Ned." But she kissed him, without giving him a second to refuse. She took his head between her palms and pressed her lips to his. His surprise was evident. He didn't exactly respond.

She grabbed bunches of that luscious hair and combed her fingers through it, inhaling his clean scent as her breath increased. Just touching him was like ingesting a potent drug.

He gently broke away and gave her a kiss atop of her head. "No need to get carried away, dear, I'm just a bloke." He resumed walking.

She longed to tell him just why she'd come all this way, through five centuries, never to see her loved ones again. But she was losing heart. He simply wasn't interested. Oh, why hadn't she listened to Dorothy and played that silly game she'd suggested? Tease him, torment him, don't look him in the eye.

Play it cool.

But to her that was sillybuggers. She and Ned were destined for each other.

Why didn't he realize that?

They reached Dorothy's house, but she'd locked herself out. Thankfully, Dorothy heard her knocking and let them in.

"I didn't even know you were out!" She belted a robe, her feet jammed into fuzzy round things that looked like dead ducks.

"She lost her way," Ned explained, but his tone confirmed his disbelief.

"Oh, no," Dorothy murmured, but her reply held a thousand more words. When she shook her head at Lisbet she may as well have shaken her finger.

"I must return, we need to rehearse some more. Good evening, ladies." He turned and vanished into the night.

Lisbet fell into Dorothy's arms, sobbing.

"What happened this time?" Her voice had a slight edge to it.

"N—naught—I just took a stroll." Lisbet wrung her hands.

"And just happened to run into him?" Dorothy's tone made it clear she didn't believe a word.

"He ran into me, actually." At least that was the truth.

"Where?"

Head down, she admitted it. "At the window of his privy."

Dorothy let out a whoosh of air. "Oh, Lisbet! What did I tell you?"

"Please don't lecture me," she implored. "But I just had to see him. Now I know the Grand Wizbar's love spell isn't working."

"Even if Cupid had shot an arrow up his arse, your forward manner is enough to scare King Kong away." Dorothy chided, shaking her head.

"King Kong? When did he rule?"

"Never mind. I told you—play it cool. You'll never get him by throwing yourself at him." Her voice calmed, her speech slowed.

"But he's a magnet, Dorothy. I can't stay away. I'm—what did you call it when you and Julianna talked about ice cream—hooked."

As Lisbet warmed to Dorothy's loving hug, she felt almost like she belonged here. This woman truly cared for her. "I know what it's like, my dear. I do know. But you've got to play the game. That's all it is, you know, a game. And you'll never win unless you play by the rules."

She gave Lisbet a copy of a book called *Men Are from Mars* to take to bed. "My goodness, they have come far in five hundred years. But Ned isn't from Mars."

"No, dear, it's a figure of speech. Just read it. You'll learn a lot about how their minds work. They're so different, they may as well be from Mars."

Chapter Seventeen

After breakfast Julianna and her visitors sat in her lounge over another pot of tea.

Richard flipped through her CDs and put on the new Silver Thunder release. Although rock music didn't quite capture his fancy, he did like this particular band. George had taken to the Beatles, while Ned preferred the soothing quality of Brahms.

"Our film needs music in the background, does it not?" Richard tapped his foot in time to the first track.

"Yes, it's called a soundtrack." She poured milk into her cup from her cow-shaped ceramic pitcher. "I reckon I'll ask Herb or Jonathan who they'd prefer."

"What about these blokes?" He held up the CD cover, featuring four hot hunks.

"Silver Thunder? Sure, I suppose their theatrical, sublime style matches the mood of the film. That'd be a great excuse to meet them, too." Her favorite band was Midnight Oil, but not for their looks.

"So when am I going to meet this leading lady of mine?" Ned flipped through his copy of the script.

Richard opened his leather folder, his copy stacked neatly inside. "She's arriving in a bit, as is that producer chap. You'll read through the script with her then." He turned to Julianna. "Julianna, I would like for you to be in this film."

"I'm in it." She opened the drapes. "I'm in it for a

quarter of my life savings and half my divorce settlement."

"I mean acting in it." He rose from the couch and approached her. Ned was studying his part, not paying attention, and George was at the bar adding a splash of whiskey to his tea. "I want you to be my Anne."

"Anne?" It was obvious who he meant, yet she had to ask, for that ultimate reassurance.

"Yes." He spoke and nodded so matter-of-factly, his eyes so sincere, as if there was never any question who would play the person closest to him.

The invitation flattered and disturbed her at the same time. "But—she died so tragically and so young. I don't know if I could handle it."

"She doesn't die in this version." He gave a faintly amused smile. "She outlives me." A smile of pride lit up his face.

She didn't have to think about it any longer. "I'd love to—I'd be honored."

"Good." That settled, he abruptly turned, and all business once again, sat at her writing desk and began scribbling notes. "Your first lines are on page thirty-four. Mayhap you'd best go over them. We can rehearse our first scene after the others arrive."

Just then the knocker clunked on the door. Ned jumped up as if sprung, flipping the newspaper over in his haste to get to the door. "'Tis my heroine, just on time!" With a brief glance in the hall mirror and a smoothing down of his hair, he swept the door open.

Julianna stood to the side, as an observer watching a play from the wings as Edward's eyes met Brooke's for the first time. They stood and stared, blinking, the threshold between them. Finally Julianna broke the silent gaping as she remembered it was her house. "Come in, Brooke. This is my cousin Cuthbert. He'll be playing the hero in the film."

"Oh, I just knew it!" She shimmied out of her buttercup yellow blazer. Julianna caught it just in time, sneaking a glance at the label. Either she trusted Julianna to keep her threshold well swept or she didn't give a fig about her wardrobe. "When you opened the door, I said to myself, 'here he is, my leading man, Arthur to my Guenevere, Antony to my Cleopatra, your name next to mine in lights.' You ooze heroism, Cuthbert, you reek of it."

"We should ooze and reek quite well together, then." He winked at her with one eye, then at Julianna with the other. She wondered how much practice that took.

"Come in, Brooke," she repeated, and Brooke squeezed past Ned, slowly, deliberately, and very theatrically, making sure their bodies brushed together.

"Take your time," he purred. "An entrance such as this can never be rushed. In fact, let's have a retake on that."

A car door slammed, then Jonathan Garrett rushed in carrying some recording equipment. "Sorry, had to get this lot out of the car." He made the visitors' re-acquaintance and settled himself on the sofa with his recorder and mike.

Julianna introduced Brooke to Jonathan and to George as her cousin Wilberforce. After the briefest of hellos to Jonathan and "Willy," Brooke stood at Richard's side, telling him how thrilled she was that he'd decided to stay and not return to the great beyond.

Jonathan tugged on Julianna's sleeve. "Great

beyond?" His eyes nearly crossed in disbelief.

"She thinks he's Richard the Third's ghost, whom we conjure up briefly every year at a séance," Julianna answered with an exaggerated shrug. She kept one eye on Blabbing Brooke, now admiring Richard's Wensleydale Ring, staring into it as if waiting for it to speak to her.

"Blimey, these history nuts." Jonathan shook his head and adjusted his sound level.

"Julianna, I told you I believe!" Brooke held up a manicured hand and daintily sat on her sofa. Ned's eyes looked as if they were going to roll out of his head and up those trim thighs. "My silence in exchange for the chance to work with a departed king's spirit. Just a few weeks in proximity to him is worth forfeiting the greatest story my show would ever have broadcast." She turned back to Richard and clasped her hands. "If only I could be there at Bosworth when you're mortally wounded in the film. Can I play the part of a water-boy—just to be near you when you go down?"

"I don't go down in this particular scenario," he replied coolly, handing her a copy of the newly printed revised script. "We've re-written history—to the extent that it could be rewritten."

"You don't say!" She shrieked in glee, plowing through the script. "Oh, that's fabulous—the Shakespeare scholars will descend upon you like a swarm of locusts, but it's worth it."

"Shakespeare scholars? Is that not a contradiction in terms?" Richard had read 'his' play three times already as well as sneered through the Olivier movie.

"Well, they still teach it in schools. I studied his plays at school, and in summer stock, I played the part of Gertrude in *Hamlet* and played Lady Macbeth."

"Lucky you." He cleared his throat and sipped at his tea. "A brief synopsis of the screenplay is at the beginning, if you care to start there."

But she was busy reading the ending. "Drama, pure drama. The critics will smear caviar on it and slurp it up. Oh, I just love the way I go riding off into the sunset to join my hero." She glanced up at Ned, who hadn't moved from his spot where he'd opened the door.

He threw her one of his trademark smiles which she didn't catch.

She was already reading her lines out loud. 'I am on my way home to you, Raymond.' The mount glides over the fields in the late summer twilight. 'Raymond, my darling, thy name is love to me.' Pure poetry. In cantering motion, no less."

"We were planning on reading it from beginning to end." Richard handed out scripts to everyone. "And I thought you might want to know our Julianna has been cast in the part of Anne Neville."

"Julianna, that's marvelous!" Brooke's eyes glittered along with the sunburst pin on her blouse. "So you've really got a stake in this. Financial and artistic."

"I guess you can say I've two shots at the big time now." Julianna smiled broadly. For the first time, she was aware of just how much this meant to her. Even if she didn't recoup her investment, maybe a big Hollywood talent scout would spot her.

Richard told everyone to sit and turn to the opening scene. Julianna checked her imagination and settled down to business.

Brooke read her lines like a pro; her limited acting

experience was certainly helping her now. Ned, lacking the formal training, made up for it in sincerity. He became Raymond, the hero. When he spoke to his heroine, Julianna could see he was living the part. Even George looked impressed, as he read the minor parts that hadn't been cast yet.

When it was time for Julianna to make her appearance as Anne Neville, she nearly froze. How could she live up to this cousin of Richard's, with whom he'd shared his childhood and loved dearly? But to give up would have been shameful, so she struggled through her lines, with Richard reading his as naturally as if he'd been there. At that moment she decided to hire an acting coach.

"Anne, my darling, I'm so glad I found you! Who did this to you? Who had you disguised as a cook-maid and spirited you off to this horrid place?"

"I never thought this would come out, Richard, because I never thought you'd find me, but it was your brother George. He's keeping us apart so he can have all of Isabel's inheritance." When no reply came forth, Julianna looked up from her script to see Richard glaring at George, who sat on her window seat, happily munching peanuts and flipping through the pages. "The next line's yours, Richard," she cued him.

His eyes beheld all the fury of a raging thunderstorm. "You fobbing fly-bitten sod," he murmured through clenched teeth. "I still can't believe you'd do such a thing to me."

George blinked. His head bobbed. "What'd I do now?" He choked out, over a shrug.

"Richard, it's only a screenplay," Julianna stage-whispered, nudging him, fully aware that Brooke's ears and eyes rivaled radar detectors. "Besides, it—" She leaned over and whispered, "It never happened, right? And it never will!"

"Not if I can help it," he mumbled into his copy of page 103. He took a deep breath and recited his lines with what she knew was forced detachment.

Richard got over his anger until Henry Tudor showed up. Not cast yet, Jonathan read the part. Although not an actor, he rattled off a few practice lines with a charming fake British accent tinged with French.

"So we finally meet, Henry Tudor," Richard recited, barely glancing at the script. *How had he memorized it all so fast?* Julianna wondered.

"And you come all this way to oust me from my throne? You wasted your mummy's groats." Richard's eyes stared daggers through Jonathan.

"Who said the throne was yours, Old Dick?" Jonathan read, cross-legged with an arm flung across the top of the couch. His poise lent a certain calm arrogance to the role.

He wouldn't make a bad Tudor at that, she thought. But she didn't dare say a word. One producer acting in the film was enough. From here on in, she wanted to recruit as many professional actors as they could afford.

"If facts serve me right, you yanked the throne out from under your nephew's tender bum," Jonathan continued. "His face escapes my mind's eye—ah, well, mayhap that's because no one's seen him in so long, har har!"

"My brother King Edward was pre-contracted to another wench at the time of his second marriage, ergo his heirs were illegitimate, ergo Parliament unanimously declared me king, 'tis thusly why I became king, and you well know it as does your entire qualling faction, you knotty-pated lout!" Richard's voice rose louder with each word. On his feet now, he shook a fist at Jonathan.

All eyes looked up in puzzlement.

Jonathan emitted a baffled "Huh?" This wasn't in the script!

"Richard, sit down." Julianna grabbed his belt loop and dragged him back down. "Will you keep to the damn script you wrote?"

He closed his eyes and bowed his head in abject apology. "I'm sorry. I just run off at the mouth at times."

"Oh, is that your mouth running off?" George drawled from the window seat. "I was about to fetch a chamber pot, thinking it was runoff of another sort."

"Oh, quash!" he ordered George and flipped the page. "Er—here we are—" he continued with his distinctive brand of poise, "My nephew is as secure in his comfortable apartments in the Tower as is my title and claim to the throne. And what qualifies you to be king, Sir Taffy? Besides your wonky claim via the wrong side of your great-great-grandfather's sheets?"

"Popularity. My followers adore me. They flock to me."

"Ah, that might very well be, but I don't believe the sheep of South Wales particularly give a bleat who's king. And er—who is it that follows whom?"

Jonathan replied, "All of Wales bows at the sight of me."

Richard shot him a dirty look. "I doubt it not. Ba-a-a-a-a-a!"

"Were this a popularity contest, I'd be choosing my

coronation robes as we speak," Jonathan recited. "But since we must vie for the crown the noble way, let us call our armies to our colors forthwith and engage in battle once and for all!"

"Sod battle!" Richard wailed. "Why waste my treasury's resources as well as the lives of hundreds of Welshmen? We shall have it out right here—so go sharpen your sword on your fangs. And wear a codpiece, if you can find one small enough."

"A duel is good enough for me, your lowness. Any particular location?" Jonathan read.

"Saint Luke's Cemetery is as good a place as any," Richard replied. "Unless of course you prefer to be buried elsewhere?"

"Just remove that white boar from your tabard unless you want to be remembered as the red boar," Jonathan read and turned his page.

"Superb. Very well read." Richard placed his script on the table and looked around. "Who pinched my nuts?"

"I have them." George walked over with a bowl of Richard's peanuts. He placed it at the edge of the table, slid it over, and scampered away.

"At ease, Willy, I'm no longer angry. I just—" Richard let out a histrionic sigh. "Please understand, I'm rather caught up in these events."

"Oh, I understand," Brooke nodded, her diamond earrings swaying. "This story will set English history on its ear, King Richard. Nobody will know what to believe about you anymore. Cheeky monkey."

Julianna rolled her eyes, meeting Jonathan's puzzled look. "Let's take ten for tea." She cast a glance at Edward ogling Brooke. "Or whatever."

****

"Can we go now, can we go now?" Lisbet hounded Dorothy as they brought their lunch dishes in from the garden.

"All right! My goodness, I'm surprised you haven't pitched a tent under his bedroom window. Uh-oh—" She shook her head rapidly, and her glasses swung on their chain. "Don't take that literally. I'll ring Julianna and make sure they're in."

Lisbet placed the dishes in the sink and dashed up the stairs to pretty up. She perused the array of jars, compacts, brushes, tubes, and perfume bottles. Her heart raced and a ribbon of sweat broke out along her hairline. She clenched and unclenched her fists. All these beauty rituals made her so nervous! She flipped to the page in the magazine Dorothy showed her about applying makeup and followed the pictures carefully, choosing her colors like a queen selecting her coronation garb. Good thing she had an eye for color.

After five changes of clothes, including Julianna's skirt that she couldn't sit in, she chose a pair of simple black trousers and white blouse. What was more basic than black and white—and she would be subtle if she had to tie her hands behind her back and wear a blindfold. No more chasing Ned!

After assuring her that she looked lovely, Dorothy brushed Lisbet's hair until it glowed, squirted some more of that white foam into it, and led her to the Jeep.

"They're rehearsing, and I'd like to see our actors in action," Dorothy said as she backed down the drive. "I have a few suggestions for some of the other parts, too. I hope we can audition them before too long."

"How did you get involved in all this?" Lisbet

asked as the Jeep bounced down the rutted lane.

"I was a drama major in college, but my interest was always behind the scenes, as a stage manager. I also did some directing. I know a few actors that have become quite famous over the years, and some not so famous. But I've always had an ambition to see my work on the silver screen—uh, that's the cinema—moving pictures—like telly, but much bigger. So I wrote this screenplay, and hoped someone would be interested in producing it—besides me, that is."

They reached Julianna's cottage, and Lisbet saw a few more of these strange-looking contraptions with rubber wheels. As they pulled in behind a large black one, she had to keep herself from dashing to the door and knocking it down.

Dorothy pushed a button and some chimes sounded.

"Come in," a voice called, and Dorothy opened the door. Edward's golden head was the first thing Lisbet saw, but she wanted to crawl under the rug when she saw what he was doing. He had one arm around a stunning blonde woman and the other holding a stack of papers. She was rubbing his neck, very sensuously.

"Raymond, facing death makes you look at things very differently," the blonde woman said.

"You needn't tell me what facing death entails, my dear," Ned replied, turning a page.

"When I thought I was dying, I prayed for a chance. Not for a second chance at life, by that time I was beyond hope, but a chance to tell you..." She swept a lock of his hair from his forehead and caressed his cheek.

He smiled brightly. "Hm, I like that. Oh, sorry." He

resumed reading: "Tell me what?"

She quit her caressing to turn a page on the table before her. "Raymond, I was as worried about you at battle as you were about me freezing in the forest. I know you never doubted my ability to take care of myself."

"Even the most rugged highwayman would find difficulty surviving in the ordeal you went through. I went to battle thoroughly prepared."

She turned sideways and Ned pressed her closer to him.

This is acting? Lisbet wondered. Ned seemed to be enjoying this immensely.

"So what did you want to tell me?" he said.

"That I no longer felt the sorrow of my own life ending, but that I was leaving you behind. Without ever having told you..."

Now Ned was planting kisses on her neck. The woman shivered. Either she was a truly gifted actress or she was enjoying this as much as he.

He still wasn't even aware Lisbet was in the room. Oh, how she wished that were she in his arms, even if he didn't mean a word of it.

"Tell me what? That you are beginning to appreciate my overbearing presence?"

"Perhaps." She pulled away from his kisses and yawned.

"You are beginning to tolerate my boorish inclinations?" Ned made another lunge for her.

"Haven't I been?" She slithered away.

"You are beginning to enjoy my company?" His hand crawled up her arm.

"I have been known to on occasion." She flicked

him away.

"Does all this mean you are falling in love with me?"

"Now are you not being a bit presumptuous?" The woman's voice turned throaty.

"Never have I been invited to be bathed by a woman who loathed the sight of me, so I think not."

She gave him a playful slap, and his mouth descended upon hers. Lisbet looked away. She couldn't watch any more.

"Tell me what is in your heart, my love," Ned breathed.

Lisbet peeked with one eye. The woman stroked his chest, her lips upon his earlobe, her tongue darting out and flicking it playfully. Everyone in the room seemed to have stopped breathing.

"Raymond, I..."

Ned rolled on top of her, still clutching the script. He supported himself on his elbows. "Tell me what you have been afraid to tell me, and God knows you must have said it in your head enough times to...oh, just tell me!"

The woman hiked up her skirt and wrapped one shapely leg around Ned's waist.

"I know what you want to tell me, so tell me. Tell me you are in love with me!"

Their mouths locked together, and they just didn't stop.

"Uh—" Richard tapped him on the shoulder. For a moment it looked as if Ned was pushing him away, but he finally ended the kiss and rose to his knees, brushing himself off.

"This is where we make love for the first time, is it

not?" Ned flipped another page over. The woman rose to her elbows and tossed a lock of hair behind her shoulder. "So we'll be naked when this scene is shot."

"Well, no, actually, you'll have body suits on." Dorothy strode up to the table and took a copy of the script. "It's not that kind of film. We're only aiming for an R rating, you know."

Ned scowled and helped his leading lady to her feet. She stood and walked away nonchalantly, passing Lisbet without a word, presumably on her way to the loo to sort herself out.

"Ah, Lisbet. How nice to see you again. I see you found your way back." Ned approached her, and she stood rooted to the floor. She couldn't move. She couldn't even raise a hand to meet his in greeting.

"Eh—I—hello, Ned."

"Er, around here I'm Cuthbert," he said out of the side of his mouth, leaning down so only she would hear. "These media people don't know I'm—we're—ask Dorothy to explain."

"Oh, she already has." Finally! Her voice hadn't betrayed her trepidation. Her body hadn't betrayed her desire to leap into his arms and drag him to the floor, much like the scene she'd witnessed. "I just—slipped. So sorry, Cuthbert."

He flashed a smile, gone in a heartbeat as he turned and began going over the script with Richard. The others joined in and she was left alone, standing at the edge of the room, feeling lost and left out. She busied herself pretending interest in the books along the wall. She plucked one out at random and flipped through the pages. It was about some chap named Thomas More.

She raised her head when she heard someone

mention her name.

"—a part for Lisbet?"

"For me?" She slid the book back into its place and joined the group. There was an opening next to Ned, but her better judgment, finally functioning, told her to stand apart from him. She wedged herself in between Richard and George.

"The heroine's sister." Dorothy nodded, flipping pages. "She has a very minor role, but I would feel so bad leaving you out. She's only got a few lines, and the rest of the time just sits there and looks pretty." She gave Lisbet a warm motherly smile. Lisbet's eyes filled with tears. *Oh, ma mère, I miss you so,* she silently sobbed.

"That would be lovely." She sneaked a glance at Ned, his gaze fastened to the blonde woman's bosoms.

"Brooke," she heard someone say, and the woman looked up from her script.

So her name was Brooke. No one had even introduced them. Lisbet didn't feel like introducing herself. For one thing, she felt very plain and inadequate next to this well-built woman who exuded charm and poise. She was the picture of confidence, from her well-articulated voice to her sweeping mannerisms and her perfectly shaped nails. No wonder Ned wanted to act out their next scene straight away.

"But the next scene is me and Anne Neville." Richard wrote with one hand and broke apart a peanut shell with the other.

"Very well, then." Ned gave Brooke's arm a squeeze and strolled out.

Lisbet managed to read her three lines quite well; with Ned out of the room, she maintained a semblance of calmness. She tried to quell her ferocious jealousy by assuring herself that Brooke wasn't a bit interested in Ned, hardly saying another word to him, despite his overt flirting and poorly concealed flattery. But, oh, how Lisbet wished she were playing that heroine's part, falling into his arms, pressing her body to his hard, demanding maleness.

In due time, she told herself. Mayhap Dorothy was right. Ignoring him was certainly working for Brooke. His attentiveness grew in inverse proportion to her aloofness.

Julianna took her aside to tell her how well she'd read her lines, and they made a date to go clothes shopping in the morning. She only wished Julianna's taste matched hers. The girl had rather appalling taste in raiment. Today, in a black and yellow striped blouse and tights, she looked a right bumblebee!

Chapter Eighteen

Brooke was the last to leave that evening, and while Ned walked her to her car, George settled before the telly, and Richard helped Julianna buff her kitchen cabinets.

"You really don't have to do this, Richard," she said, wringing out a sponge. "I just felt the need to do something mundane, in contrast to all the extra-worldly things that have happened to me in the last few weeks."

"No hardship, I enjoy it. 'Tis refreshing to do things for myself for a change." He rubbed a door till it gleamed like a mirror.

"You're quite an artisan."

"Most likely what I would have been if—oh, let's not 'if.' Let's put 'if' out of our vocabulary for the next fifty years." He wrung out his sponge.

"I hate that word myself," she agreed as the phone rang. It was a bloke named Herb LeFranc, Jonathan Garrett's choice of a director. After a nice chat, she told Richard the director's plans. "He's coming over tomorrow and wants to start doing the location shots as soon as possible. He's got another film to shoot in three months."

"So what does this chap know about directing?" Richard polished her utensil drawer, not missing a stroke.

"Dorothy showed me his résumé. He's got an

impressive track record. Directed a few films that did quite well. Did a lot of Shakespeare theater before turning to film directing. Rather flamboyant, she said, and he sounds so over the phone. But sounds creative as anything."

"He'll do, then. I trust her judgment if you do." Richard stood and stretched.

She put the kettle on and motioned for him to sit. "You don't have to kill yourself." She brought out the cups. She also reached for the whiskey bottle she kept in the cupboard and poured herself a neat one. "It's been a long day and I'm knackered. I can sure knock back a few. You really ought to unwind, too. Have a drink."

"I just want to keep busy." He resumed rubbing.

"Isn't all this writing and rewriting and rehearsing exhausting enough? I'm knackered." She eased into her cushioned kitchen chair.

"Nay, I'm most energetic these days. I've got energy to burn I can't even talk about."

But she knew what he meant. Why did she feel guilty? It wasn't like she was deliberately holding out on him.

"Richard, I went through a horrid, hateful divorce, and he was a real scumbag and I haven't been involved with anybody since and—"

"Whoa!" He tossed the sponge into the pail. "Somewhere there was a segue I missed. Or is this a modern ritual, spill your guts at nine p.m. on Thursday? A form of modern confession mayhap?"

She smiled. "No, of course not." He declined again when she offered him some whiskey. "I just thought— sorry, I jumped to a conclusion."

"Jump anywhere you want." He sat across from her, pouring the tea through a strainer. "Carry on," he prompted her.

"I just—thought you might want to know. I'm not just putting you off."

"You explained it well enough that night on the sofa. I took your explanation at face value and, well, there it is."

"Besides, I think you're still hung up on Anne Neville."

"Hung up?" he repeated slowly.

"Stuck on her, smitten, you've still got feelings for her."

"That would be rather futile, wouldn't it?" He cast her a wary glance, his eyes narrowed. "She's been dead five hundred years."

"Not from your perspective. You only left her a few weeks ago."

"She left me. We had a row over another lass and she called it a day. So what's done is done. She must realize that as well. I mean, she must have realized—I mean—oh, blast it. None of this matters. It was five centuries ago. Why are we talking about this?"

"I don't want to get involved with someone who has feelings for someone else," she stated.

He halted his cup midway to his mouth. "That's what's stopping you?"

"It won't be the first time for me. I married a guy who never gave up on his ex. I thought I could change things and make him fall in love with me, but I was mistaken. I wasted ten good years of my life trying. He finally left me, with a house and a stock portfolio, but very little dignity."

"I do not have romantic feelings for Anne Neville, Julianna. We're longtime companions, as an heiress she'd make a fitting wife, although we'd need a dispensation, being cousins, but I never felt that way about little Annie. Even if I had developed romantic feelings, she's in the past. If I can let go of my past, you can certainly let go of yours." He fiddled with a fork.

"This advice from someone who's rewriting history." She gave him a lopsided grin.

"'Tis fiction, Julianna, although I admit I forget now and again. Just a way to enlighten the world and entertain it at the same time. The events in this film won't change what happened. The only way to do that would be to travel backwards in time and live it over again. And we now know that's impossible. Lisbet explained it all to us. She can't go back, none of us can ever go back."

"You don't know that. You only have the word of that silly wizard. What does he know?" She needed ice in that drink, but didn't want to move.

"He knew enough to be able to send us here. And unless we get a visitor from the far future who knows how to manipulate quantum physics, I somehow doubt I'll be able to procure passage back to the fifteenth century."

"But if you get the chance to go back, will you?" She drained the glass without looking at him.

"Not if I have anything—or anyone—to leave behind here."

She stared into her empty glass next to her full teacup, but felt his eyes blazing into her. Not wanting any tea, she poured herself another neat whiskey. It started to talk for her.

"I don't want you to leave. Ever." The whiskey said what she'd been afraid to admit. It said it all for her. "I'm so selfish. It's not in your best interest. But that's how I feel. That should be enough to scare you away."

"Are you one of those sincere drunks?" He drew his chair close to hers. "Or one of those gobshite drunks?"

She started laughing and knew she looked ridiculous. But it felt good to laugh, so she went with it. If sober, she never would have cracked a smile. "What do you think?"

"I trust you're being sincere, as always. I admire anyone who can admit to being selfish and acting in their own interests. I admire anyone who can rattle off their faults and shortcomings so."

"You might admire it, but—*hic*—could you fall in love with it?"

"We're all selfish, my dear." He glimpsed his reflection in a silver knife. "We human beings love each other despite what we are more than because of it."

"But love is putting someone else's needs before your own," she argued.

"Just because you don't want me to leave doesn't mean you would physically stop me."

She nodded. He was right. "Right. You're right. I wouldn't try to hold you back. But I don't want you to go, ever," she pleaded. "I want you to stay here. With me. For the rest of my life."

"Mayhap we could compromise," he offered. "If it ever came to it. But it won't. We're talking sillybuggers now."

"Compromise how?" She hiccuped again and poured herself another glass.

"You could come with me." He placed his elbows on the table.

"Oh, God!" She shook her head. A strand of hair flew into her mouth. "Me in the fifteenth century? With no indoor plumbing? No modern medicine? No *Star Trek*?"

"Everything's a tradeoff."

She thought about that and looked into the eyes that she knew had been trying to capture hers. They clasped hands over the table. She knocked over the whiskey bottle and he caught it just in time.

"Shall we go together?" he asked softly.

"Oh, I don't know, Richard." She suppressed a shudder. "The fifteenth century's such a dirty, smelly, dangerous place—"

"I meant upstairs."

"Oh." Now she needed that good strong tea. She took a mouthful. "Let's go outside instead. I know a lovely spot just beyond the garden."

They went out the kitchen door and walked arm and arm toward her garden gate. She led him to a narrow stream where she loved to sit anytime during the day or night. It was so peaceful here, with the gurgling water providing a soft backdrop. As they sat on the grass, she heard something. It sounded like a woman laughing. Before she could register another thought, two figures emerged from the shadows.

Richard halted in his tracks. "Ned—Cuthbert— what the hell—"

"Oh, sorry, Ri—"

"God's foot, how long have you been out here?"

Richard screwed up his face as if he smelled burning rubber.

Ned and Brooke stumbled up to them, trousers and shirts and blouses and shoes bundled up in their arms. A bunch of crumpled candy wrappers fell to the ground.

"Uh—we were just rehearsing some more." Ned reached round and plucked a twig off his backside.

"Glad to see you no longer need the script, then," Richard commented, dismissing them with a casual nod as he took Julianna into his arms.

****

After breakfast the following morn, Lisbet settled in to apply her makeup. She was getting quite proficient at stroking the right amount of shadow on her lids, unclumping her mascara and blotting her lipstick.

Dorothy called up for her to hurry; they were gathering at Julianna's again for another reading of their parts. She'd spent nearly the entire previous night reading, but not the script. She'd devoured all the relationship books Dorothy had piled on her nightstand, and in summary she realized they all said the same thing: do exactly the opposite of what she'd been doing. She now realized that silly wizard was full of wind and piss. She'd have to win Ned on her own power. But, oh, how she adored hurling herself into his arms and bringing his lips to hers. Even sneaking up to his window had been impulsive and romantic. But no more of that. She wouldn't give him the time of day if she was carrying Big Ben on her back.

Her heart leapt at the thought of seeing him again, but acting aloof—and acting it would be. More painful would be sitting quietly like a professional when he read his lines with that woman, and writhing out all their love scenes. This was going to be the true test of her acting ability. But she wanted so badly to be part of this production. The films Dorothy had shown her on telly entranced her; she was enchanted with the idea of moving, talking pictures, and was thrilled to be a part of it.

"You've got to be poised," Dorothy advised in the Jeep on the way to Julianna's. "That's the word. Poised. Keep that word in your mind at all times, even if you have to write it on every page of the script. When you look at him, think poised. When he talks to you, think poised."

"How about after I get him where I want him and he's mine, God willing?"

Dorothy took her hand off the long skinny handle and squeezed Lisbet's arm. "Then you can jump him whenever you want."

After lunch, of which Lisbet couldn't eat a bite in his presence, they stood about in Julianna's garden and read their parts. When they got to Ned and Brooke's love scene again, Lisbet excused herself and stayed in the lounge until it was over. But she made sure she exited—and re-entered—with poise.

In her only scene with Richard, they discussed the Battle of Barnet. "And did the Yorkists emerge with much poise—er—" she sputtered and stammered and lost her place in the script. Then she dropped it and retrieved it, only to spill tea on it.

Richard suggested they start at the top. Poise was embedded in her brain. But Ned was embedded in his leading lady's bosom. She turned away, only to catch George regarding her with deep compassion softening his eyes. He understood. He knew his brother. How he detected her despair, she didn't know. But the smile they exchanged was one of mutual understanding and secrecy.

After they rehearsed and dispersed to head for the pub, George took Lisbet aside. "Any time you want to talk out your pain, just come to me. I know him better than anybody."

"But how did you know—" She threw a glance in Ned's direction, knowing she didn't need to complete the unspoken thought.

"The very flies on the walls must know. You're deeply enamored of Ned, and he's fawning all over that buxom varlet. But fret not, my dear. 'Tis simply not your time yet."

"When will be our time?" Mayhap he was prophetic, as well as wise beyond his years, which he'd exhibited whilst reciting his poetry, rich with profound insight only one with a fierce passion for living could convey. If anyone could tell her what the cosmos had in store for her and Ned, it was George.

"I know not exactly. But he's not unaware of your beauty. I saw that spark in his eyes when he beheld you. He'll soon tire of the actress wench. She's a ball of fluff. But you—you're as solid as the earth on which we stand."

"What do I do in the meantime?" she had to whisper, as they'd now joined the others, busy deciding who would ride with whom to the pub. She wondered if he'd have even more sage advice than Dorothy's and in those books of rules, which to her were rather pedantic. Who wanted a textbook romance?

"Meantime? Knowing Ned? First, let me get to know you better. Let us talk and read and mayhap even dance together. He's not ready for you at present, and I can share your burden whilst you await him to come to his senses."

"But George, I don't want to use you to make him jealous."

"You won't be using me. I'll savor every second in your company." He took her hand and kissed it so swiftly and discreetly, no one even knew they'd exchanged a word.

She rode to the pub with Dorothy and Julianna, but contained her thoughts, not exchanging any words with them. George was by far the scholar of that family. His intelligence surpassed Ned's by bounds. He had not Ned's commanding presence or captivating charm, but a more subdued charisma that took some probing to unearth under that bawdy exterior. His tongue was of the purest silver, and even more genuine. When Ned flattered, she melted, yet inside she knew 'twasn't coming from his heart, but his head—and which one, she didn't want to guess. When George spoke, he'd already formed the words carefully and lovingly in his heart. She liked him. She could never love George, but she liked him. It was Ned she loved. Yet she could never like him.

As the group took their seats around the long table in the pub, it was George who held out her chair and sat next to her. They spent the entire meal engaged in conversation about their journeys here, the emotional upheaval the decision had caused, and lighter fare, like poetry and music. Her eyes barely left his all evening, except to glance over at Ned, who was gaping at George, a mixture of bewilderment, respect, and a pinch of resentment flustering his features. *A-ha. There it is*. She slung him the most impassive of smiles and went back to discussing Chaucer.

"You and George looked mighty cozy," Dorothy commented as Lisbet brought down the pile of books later that night. "Looks like you were having the most intense of discussions."

"He's so dear." She replaced the books on the shelf. "He understands me. And he understands Ned."

"Ah, when you find that combination in one person, you've got a friend for life." Dorothy held up her brandy glass and saluted her.

"But you'll always be my closest lady confidante," she assured her combination landlady, advisor and friend. "I fear I can never discuss certain things with George."

"Of course not. But seeing you huddled at the end of the table with me won't ever turn Ned's blood green!"

Chapter Nineteen

The casting was finally done. They all sat around Julianna's fire on a cool crisp autumn evening sipping hot cider.

"Where is he? He should've been here half an hour ago," complained Jonathan of their director, Herb LaFranc, as he glanced at his watch.

"He likes to arrive fashionably late," Brooke replied, not looking up from her nail filing. "I know him, he's positively brilliant, but not the most reliable chap."

"Well, I hope so; when you think of what this is costing—"

The doorbell shut Jonathan up. He nodded in relief and took to his lager and cider.

Julianna opened the door to not one, but three, standing at her doorstep, dressed exactly alike, in matching fur-trimmed parkas, snow boots, and leather gloves—and it was only October!

"Evening, darlings, hope we're not too late, had to pitstop along the way, you know how it is when you've got youngsters!" He burst in, followed by two grinning, gurgling chimpanzees who headed straight for the telly, removed their coats and plopped themselves on the floor crosslegged.

"Bubble and Squeak won't be any trouble, I assure you." Herb tossed his parka over the sofa back and peeled off the gloves. "I brought all their goodies, a jar of Horlick's, a tin of chocolate bickies, and their favorite cherry lollies, so you won't hear a peep out of them, maybe just a slurp. Toss them the remote and they'll be quiet as mice."

"Hello, Herb. Hello Bubble and Squeak. I trust they're trained."

"Better than some people, ducky." He stared her down.

Julianna motioned for him to sit, but first he made the rounds, shaking hands with everyone in the room, kissing the women's hands. The women, as always, seemed happier to see him than the men. Maybe it was in the greeting.

"So how do you like your Henry Tudor, Johnny? Doesn't he just make you weep with pathos?" Herb sat, slipped off his shoes, and crossed his legs. His socks had toes.

"He's perfect for the part," Jonathan replied. "I wouldn't have auditioned anyone else."

The chap playing Tudor was an actor named Crispin Q. Walther II. Richard had requested someone outrageously ugly, but Herb explained that they could make him ugly easily enough; they were going for acting ability first. "Uglifying an actor is nothing. Look at the job they did on Olivier in *Richard the Third*."

"Oh, yes, of course." Richard nodded, agreeing wholeheartedly. So Crispin'd spend an extra few hours in the makeup chair every morning getting uglied up.

****

The first few weeks of shooting went rather well—for the most part.

"Cut!" Herb yelled into a gold-plated megaphone

emblazoned with his initials. "Tea time!"

Richard strode off the set, resplendent in his fifteenth-century raiment. He took Julianna's hand and she bobbed a curtsey. "Oh, you are truly a king," she sighed as they headed for the trailers.

"Shall we lunch at the Hare 'n Hounds?" He entered his trailer and retrieved his new wallet, sufficiently stocked with modern British sterling. She'd sold some of the gold Ned had given her and disbursed the proceeds among them.

"We should change out of these costumes, Richard. These skirts are so cumbersome." Once again, she'd nearly tripped over the voluminous velvet skirts sweeping up the castle grounds. "Not to mention hot as hell."

"You may change. I prefer this raiment."

They left the grounds of the stately old Caernarvon Castle and headed up the high street to the pub.

Richard stroked his velvet rolled-brim hat sporting a long ostrich feather. "I prefer walking around like this. I feel right at home."

As they walked, they passed a small group of camera-wielding tourists. Richard halted and posed so one of them could snap his picture. "Oh, if only they knew who you really were," Julianna leaned over and whispered in his ear as they parted company with the still-gaping, marveling tourists.

"The world's loss, is it not? However, purely their own fault." He straightened his doublet as they walked.

Once again she held her skirts up, amazed that women's gowns in those days didn't turn brown after one wearing. "I'll never get used to people stopping us on the street. It makes me feel like a movie star. The production's going great so far, isn't it?" she asked as they approached the pub entrance and he stepped aside to let her pass.

"Swimmingly, except for those few mishaps."

"Oh, well, every project has its goofs and its gaffes. As long as nobody gets seriously hurt." The pub's warmth enveloped her.

"But 'twas one thing after another for a spell." They sat at a small table in the darkened pub and browsed the menu board above the bar. "George flubbed his lines, that entire prop came crashing down, the camera ceased to function—'twas as if it were jinxed."

She tried to remember just what scene they were shooting when it all went wrong.

"What do you fancy?" he asked.

"Hey? Oh, uh—pie and chips and a pint is fine," she replied distractedly.

As he went to the bar to order, she went over the scenes of those few days in her mind. Henry Tudor's mother Margaret Beaufort was spying for her pretender son, gathering intelligence as well as an army to oust Richard from England's throne and put her Henry there. Richard performed the scenes with a sincerity she'd only seen in seasoned, gifted actors. She knew it was because there was very little acting involved and these were his true emotions coming through. She shook her head and pressed her thumbs to her temples as she did every time she began thinking too deeply about the events of the last few months, the astonishing potency of the universe, and how her life changed forever. Richard brought her pint over, and not a second too soon. She took a generous gulp as soon as he handed it to her.

"Oh, I needed that," she groaned as he sat next to her with his pint of ale.

"Why? Are you expecting another volley of mishaps?"

"I hope not. But we can't rule it out. Remember what you said about there being more dead people than live ones who'd like to do you in?" She took another indulgent sip.

"It occupies a great deal of my time, waking and sleeping."

"I just remembered," she said. "The days when everything went wrong, we were shooting the Margaret Beaufort scenes."

"I thought I'd had my invisible adversary narrowed down to Tudor if anybody."

She shook her head and hastened on. "Then I thought of the times my poltergeist Galahad acted up since you've been here, breaking things in my house, blowing all those papers around, tripping Ned in front of Brooke."

"But that one backfired, as he fell straight into her arms and took great advantage of the pratfall, the prat." He chuckled.

"Yeah, but this can't be coincidence." She took another welcome swig of lager. "I think I have my prime suspect in place now, and it's not anybody as obvious as Tudor. Although he was the most obvious suspect, I can pretty much rule him out."

"Then you think it's his shard-borne mother?" He studied the menu.

Before she had a chance to answer, Richard began squirming in his seat, not noticeably at first, but soon he was fidgeting like his chausses were crawling with fire ants.

"Richard, what is it?"

"I've—" he grimaced, took a furtive glance around, then started thrashing about as he groaned in exasperation. "I must see a man about a dog—or a pack of wolves—be right back!" He dropped the menu and dashed toward the men's room.

"What was that all about?" she muttered to herself as she took another swig of lager. She hoped it wasn't serious, with more members of the cast and crew beginning to fill the pub. She didn't want them to see their star wriggling his bum in his seat all through lunch.

When he returned, he looked noticeably relieved. "I'm still apprehensive that I'll suffer that discomfort again before too long."

"Richard, what was it? You sit on something?" She leaned forward.

"Nay, just—" He nearly drained the entire pint. "I cannot talk about it."

"You can tell me. Are you in pain?"

"Not anymore." He shook his head and took up the menu.

"Well, what is it?"

"'Tis nothing, Julianna, may we just put a lid on it, as you say?"

She wondered if it was another of those mishaps. Might Margaret Beaufort be up to her pranks? What had they said to rile her so, if indeed it was Margaret Beaufort whom she'd dubbed Galahad ten years ago? "Did we say something to cheese Margaret Beaufort off?"

"I didn't say aught about the pr—oh, no. I shan't say another word. I don't want to go through that again." He held up his hand. "I'll have fish and chips."

"What again?"

His lips compressed into a pencil-thin line. "'Tis a male affliction. But I trust it's fixed."

"She pinched you or something?"

"Very well, I'll level with you. A wire brush with extra firm bristles would have been a welcome accessory." He grimaced.

"She made you itch down there?" Julianna plucked up her pint glass and pressed it to her lips to keep him from seeing her laugh. A dose of itchy balls, what would the old harpy think of next? "I remember now, you'd called her a name. And it happens every time. In my house, on the set, now here. We've just got to be very careful how we treat her. Maybe we'd better change the script a bit."

"Alter history to suit the whims of an old cod—ugh, God's truth, there I go again! Please—you must stop me in time lest she wreak havoc upon my nether region at an even more mortifying moment." He glanced around the now-crowded pub.

"Sorry, Richard. But maybe we should change things to suit her. If she's an angry poltergeist, this could be just the beginning. She can sabotage the whole production. We'd better appease her."

"'Twill muck up the entire storyline. Nay, I refuse." His fist slammed down on the table. As if aimed, his pint glass pitched forward, throwing a generous splash of ale into his face. "Damnation!"

She fished out a tissue and handed it to him. "I think we'd better give that script another going-over, unless you want to be up to your crotch in cornstarch for the next two months. Try explaining the reason for that to the urologist."

That night, when Julianna and the three brothers were alone sipping brandies by her fire, she voiced her suspicions. "I've had a poltergeist in this house since the day I moved in. I named him Galahad, and he pulled silly pranks, like hiding things and turning my radio on. But I believe Richard and I have just come to a logical conclusion."

"Poltergeist?" Ned looked around and gave a little jump. "Hey, he pinched my bum! So he's that kind of poltergeist. You think he'd go after that director woufter."

She could tell Ned wasn't serious by the way his eyes twinkled. After Richard's calamity in the pub, she wasn't up to joking about it. But she didn't mention it out loud. Richard would have died of mortification, even in front of his brothers. "Actually, it's a she, Ned. And I think I know who she is."

"A she, hmm?" Ned cocked a brow. "Send her to my room, I've never tumbled a ghost before."

"For once it wouldn't matter if she looks like a warthog, Ned," George said.

"I don't think so," Julianna replied as Richard refilled their glasses. "She's Margaret Beaufort."

"Why would she haunt us?" Ned asked.

"Why wouldn't she? We're not making too flattering a portrayal of her or her son," she said.

"Mayhap that's what she's getting so ugly about," Richard said. "She wants to see her Taffy son on my throne, not run through the culls with my sword, which I don't even care enough to keep afterward, but cast off to a Shoreditch cook-maid to slaughter hogs."

"The actress portraying her seems to fare well enough," Ned said. "Has any unfortunate accident befallen her?"

"Not that I know of," Julianna replied, "but it's not the actress she's got a grudge against. It's the creators. Us. I'm just afraid she's going to ruin the whole thing, or even worse, it'll premiere and flop and be a financial disaster and an artistic embarrassment."

"I've already made up my mind I'm going to appease her." Richard took his script from his folder. He started scribbling notes.

"Oh, come on, you two, you can't believe that drivel. Minor mishaps take place all the time. The idea that it's her ghost is preposterous." Ned twirled his glass, shaking his head. "Sounds like the kind of drivel Brooke spews forth."

Richard stared at his brother. That unwavering look always unnerved everyone but Ned. "I have irrefutable, indisputable, undeniable proof of which I care not to divulge any detail, Ned."

"Why, Dickon? She make your tarriwags itch?" George helped himself to a refill. As he shot George the same deadly glance, George's face shrank behind his personalized extra-large snifter.

"Instead of hurling Taffy Harry into the dungeon, I'm bringing him to court." His eyes narrowed into semi-sinister slits.

"To court?" they all sang in unison.

"Aye." Richard nodded as he wrote. "And giving him quite a prominent position there."

"I'm afraid to ask which position," Julianna said. "I don't want my house to blow away and wind up in Oz.

I just hope you know what you're doing," she warned him.

"His mother Lady Beaufort will be quite flattered. Compared to what he deserves, this is overly generous."

"Your calling her a lady is overly generous," she remarked as they shared a smile.

****

Late that night Julianna tiptoed downstairs and sneaked a peek into his folder. He'd brought Tudor to court, all right—as the king's private fool. She took a cautious look around. Nothing had flown off the shelves, the rug wasn't folded back ready to trip someone, and her door wasn't flapping open. Whew! She let out a relieved whistle. Maybe Margaret Beaufort's spirit was flattered—after all, in real life, she'd been at Richard's court for a while. And she did love her fool son to pieces.

Julianna heaved a relieved sigh and went back to her room—then on second thought, slipped into the room where Richard slept. They were all too tired for recreation lately except Ned. Besides the regular romps with his leading lady, he'd slipped off the set with two extras and the court washerwoman.

****

Julianna's cell phone ring tone of "Now is the Winter of Our Discontent" from the 1995 Ian McKellen movie *Richard III* jarred her awake the next morning.

"It's time to go public, Jules!" Brooke's chirpy voice pierced her eardrum.

"What?" she mumbled, glancing at the clock. "At seven in the morning? Can't you wait until normal business hours like a normal person? I'll be groggy for the next two hours."

"I didn't get where I am by letting grass grow under my feet. This coming week I'm devoting every episode of *The Royal Issue* to coverage of the filming. I want you and Richard at the studio tomorrow at nine for interviews."

Julianna emerged from her fuzzy state, pushed hair from her eyes and yawned. "Oh, sorry, but I'm really beat. I shouldn't need to ask you this, but you haven't uttered a syllable about who you believe Richard really is, have you? I know what you've done in the past to get ratings."

"Of course not, even I know better than that. Being a ratings hound is one thing, being branded a nut is another. No, the public is nowhere near ready to hear the truth about our Richard. The film's going public, not our secret. So don't lose any sleep over it."

"Good. See you tomorrow." Her mind at ease, she did what Brooke told her to do—she rolled over and went back to sleep.

****

George escorted Lisbet off the set at the end of a long day's shooting. Tired as she was, she wanted to hear more of his improvised poetry. It relaxed her after being in such an emotionally charged atmosphere. Not to mention Ned's scenes with his heroine, which she knew he must purposely flub in order to shoot retake after retake—especially the ones where he gives her a tumble.

But Brooke didn't seem to mind. After each scene, she simply dusted herself off, adjusted her chemise, and glided off the set to her dressing room, leaving Ned glancing round to make sure everyone had seen their expertly choreographed tumble.

"Shall we stroll down to the waterfront?" George suggested as they left the castle grounds. Lisbet held on to him for fear of falling in the high-heeled footwear she was determined to master.

"Sounds lovely, George. 'Tis such a clear, crisp eve." She gazed up at the stars appearing one by one. "Will you recite me a poem about the heavens?"

His eyes swept across the heavens. "Its infinite vastness perplexes me. I never know where to begin or where to end."

Aware that someone was watching them, she glanced over her shoulder to see Ned atop one of the castle ramparts, resting on his elbows. He gave a casual wave. "Ned's watching us," she commented as they crossed the street and headed for the quay.

"He's been watching us for the last six weeks. Haven't you noticed?" George looked ahead and gave his brother a wave, which he didn't return.

"Of course. But I have enough diversions. I'm too busy marveling at all the enormous machines that make this production possible. It overwhelms me at times." She smiled up at Ned, knowing he was too far to see her face. "But I derive a smug satisfaction knowing he's showing some interest. Especially since Brooke has been spending her spare moments with that Tudor chap."

"Ah, yes." George snickered, taking a swig from his flask. "Crispin is a gifted actor indeed. He certainly ruffles Richard's feathers when they do a scene together. Crispin and Brooke go quite well together, do they not? I'd suggest they work a romance between those two into the script, but I reckon history's been tweaked enough. Seems all their chemistry's off the set.

It may not be magic at all before the cameras."

"Do you think this bothers Ned?" she asked.

"Not much at all bothers Ned. But I believe it's just a matter of time before he begins wooing you. Now that his heroine's attentions have turned elsewhere, he's bound to appreciate the subtle loveliness that's been before him all this while." He offered her a sip from his flask as they walked along the sea wall.

"Nay, I shall do something silly. Even mead has had some sillying effects on me." She let out a delighted giggle.

"Nonsense, you're no doubt even more of a delight with a tipple in your tum." He smiled down at her.

"Oh, George, cease." She playfully slapped his doublet. Just then she stumbled backwards and would have tumbled into the sea hadn't he caught her just in time.

"I've got you, I've got you!" He pulled her to her feet, his hands firmly clamped to hers.

She leaned against him, panting with fright; she could have been swept away under those crashing waves. "'Tis all right, my dear. Just a little slip. You must get a pair of those trainers they're all wearing. Just wear something less slippery on your feet in future."

She finally pulled away, realizing he'd been holding her a tad too tightly—or was he simply trying to protect her? "George—we should take our leave and return to the hotel. The others must be wondering where we are."

"Any one of the 'others' in particular?" He gripped her arm to further steady her and held her fast as they retraced their steps.

The commanding figure stepped directly in their

path. The darkness obscured his features. Yet the golden head glowed.

"As I live and breathe. Why, Ned, we were just talking about you, and how you seem to be everywhere," George commented.

"Ah, just going for a stroll." Ned's airy tone floated toward them. She reckoned he was forcing nonchalance into his voice. Her heart tumbled over a thrill. *Does that mean he's beginning to care?* she begged the great unknown.

"What an amazing coincidence," George observed, and she knew he didn't believe a breath of it. "Did your heroine and Henry Tudor abscond back to France to plan the final invasion? I suppose France is a bit far for you to tail them."

Ned didn't give his brother another glance. His eyes fixed on Lisbet. She looked up at him, trying to discern the amount of interest he harbored. But she didn't try to hold back her satisfied grin.

"I walk out this way quite often. I wouldn't have escorted a lady out here and let her nearly tumble into the vastness of the sea. You clumsy ox." He threw another glance at George, who licked the drops off his flask's mouthpiece.

"Oh, no, 'twas entirely my fault. I'm the clumsy one!" Lisbet insisted.

"I was just about to take my evening repast. Would you care to join us, George?" Ned asked, holding Lisbet's gaze.

"Us?" George looked round.

"Myself and Lisbet." Ned held out his arm to her. She glanced at George and splayed her hands. He gave a quick wink and a nod, as if to say, 'You got him!' She took Ned's arm and her entire body warmed at the physical contact. The rising wind now felt like the most soothing summer breeze.

"I shall vanish, then." George turned to leave.

"Nay, George, do join us." Badly as she wanted Ned all to herself, she felt terrible leaving George alone like this.

"I wouldn't dream of it!" He gave an emphatic shake of his head. He vanished before either of them had a chance to say good night.

She looked up at those heavenly eyes into which she could see eternity. He returned her gaze with that same covetous sparkle she saw him give his fictional heroine—and there wasn't a script in sight! Was it possible—finally?

Smile met smile and he bent down to touch his lips to hers. Her knees wobbled, her balance nearly left her, and this time she didn't care if she slipped into the sea.

George headed for the pub, his heart a bit lighter now that he knew Lisbet was finally where she belonged—with her beloved. Now all she had to do was keep him interested, a feat no woman had ever managed to accomplish. Now that his work was done, he looked forward to a good strong pint.

He noticed a figure sitting huddled on the pier, looking forlorn and empty, so small against the vastness of the sea beyond. If it was a film crew member, George would be happy to invite him for a pint and a round of darts. But as he approached more closely, he could see the figure was a woman's. Her long blonde hair tumbled over her shoulders, shielding her face from view. As he saw the glint of an earring and the bit of stocking top showing, he knew who it was. Why, it was the star of the show, the last person he thought would ever spend a moment alone like this, looking like her adoring world had abandoned her.

"Brooke," he called out softly and sat by her, holding out his hand to clasp hers. It was like ice. He swept off his jacket and draped it round her shoulders. She looked up at him, a different person without all the paint covering her eyelids, cheeks and lips.

"Ta for the jacket. Although I wasn't really feeling the cold. I'm a bit numb at the moment."

"Is anything wrong? Are you ill?"

She shook her head, inching closer.

He leaned forward, wrapping his arm about her shoulders. "Just wondering where I went wrong—again."

"Wrong? How?" How could she do anything wrong? "You're the picture of perfection, in every line you speak, every emotion you bring forth before those cameras, every movement in the love scenes under the glaring lights."

She heaved a sigh. "Crispin and I had a falling out. He told me it's best we just work together on the set; we weren't meant to have anything more than a working relationship. He said in his theatrical way that he can't stand my guts."

"Bosh. You're a beautiful, desirable woman."

"Apparently it's not enough for him. Said I was too egotistical. Always vying for attention, the limelight, the main event. Little did he realize he was describing himself, the conceited oaf!"

"That does happen at times." George offered her his flask, which she took and drained. "When two heads butt a bit too forcefully, no one wins. I've seen it before. It's a simple scientific principle. For every reaction there's a reaction. You can't have two actions heading for each other with no resistance; they'll collide, and quite violently."

"You're right, we're too much alike. But I thought we had a real chemistry going there. And he's a movie star. Just what I'm looking for. But I never seem to click with actors. Why don't I ever learn?" She gazed up at him as if searching his eyes for the definitive answer.

"Have you ever been attracted to a man with a bit less drive, less push to succeed and be the best?" he asked.

She shook her head. "Nah. I didn't think that type would interest me."

"Would you be willing to try it—just once?"

She regarded him as if she'd never seen him before, then a slow smile lit up her face. As if she was becoming more intrigued by the second. "With a guy who's got no drive, no ambition, couldn't care less if he walks in my shadow, with hardly any ego?"

"Try no ego."

"But guys like that don't go for feisty women, who take total charge of their destiny."

"Ah—well, I do. I'd like to be with a woman who's in charge of her destiny. I'd like to be with a woman in charge of my destiny. I've floated through life, all the way through—and I've enjoyed it. If there's a fork in the road, I turn round and go back the way I came. 'Tis easier than deciding which road to take. There's a certain enchantment to seizing the moment and living it as if it will last forever." The wind blew hair into his face and he pushed it back. "That's what my life has been—one long, continuous moment. I don't even think in terms of months or years. I've never owned a calendar. A clock is as far as I'll go. Twelve hours ahead is even too far to contemplate. But to have a year mapped out before me"—he shuddered—"gives me the willies."

She laughed and leaned into him, nestling her head on his shoulder. "I need to be more like you. Seizing the moment." She squeezed his arm. "I like that. I've heard 'seize the day' but 'seize the moment' is so much more intense, so much more passionate—like it might end any second, so go for it!"

"Shall we?"

She looked up. "Shall we what?"

"Go for it. I can give you a moment if you wish." He tipped her face toward his with his fingertip. "A long, languorous moment that might even seem like hours. Mayhap if we're lucky it will be hours. I like to live my moments so that they seem longer."

"You've a way with words, Willy." The wind carried her words away.

He leaned over and whispered in her ear, "Why don't you call me George?"

"George? Is that your middle name?"

"Nay, I just like it. Sounds stronger than Willy. I'm really not a Willy, am I?" His look dared her to say yes.

"No, I'd say you're a George, if anything."

He helped her to her feet and they headed back toward land. "George. Yes, definitely. I hope I don't slip and shout out Willy in the throes of passion."

"Shout out anything you like. As long as it's not Crispin."

****

"I'm in love, Dorothy, I'm madly and passionately in love!" Lisbet burst into the kitchen. "He looked at me, he took my hand, he kissed me!"

This was enough to make Dorothy halt her scone-mixing. "You are talking about Ned, I trust?" She wiped her hands on a tea towel.

"Of course! Who else? The reason I'm here, the reason I traveled five hundred years, the reason I breathe!"

"What happened?" She banged the spoon on the side of the bowl.

"George did it."

"Ah, George the eloquent, with his silver-laced tongue. Did he recite a sonnet about you that captured Ned's fancy?"

"Nay, not a word." She flitted around the kitchen. "He simply showed interest in me, and I daresay it wasn't all acting, either."

"I can't see why any man wouldn't be interested in you. You're a lovely lass. So, where did you and Ned leave things? Has he pledged anything? Or shown you anything besides this sudden interest?"

Lisbet's cheeks burned. "Well, what he wanted to show me would have put our relationship on another level altogether. Suffice it to say I saw enough of it whilst glimpsing him in the crystal ball."

"Oh, that." Dorothy nodded. "A word of caution, Lisbet. Ned is a fast worker. You know that book that says men are from Mars? Well, Ned's from a galaxy all his own, with a rocketship that's faster than the speed of light. Don't let him offer you a ride on it until you're ready. And I trust you understand the space-age metaphor."

"I'm not a mere lass, Dorothy. I've been married. I can keep up with Ned, don't worry about me."

"Care for some scones and tea? I'm making your favorite, banana and currant." She resumed her mixing.

"Nay, Dorothy. I need to watch my waistline." She skittered off and drew a bath, dumping in all the sweet-fragranced salts, gels, beads and oils she had. Ned had commented on how sweet she smelled—and she hadn't even used her feminine wipes today!

****

Julianna and Richard sparred in a late-night game of chess when a pair of headlights shone into her front window. A moment later Ned let himself in.

"The pumpkin coach is a bit late this eve, is it not, King Charming? And where did you dump Cinderella?" Richard asked without looking up.

"'Twas a taxi, and my Cinderella is safe at home," he replied, already tearing into a protein bar.

"Did you and Brooke have a nice evening?" Julianna swiped Richard's remaining rook.

"I had a wonderful evening. I know not if Brooke did. 'Twasn't she I was with." He bit and chewed.

"Who was it this time?" Richard moved his queen to the other side of the board. Julianna wasn't sure if his brother's escapades truly intrigued him, or he was just making conversation. He maintained that deadpan quality no matter what his level of interest. "Or do you prefer not to reveal the participants' names?"

Ned chuckled, popping the last bite into his mouth. "'Twas only one partner this eve. I agree with you, I must curb my excesses lest I pop my clogs even younger than I did in our alternate destiny."

"So who did you see tonight, Ned?" Now Julianna

was curious. Who hadn't he been with from that cast, including extras?

"Lisbet."

"Lisbet?" Both Richard and Julianna said in unison.

Richard finally looked up. "She's been here nigh on two months now. What took you so long?"

"I didn't tell you, but she'd pursued me relentlessly when she first arrived. Wasn't exactly subtle about it, either. Made me wonder if she'd traveled through time just to follow me." He raised his head, licked a forefinger, and drew it over his brow.

"There he goes, on his cuckoo cloud again," Richard muttered. "Bring a brolly this time, Ned, the cloud's about to burst."

"Nay, really. She crept 'neath my privy window one eve, threw herself at me, nearly ransacked me on another occasion, blurted that she loved me madly, and gazed at me with the longing of a star-crossed damsel out of a Greek tragedy."

"And what finally drew you to her?"

Ned peeled off another protein bar wrapper, looked up and paused. "She stopped," he stated simply.

"What about Brooke?" Julianna asked. "I thought you two were setting off sparks."

"The occasional spark still flies." He sat on her sofa and stretched his legs on her hassock. "But our liaisons are purely recreational. I thought it time to set my sights farther afield."

"Aye. Since Brooke started cavorting with Crispin," Richard remarked as Julianna's pieces chased his queen around the board.

"I believe Crispin got the boot this eve," Ned said.

"How do you know?" Richard moved his queen out of her way.

"Someone new has struck her fancy, by the looks of things. And I was the one doing the looking, so I know. Someone handsome and charming and far more suitable than that affected screen siren."

"Who?" Richard looked up just as Julianna swiped his queen with her rook.

"I'll give you a hint. He's related to me. And 'tis not you, before you ask."

"George? George managed to snag Brooke?" Julianna's eyes widened in wonder. "I've seen Brooke give George the come-hither many times, and he simply smiled it off, more interested in what was in his silver-plated flask."

"They came into the pub, where Lisbet and I had our evening meal. They stopped by to say hello, then huddled in the corner like two vines twined round each other. George said not to wait up for him. Not that I would have anyway." He licked chocolate from his fingers slowly and sensuously, like he was enjoying that as much as the bar itself.

"What happened to Crispin?"

He waved a hand. "Oh, he was at the other end of the pub, entertaining the lasses that play that bevy of maids in the film. 'Twas George our star was wrapped round. Like a ribbon round a present."

Richard shook his head as Julianna announced checkmate. He said, "I don't know where you two rakes get it from. Certes not from the Plantagenet side."

"Wherever it came from, you weren't there to catch any of it, lad." Ned leaned his head against the sofa back.

Julianna was thankful for that. She could never tolerate someone with such a wild streak in him. Richard was perfect for her—yet something still tugged at her heart. He could be whisked backwards as fast as he'd come here. Once again, she pushed the haunting thought out of her mind.

She poured each of them a nightcap and sat on Richard's lap in her easy chair.

"I know it's rather late to talk about anything serious, but I have a feeling I know who ratted on us to the media and got Brooke pounding on the door with her cameraman in tow," she said.

"Another of your poltergeists?" Ned set down his brandy. For all his wild ways, he wasn't much of a drinker.

"No, actually the same one," Julianna replied.

"Margaret Beaufort?" Richard twined her fingers with his.

"Who else? She's been trying to sabotage this thing from day one. She must've tipped Brooke off."

"How?" Richard's eyes widened. "I didn't know ghosts had Internet access."

"She could've dropped her an anonymous note. A phone call, maybe. Ghosts have been known to make phone calls. One of Brooke's shows featured a ghost who haunted a boat, and she always contacted people by phone, no other way."

"Why don't we just ask her? She knows us well enough to divulge her sources. Or has she already, Ned, in one of your passion-induced sessions?" Richard asked.

"We never discussed it. Never discussed much of anything, come to think of it. Only the earthy basics, if you know what I mean, Richard—or do you?" Ned displayed his teasing smirk.

Oh, no, she thought. *Another barb-trading match.*

"It matters not how she found out. It's worked for the better, hasn't it?" Richard stretched his arms over his head. "She's a fitting heroine. Not as fitting as you would have been, but I'm even happier having you play my Anne."

He stroked her cheek and a burst of emotions flooded her heart. Was she a substitute for Anne Neville? she wondered once again. And once again, she pushed it aside, determined to live for the here and now.

"I'm all in." Ned yawned as he stood. "You lovebirds carry on; my pumping station's off for the night." He lumbered out, and as if he'd read her mind, he turned out the light, leaving her and Richard in pale moonlight.

Chapter Twenty

"It's a wrap!" Julianna heard the words she'd anticipated and dreaded at the same time.

Thundering applause surrounded her. The last scene, with Brooke alone on horseback riding off into the proverbial sunset, was over.

The heroine cantered back to the director, dismounted, and hurled herself into his arms. "What a tremendous success!" she sang in her trained broadcaster's voice. "Hollywood, here we come! Dust off your mantel, Herb, an Oscar is a-comin'!"

Julianna sat in her chair, watching all the hoopla around her. She felt detached, like she wasn't there. Somehow she didn't feel like a part of this wrap hysteria. She wished it could have kept going, on and on. She wished the film had been real life and she'd been Anne Neville.

Richard glided over to her, twirling his sword, and asked her something about the caterer for the wrap party, but she'd barely heard him.

She didn't want to go back to the twenty-first century, not just yet.

She wanted them to be Richard and Anne for just a while longer.

Finally she stood, taking him by the arm. "Let's go for a walk. Just for a little while."

"But the party—"

"The party will be going on till the wee hours. You can certainly wait a few minutes to make your grand entrance."

"I like to be prompt." He squared his shoulders and stood at his full height.

"Not to a wrap party, Richard. The thing to do is arrive fashionably late."

"With the most beautiful actress in the film." He hugged her close.

She was really fighting tears now. "Oh, Richard, I didn't want to see it end."

"A week ago you were complaining you were dying to take a few days off because the schedule was killing you. Now you want to do the sequel. Don't you think you should take the few days first?" His smile, so genuine, made her want to cry harder.

"I don't mean shoot a sequel. I mean just being. This whole medieval world, these costumes, the beautiful story—it's just sad, that's all."

"You, who can't live without your e-mails and running water and blow dryers—even getting me using those—want to carry on living in my times?" He shook his head. His hair glinted with blue highlights in the late afternoon sun. "And just as I'm getting used to all this modern garb and grub and learning where not to stick my finger when the switch is on."

They left the set and walked down the road leading to the local pub. Car engines roared all around them as the cast and crew dispersed, to reconvene later at the party in a rented hall.

"It's over, Richard, and things will never be the same."

"Why do you say that? We have the premiere, the

reviews, Brooke's show, the interviews, the publicity— we'll be busier than when we were doing all this writing and shooting." An enthusiasm crept into his voice that she'd heard only a few times before—when he changed Tudor's role in the story and when they'd hired lawyers to draw up contracts. Deep down, Richard was ambitious, caught up in the fame and wealth and acquisition of more of it all. He'd been like this in his own time, too, she knew. Why would he change now?

Still, it troubled her.

"I don't want to be a celebrity, or a movie star, or hounded by cameras and reporters." She tucked her hand in the crook of his arm. "I just want to go back to Yorkshire and live quietly, as an officer of the Richard the Third Society and write my history books. And have you with me."

"Well, that's fine. Who said you can't?" He pulled her closer.

"We can't lead a quiet, private life if we're caught up in all this promo stuff."

"Certainly we can. This won't last forever." He waved a hand at their surroundings. "Then we can retire to our cozy little hamlet and raise lilies. But we must do our bit while we can. I want to make sure the world sees this. This is the closest I can ever come to changing history. I want to make sure my efforts, not to mention yours and everyone else's, weren't for naught. All the adulation will subside soon enough, trust me."

That sounded prophetic. "Then what? Is there something you're not telling me? Something that wizbar chap told you, or cooked up? That sounds ominous."

"No, Julianna, I know as much as you about what the future holds. I'm only going on the principle of making hay whilst the sun shines, going back and correcting past mistakes. Something I didn't do in my first life. Now that I know how that ended. I have the chance to do it right this time, and that's what I'm doing."

"I'm still afraid someone's going to expose you and your brothers as time travelers and make a big mess for all of us." She shivered as the wind blasted past them.

"Who?"

"You never know. George or Ned or even Lisbet might slip to Brooke or some reporter. Another time traveler could expose you. You don't know how many of them are walking around. And of course, there's always the obvious. Margaret Beaufort."

He chuckled. "Ah, yes, Maggs. She's quite appeased, by the looks of things. I brought her son out of exile, let him into my court, and as my private fool, he was the hit of the show! Crispin may have a brilliant comedy career ahead of him. Lord knows, this country can use all the laughs it can get these days."

"I don't know if she's finished with us," Julianna said. "There's still the box office to contend with, you know."

"I don't think we'll hear from the old harpy again. I gave her much more than she ever deserved, considering how she handled things the first time round. But I'm satisfied with the results, and if she has the sense of a rocking horse, she'll be, as well."

Just then Richard stumbled and nearly fell flat on his face. "That reeky old clapper-clawed moldwarp!"

He regained his balance and his gracefulness at once, then shook his fist in the air.

"Uh—Richard." Julianna pointed downwards. "Don't go blaming the old moldwarp so fast. You're the klutz this time, I'm afraid."

He looked down and with a growl, kicked the rock out of the road, the very solid, very earthly object that had tripped him.

****

Julianna invited Dorothy, Lisbet, and the other producers over to watch the first episode of *The Royal Issue* featuring their film. The director, Herb LeFranc, got wind of her little get-together and showed up an hour early, with Bubble and Squeak in tow, and fruit baskets for everyone. Although it was only 6 p.m., the wine and lager already flowed, more to calm nerves than for social reasons.

Richard reclined in her loveseat. Julianna sat on the floor, her head resting against his knees. She was too nervous to sit on the loveseat with him. So Ned was in her usual place there, with Lisbet on his lap. George was in London with Brooke, who had insisted she interview him live on her show.

"Why?" Ned had inquired of that decision with cocked head and brow. "He only had a minor role, spent mostly in leg irons. Why not interview the hero?"

"Because it's her show, and she's not gaga over the hero the way she is over the chap with the minor role in leg irons," had been Richard's calm and, of course, straightforwardly frank reply.

So they watched as the opening sequence flashed across Julianna's telly screen. Then Brooke and George appeared in period costume, George still in his leg irons, a backdrop of Caernarvon Castle behind them. The only modern instruments were the body mikes clipped to their collars.

Brooke opened with her trademark greeting: "Evening, fellow Brits, and welcome to *The Royal Issue*. I'm Brooke Hill, of course. All week we have a special edition of the show, to introduce you to the historical film which I helped produce and also starred in, *Home of Thy Heart*. This charming and stunningly handsome man beside me is Wilberforce Hammond, who portrayed George Plantagenet in the film." She went on to gush about the quality script, the first-rate acting, the insightful direction. George hardly said a word, just sat there looking smug.

"What kind of interview is that?" Ned spoke around the mushroom turnover he was chewing. "He's clammed up like a dead oyster."

"She hasn't asked him anything yet," Julianna replied. "Maybe she just wanted him there for a prop."

"...and I want to take this opportunity to make a very special announcement." Brooke clasped George's hand and they both stood. He stumbled in the leg irons, but she righted him, and his appreciative smile flashed across the screen. "Wilberforce and I are engaged to be married. And we'll cover the entire event right here on *The Royal Issue!*"

Ned almost choked on his turnover. Richard's tankard froze halfway to his lips. Bubble and Squeak, following Herb's squeal of delight, clapped their monkey hands.

All Julianna could do was shake her head and keep a straight face.

****

"Dorothy! He asked me to marry him!" Lisbet twirled through the room clutching several bridal magazines she'd snapped up at the newsstand.

"When?"

"As soon as possible. And this is the wedding dress I want." She opened the top magazine to a centerfold spread featuring a lavish French designer creation.

"I mean when did he ask you? He only started noticing you exist less than a week ago."

"Last eve, after our little gathering dispersed. He said he can't have George being wed before him. I suggested a double ceremony, but he flatly refused. He wants our wedding to be the wedding of the century. Fit for a king and queen. Dorothy, 'tis finally going to happen!" She twirled like a ballerina, crashing into the utensils hung on the wall. "I'm going to marry my king!"

"Only he's no longer a king, just remember that," she warned, handing her back the magazine. "You'll be just another British couple. You may even have to get jobs if the film isn't the blockbuster we expect it to be."

"The gold I brought with me should sustain us, combined with Ned's gold. It matters not, I'll scrub privies if it means being with my beloved Ned," she gushed, flipping through yet another bride magazine. "And these shoes—how much is four-hundred-thirty pounds, Dorothy? Is four-hundred-thirty pounds a lot in modern terms?"

"For a pair of shoes, yes. But for an engagement ring, nowhere near enough."

"Thanks, I'll note that." Lisbet ran her fingers down a photo of a frothy bridal gown. "But Ned is no cheapskate."

****

"Two weddings now. And the film hasn't even premiered yet." Julianna flipped through her mail while Richard read the reviews of the sneak previews in the trade papers.

"Ah, this one says 'Anglophiles will enjoy the depth of detail and the large cast of historical personages. We meet kings, queens, nobles and commoners, in this colorful tapestry. Yet the jumbled details and huge cast of players make it difficult to sort it all out.' Bosh! Where was this bloke during the film? In the balcony choking his gopher? The story is so coherent, even a Tudor can follow the plot."

"Oh, don't put much stock in reviews, Richard. Some of the greatest masterpieces get panned. As long as they spell your name right, as they say."

"And look at this bit. 'The actor portraying King Richard looks so much like him, it's spooky. I was expecting him to typically shoo his nephews away to the Tower any minute, and quite frankly, was surprised, but mightily pleased the lads didn't perish at their uncle's wicked hand, a soul who turned out to be quite benevolent indeed. Quite a departure from what we've been fed through books and theater over the last five centuries.' He slammed his fist on the table. No tomatoes got in the way this time. "Cobblers! Why don't they get some real historians to review the film instead of these scoffers?"

"That's encouraging, Richard." Julianna peeked at the review. "Shows they're picking up on what we're trying to do. He says he's pleased the story turned out differently than the way the other hacks wrote it, posing as historians. This is the beginning of the debunking of those earlier theories. When the film comes out and the critics review it en masse, you'll be a hero."

He scoffed. "Aye, albeit in a film. Oh, if only—"

She held up a hand. "Don't start 'if only'ing again, please. We've done our very best. Unless another inexplicable phenomenon takes place, this is all we've got. And frankly, I don't know if I can handle any more of those."

He nodded and put down the trade paper. "'Tis all we can do. Who is going to review it for the Richard the Third Society?"

"We'll get the Society's patron to do it, that would be quite an honor coming from him."

"Ah, yes, the Duke of Gloucester." Richard's eyes focused on a faraway thought. "I hope the chap appreciates the title that's been bestowed upon him. I wonder if we have anything else in common, besides the title, and the striking good looks."

He cast her a sideways smile, but she pretended not to notice. She was afraid if she gave in to his peculiar brand of humor at times such as this, it would go to his head and he'd wind up like his self-infatuated brother.

"Getting back to the weddings—" She held up the invitation she'd received the other day from Brooke's parents, declaring in raised script on 48 lb. cream parchment, their 'joy and jubilation' over the nuptials of their daughter, Brooke Eloise. "They set the date for the ninth of April."

"The day Ned dies, in our former life." His voice saddened. "Just another demonstration of George's unequivocal paucity of couth."

"You think Ned will notice?" she asked. "He's really good with dates."

Richard gave a definite shake of his head. "He will neither notice nor give a whit. Nor will he ever let himself be upstaged by George's antics. I guarantee you, Ned's trip down the aisle will take place first, and on a much grander scale. I would prefer an elegant and understated gathering, wouldn't you, Julianna?"

Her heart lurched. Was that his way of proposing? "Uh, why—yes, of course. I would prefer a small, intimate gathering, Richard." She went over to sit next to him.

He tossed the papers on the floor and brought her to him. "Would you mind waiting till after the other two jubilees have faded into memory? Let's not even tell anyone."

"You mean elope?" Her voice and her hands shook. She swallowed a lump.

He shrugged. "Why make a three-ring circus out of it? When I read about my coronation feast, it surprised me that I'd have allowed such a loud, conspicuous affair. Parliament must have pressured me into it because a gala on such a grand scale isn't my style at all."

"Richard, am I correct in assuming that you just asked me to marry you?" She pulled back to see if anything was troubling his eyes. They were as clear as the midsummer sky over the moors.

"My only regret is that you'll never be queen. Would being my wife be enough?"

She fell into his arms. "Oh, Richard, I couldn't ask for anything more! I love you so very much!"

"And I you, my darling." He nuzzled her earlobe. "Shall we engage the services of a jeweler to custom design you a dazzling betrothal ring?"

She shook her head and pushed a stray lock behind her ear. "No, I don't want anything like that. Even if the film makes a trillion pounds, all I want to do is live in Yorkshire in our little cottage as a married country couple, with life's simple pleasures."

They pulled apart and she gazed into his eyes in all their blue beauty. "My wish exactly. When shall we start digging the moat to keep the fans and the media out?"

He smiled and they looked down at their clasped hands as he slipped the Wensleydale Ring on her finger. "Now this ring has more meaning to both of us than ever before. It makes you a true Ricardian."

****

Home of Thy Heart blazed across the marquee of the West End's Majestic Theater. Brooke certainly had done her job in reaching the masses, now wrapped around the block and thronging Leicester Square in hopes of copping a ticket or glimpsing the stars.

Julianna watched from the theater entrance where they'd been signing autographs as a white stretch limo pulled up. "What's in that thing, a swimming pool?" she asked Richard.

An usher opened a back door and Ned's huge form unfolded, sporting a perfectly tailored white tux. He turned and helped Lisbet out, swathed in dark blue sequins, glowing like an Olympian goddess. In contrast, Julianna's simple black sheath merely boasted sensibility.

"Once again, Ned had to make the grand entrance," Richard commented as the crowd roared, watching their hero stroll up the red carpet, waving and blowing kisses like a king at his coronation. "I'm surprised he didn't arrive on a caparisoned white stallion."

"Or in a coach and six," she added. "Maybe that's how George will come."

"Nay, he already told me his preferred mode of transportation. And there he is." Richard pointed as Ned's limo pulled away. She couldn't see over the crowd mobbing Ned.

Police cleared the way and a bright yellow convertible pulled up to the curb. The door fell open and George tumbled out, waving to the onlookers with an open bottle. He shook it and released his thumb from the top, shooting a stream of foamy champagne into the squealing, clamoring crowd. The convertible drove away and a limo with "*The Royal Issue*" splashed on the side pulled up.

The crowd hushed as if a church service were about to begin. They held their collective breath—what would their exalted *Royal Issue* snoop be wearing? Brooke hadn't divulged one iota of information on her show, or even to Julianna or Dorothy, about the designer or the design. She had the *Entertainment Now!* staff sitting on their haunches. The door opened and Brooke stepped out, in the costume of a fifteenth-century queen, dripping in gems and satin skirts, a steeple headdress tipped back at a sharp angle, from which flowed a gauzy veil.

"Leave it to her to remember tonight is Halloween," Julianna remarked as the crowd roared their adoration and approval.

Followed by a retinue of *Royal Issue* cameramen, Brooke handled it all with gracious aplomb, stopping to sign autographs and handing out 8x10 glossies of herself.

"I know I should have worn my White Boar-embroidered velvet doublet and jeweled sword," Richard lamented.

Julianna shook her head. "No, I'm glad I talked you out of wearing period raiment. Despite all the attention Brooke's attracting, she does look a tad farcical. But that's Brooke, always having to upstage herself."

After one final wave to the crowd, the cast entered the theater. In the lobby, Julianna tugged at Richard's sleeve. "Look, doesn't that look great?" She pointed to the display of posters, CDs of the soundtrack by Silver Thunder, and applications to the Richard III Society.

He walked over and moved the applications to the front of the table.

Dorothy had suggested Julianna display copies of her books here as well, but she vetoed it. The idea seemed tacky, like selling Richard memorabilia on a home shopping channel.

The curtain went up and the opening credits began to fade in and out, accompanied by lush orchestral music. Her heart pounded. She grasped Richard's hand so tightly, he yelped in pain.

Then Brooke's lavishly gowned, head-dressed, expertly-made-up image filled the giant screen as she climbed the north gate of Westminster Palace to better see the victory parade, marching home from the Battle of Barnet. Ned pranced by on his gray stallion and halted before the maiden's adoring gaze.

So began the fairy-tale romance that wove through the wicked politicking, posturing, and sneak invasions that characterized the late middle ages. By the film's end, Julianna juggled a jumble of emotions: tears of happiness and sadness streamed down her cheeks. Her heart burst with pride as the crowd sustained shattering applause.

"We did it, we did it, we did it!" She rose, hugging her cast members and fellow producers. Herb LeFranc, seated with his own entourage including Bubble and Squeak dressed in black tie and tails, waved to them and blew kisses all over the theater.

Capping it all off was seeing every Richard III Society application gone on the way out.

The after-party was almost anticlimactic, celebrity-studded as it was. All Julianna wanted to do was take her shoes off and relive the emotionally charged events of the last several months in her mind.

Several big names in the entertainment world, as well as a few Royals, came to rub elbows with the artists who so beautifully portrayed a period of English history once regarded as dark.

Julianna was thrilled that Silver Thunder had graciously agreed to play the soundtrack in its entirety. The musicians cut quite a striking appearance in their formal attire. Nicholas Coventry, the keyboardist with a double handful as well as an earful of rings, asked Julianna to pose for a photo with him. So she stuffed her feet back into her shoes and obliged. She really wanted a photo with him and the lead singer, Ian Arnold, whose basic black tux made his hair glow like polished copper. So she and the two babes posed in different combinations for the band's photographer. She'd never met a rock star before, so this was rather a thrill for her. Julianna asked Nicholas to send her the negatives. She knew just where the framed enlargements would go in her study. He agreed, in his soothing southern American drawl, earrings dangling and throwing off bursts of light.

Brooke, obviously the star, swept around the dance floor with every admirer who dared approach her as her fiancé threw his own party at the bar.

Ned pranced up to Julianna with a dazzling blonde beauty on each arm, his betrothed nowhere in sight.

"Where do we go from here?" He clinked a passing admirer's champagne glass with his personalized tankard. "Where *can* we go from here?"

"Ned, I haven't even thought as far ahead as getting milk for tomorrow's Weetabix. I'm so thoroughly immersed in the moment. Where's Lisbet?" She peered around the trophies at his sides.

"In the lobby with Dorothy. She got some urgent messages on her smart phone or smart pad or whatever it's called, about wedding garb from some dressmaker in London."

"Oh, how exciting to be a bride!" A thrill of anticipation made her heart dance a little jig. She had her own wedding garb to shop for! "Well, don't you dare peek at what she chooses. I don't know how far back the superstition goes, but in our times it's bad luck for the groom to see the bridal gown before the wedding."

He chuckled. "With the number of disastrous marriages I've witnessed, I trust that superstition's been violated divers times." He strolled away, his fawning admirers trailing him on his heels.

Richard brought her a white wine and sat next to her. "Where's Ned prancing off to?"

"It better not be to peek at Lisbet's choices of wedding gowns." Julianna sipped her wine. "She's with

Dorothy looking at gowns online."

"And why are you here instead of in on the gaggle to cast your votes?" He leaned into her with a smile.

"Oh, I'm not much on fashion. I'll need a consultant when it's time to decide what I'm going to wear to our own wedding."

"Even in a potato sack, you'd be a stunning bride," he assured her as their lips met in a feathery kiss. "But why all the urgency with Lisbet, rushing off to look at gowns online tonight?"

She rested her head on his shoulder. "I have a feeling it's Ned who did the rushing, giving her a nudge so they could be married before George and Brooke."

"By the looks of things, she was as anxious to get her talons into his hide," he half-whispered.

"Oh, Richard, I knew they were meant for each other. Her coming here was meant to be."

Richard put down his glass of milk and focused on her. "You're not in haste to beat the four of them to the altar, are you?"

She shook her head. "No, we agreed—it's better if it's long after the other two weddings." She felt like teasing him. "Even if our daughters have to be the flower girls."

His eyes widened and a brow shot up under his fringe. George came lumbering up to them just then. "Have I got some news for you-u-u-u!" he slurred, swinging his champagne glass like a pendulum.

Richard gave an exaggerated wave of his hand before George's mouth. "You're officially more polluted than the Thames?"

He shook his head rapidly. "Nope nope nope nope nope." He did a little jig, splashing some bubbly onto

Richard's jacket.

"George, will you mind out my way, you lummox!" Richard blotted the drops with a linen napkin. "If you're not spilling one thing, it's another."

"See that bloke there engaged in discourse with my glamorous bride-to-be?" He pointed with a wobbly finger at a heavy-set man in a black suit talking to Brooke, or rather, being talked at by her. She pointed and gestured as if giving directions.

Richard and Julianna nodded.

"He's gonna marry me."

"Hey?" Julianna didn't think she'd heard correctly.

Richard countered, "I wouldn't advise that, George. He looks like he'll want to wear the pants in the family."

"Nay, I mean—me and Brooke. He's a justice of the peace! We're getting married here—tonight."

"Brooke is breeding?" Richard asked. George looked at him cross-eyed and galloped away to join his betrothed and the man who would soon join them.

"What do you think of that? An impromptu wedding. Leave it to George." Richard shook his head and drained his milk glass.

Julianna let out a loud hrmmph. "This wedding is as impromptu as the building of the Great Pyramid. And I'm sure George didn't know about it till five minutes ago. Brooke must have had this planned even before she bought herself that engagement ring."

"Ned isn't going to like this." He shook his head, lips pursed.

But Ned was too surprised to even protest that his brother was upstaging him.

George threw a surprise wedding complete with a

ready-made Who's Who guest list and more television cameras than bartenders.

Ned stood up for his younger sibling, who emerged from a back room and trotted up to the makeshift altar in fifteenth-century nobleman's raiment. Although far into his cups, George made a striking bridegroom, despite continually tripping over the sword dangling from his belt.

Finally Ned snatched it away from him. "You'll enter wedded bliss a gelding if you fall over that weapon the wrong way," Ned said as the crowd gathered and hushed.

As the band broke into "Here Comes the Bride," Brooke glided over a petal-strewn red carpet and joined her groom.

Cameras covered the short ceremony for broadcast on the next *Royal Issue* as confetti fluttered through the air, along a flood of balloons released from nets suspended from the ceiling.

Impromptu, huh? Julianna snickered. Brooke nearly had to carry her new husband, who stopped at the bar for one last nightcap.

"Talk about ironic," Richard uttered as he helped Julianna on with her wrap. "The star of her own royals-hounding show is married into royalty and doesn't even know it."

****

Dorothy gave Lisbet some soda crackers to calm her nausea and put her to bed. She then shucked off her evening wear and slipped on her comfy old robe. Heading for the kitchen to make a late-night pot of tea, she glanced at all the materials piled on the table, mementos from the most memorable night of her life.

She picked up the orchid corsage Herb LeFranc had given her and inhaled the last traces of its sweet fragrance. She made a mental note to press it into her Richard III Society keepsake album.

Before putting the kettle on, she went out to her garden and gazed up at the heavens. There was something she had to do; someone she had to thank. She knelt on the ground, near her marble Richard III statue, clasped her hands and closed her eyes.

"I summon my spirit guide to appear before me. I summon you, O great one. I beseech you, come to me, appear before me." She opened her eyes, yet no one had come forth. The Richard statue glowed in the moonlit night. Well, she knew he wasn't going to start talking.

Squeezing her eyes shut again, she concentrated all the harder: "Please, come forth. Come forth, Will Shakespeare. I simply want to thank you for leading the way and making this dream come true."

She opened her eyes and strained to see a blurry figure next to the statue. He slowly came into focus, dressed in a ruff and well-tailored suit, his beard trimmed into a perfect fork. He took a casual stance, legs crossed at the ankles, an arm slung over Richard's shoulder. "Good eve, My Lady. You spurred my presence forth?"

"Ah, Will, my beloved Bard. You are as handsome as ever, even in ghostly translucence."

"Handsomer than old King Crouchback, I trust?" He regarded Richard's features with a scowl and smacked the marble cheek with his gloves. "He appears rather symmetrical this eve. Did you chisel the right shoulder down to match the left?"

Dorothy shook her finger at him. "Will! The

premiere was a smash. The world will grow to love Richard just as the Society does. We made many changes, just as you'd suggested, and the end result was a portrayal of Richard as the kindhearted, noble king he really was. And all because of you. Isn't life ironic?"

"Ah, Lady Dorothy, I always knew Dick wasn't the wicked ogre of yore; I just needed to make a few quid, what with my Anne breeding and that big cottage to pay for—a bloke has to make a living." He stroked his silky beard. "I always wanted to portray him as he really was, but nobody cared to see that. Good Queen Bess insisted that I melodramatise the whole story. Clever bird she was; she knew what would sell. But these days, folk are much more sophisticated and should see Dick as he really was. 'Tis about time we shed light on such a crucial part of our history and tell the world that Dick was the good soul and Tudor the evil one, not the other way round."

"You watch that forked tongue of yours, Bard, or I'll slap a libel suit on you so fast, you'll not sell another word of your base-court fiction!" came a screechy voice that grew louder with every word.

"Who the bloody hell is that?" Dorothy looked round, stumbling backward into her birdbath as another ghostly image appeared nose to nose with Will.

"Ah, Maggs, pizzle off, won't you? This is a private conversation. Go haunt George if you want to create mischief, 'tis his wedding night."

The second figure formed more sharply now and turned to Dorothy. Dorothy moved away from the birdbath. She rubbed her eyes, polished her glasses on her robe, and put them back on.

"Margaret Beaufort? You finally decided to

appear? After years of tormenting poor Julianna with your sillybuggers and wreaking havoc on our production? So now that you're here what have you got to say for yourself?"

"I do grudgingly admit I'm impressed you folk deduced 'twas I who was conjuring up all that mischief. Considering the hordes of enemies Richard the Turd has, the parade of names must be longer than the civil list," she cackled.

"Julianna reckoned it was you, as every mishap occurred just when someone made a disparaging remark about you or your son, or changed the script to portray him in a less-than-flattering light. But we just wanted to portray these chaps as they truly were, Lady Beaufort. Nothing personal," Dorothy said.

Will jumped down from the statue's base, plucked a twig from one of the hedges and started picking his teeth. "Yeah, Maggs." He nodded. "My Lady here and her mates cut your son a good lot of slack, considering he was naught more than a fraud, frauding his bloodline, frauding through France, frauding over Wales, frauding round England, frauding right up to Bosworth, and frauding his bum onto the throne."

"He had as much a claim to the English throne as anybody!" Margaret shrieked.

"Anybody in Tunisia, maybe," Will scoffed.

"His great-great grandfather was—"

He cut her off. "Frauds, the whole lot of 'em."

"—from John of Gaunt—"

"Fraud, fraud, fraud," Will sang.

They stood nose to nose again, fists balled, Margaret Beaufort on her toes, as the shouting match ensued. Dorothy was afraid they'd wake all of

Yorkshire.

"Shhh!" Dorothy put a finger to her lips and the sparring ghosts ceased.

"My apologies, Lady Dorothy, but some of us here forgot we were a lady," Will jeered.

"My son began the dynasty of Tudor, from which spawned Queen Elizabeth the First, the greatest monarch this realm has ever known." Margaret orated. "Had I not married Owen Tudor and taken the great risk to birth my son at the tender age of fourteen, the kingdom would never have bowed before our great Elizabeth."

Will nodded in certain agreement. "And poor Anne Boleyn and Cathy Howard would never have bowed before a chopping block."

Margaret shrugged. "An unfortunate snag in our history's rich tapestry. However...in actuality, 'tis I who began the majestic and enduring Tudor dynasty. My bravery, my faith in my son, my love for my realm."

Will stifled a yawn and turned to Dorothy. "Methinks the lady protesteth too much, do you not agree?"

"I resent all the horrible things you had Old Dick do to my son in that beef-witted piece of fluff you call an historical film!" Margaret spat, causing Will to wipe his face with his glove.

"Yes, Maggs, but in real life, 'twas the other way round. Hence, were I you, I'd shut up," he replied evenly.

Margaret scowled, then twirled round and crossed her arms. "I've naught else to say to you, you ha'p'ny hack."

"Ah, the best tidings I've heard in a century." He

bowed, doffing his hat. "May I quote you on that, Madame Taffy?"

"Enough, both of you!" Dorothy held her palms to her ears. "We must all learn to get along. We'll be together through all eternity, so let's get a head start by acting like adults now, shall we?"

"Only if this addle-pate does first," Margaret snapped over her shoulder, trying to keep a girlish grin from spreading across her face.

Will turned around and peered over Margaret's shoulder. "You're rather titillating when you're mad, Maggs. I may pen my next romantic drama round you. Peppered with caustic wit and delightful humor, of course. In fact, I feel an opening hook coming on. A rose by any other name—uh, no, I've done that one already..." He tapped his pointer finger on his chin. "I'll produce something so profound, no one will know 'twas my brain what created it!"

"About me?" Margaret spun around, affecting a swoon into Will's arms. He caught her by the elbows. "Would you portray me as comely as that Juliet lass?"

"I shan't even need take my usual drastic artistic license, my dear." Will took her hand and kissed it.

She tittered.

"You're what these modern folk call a foxy chick." He gave her a wolf whistle and glanced over at Dorothy. "Will you excuse us, My Lady? Maggs and I have some history to make."

They vanished into the night, leaving a residual mist in their wake, which dissolved with the next gust of wind. Dorothy shivered, pulling her robe closely around her as she headed for the house. "Well, now, how about that." She shook her head in wonder.

"Shakespeare in love. Wouldn't that make a great film!"

****

"Yoo-hoo! Julianna! Richard! Anybody?" Dorothy peeked in just as Julianna came round the side of her house.

"Hallo, Dorothy. I was just hanging out some wash. Taking advantage of the last of this Indian summer. Cup of tea?"

"That sounds lovely, dear, but I've come to deliver some news; I couldn't tell you over the phone."

"What?"

They went through the front door together just as a series of howls came through from her study.

Dorothy jumped.

"That's all right. Just the boys playing Doom again." Julianna waved at the whooping brothers. "They're crackers, the lot."

"I need to gather you all round for this!" Dorothy announced.

"All right, I'll get them." Julianna called Richard and Ned away from the computer. "Dorothy has something to tell us." She clasped hands with them both, at that moment feeling an intense surge of love. These men had become such a big part of her life, she couldn't remember what it had been like before.

Dorothy stood in the center of the room, reminding Julianna of how she stood every year at their séances. But this time she didn't have to bring Richard back.

"I summoned Will Shakespeare last night, and he came to me. Our conversation also provoked the appearance of another entity, and I'm going to let you guess who it was." She clasped her hands together and looked from one to the other of them, her face displaying pure delight.

Ned shrugged. "The chap who really wrote the stuff?"

"No!" She turned to Julianna. "Guess!"

She shook her head. Knowing Dorothy it could've been anybody from Caesar to Churchill.

"Very well, I'll tell you. Margaret Beaufort!"

"Why, did you call her a name?" Richard's eyes swept around the room. Just then Julianna noticed he gave his crotch area a fleeting glance. That last itching incident wasn't one a guy would forget in a hurry, she reckoned.

"No, but Will said something that brought her roaring back," Dorothy proclaimed. "And once here, she admitted it was she who was responsible for all that horseplay and tomfoolery. She even commended you, Julianna, for figuring out it was she."

"Well, after a while it seemed obvious. You don't need a doctorate in rocket science to figure that out."

"Only a thorough knowledge of English history, mayhap," Richard said, his tone tinged with pride.

"And they started bickering, but not that usual bickering, you know, bickering when you know there's something smoldering. And sure enough, they took off together. They're bonkers for each other. Will told her to shut her cake hole when she started complaining about her son Harry. So it looks like she won't be bothering us again." Dorothy raised her arms and dropped them to her sides.

"Will Shakespeare and Margaret Beaufort?" Julianna mused, smiling brightly. "That would make a great play."

"Or maybe even a film," said Dorothy as Ned handed round truffles.

"Well, that's certainly something to celebrate. Especially you, Dickon." Ned handed a truffle to Richard. "You won't have any more of that itch—"

"Er, right, Ned," Richard broke in. "Let's not push our good fortune to the limit, shall we? Let's just hope the two of them will be very happy together, and if they care to see the film, we'll leave them two comp tickets at the will call."

"He said he wanted to pen a drama with Margaret as the heroine," Dorothy said, "and all night, I had dreams of storylines going round my head. He's doing it again, he's guiding me. Julianna, let's take down some notes. This can be our next film."

"Didn't he ever write novels?" Julianna asked a bit wearily. "I don't think I'm ready for another screenplay yet. I'd like to write in prose form and see it published as an e-book. That's the wave of the future, you know."

"Oh, absolutely." Dorothy nodded in agreement. "I just downloaded three of them this morning from The Wild Rose Press. They got rave reviews."

Richard went over to fetch his leather folder. "They say you're only as good as your last hit. Let's have a go at it, shall we?"

So Julianna plugged her laptop in and they brainstormed as Ned took a stroll down to the market to fetch some more bananas—tonight was pizza night.

Chapter Twenty-One

The mail landed on her floor with an extra-hard thud. Julianna put down her teacup and retrieved it. It was a large envelope forwarded from the post office containing several smaller envelopes. She shuffled through them. They were from all over Britain. Then it hit her. Her first sack of fan mail!

"Richard! Ned! Look!" She spread them out all over the floor and they tore into them like Christmas presents.

"Hey, this one's addressed to me! Cuthbert Hammond, Esquire!" Ned held an envelope up and slashed through it with the jeweled dagger he'd worn in the film. Now it served as a combination steak knife/letter opener. "'I loved your bravery and your chivalry. Your last scene with the heroine brought me to tears. Not to mention the fact that you're drop dead gorgeous. When will you make your next film?' He folded the paper and pressed it between his hands. "Hey, Julianna, do you have an extra picture frame? I wish to hang this over my bed."

"Oh, I'm sure there'll be plenty more to come, Ned. You think you can handle being a movie star?" She grinned at him and his eyes twinkled. "You'll be getting offers now. You'd better get yourself an agent."

"In due course. First things first. I need to find a home for myself and my bride, of course." He stripped the wrapper off a protein bar in that slow sensual way of his, like undressing a woman.

"George seems to be settling quite nicely in Brooke's flat." Richard tossed aside the mail, none of which had come to him. "She hasn't even turfed him out yet."

"Nah, she's keeping him in the style to which he's accustomed." Ned thumbed through the rest of the letters. "Why isn't there any for you, Dickon?"

"I get mine sent through the Society," he replied loftily, with a wave of his hand. He now had a matching replica of his Wensleydale Ring. "Do you believe people are writing to me?"

"Nay, can't say I do," Ned drawled. "You can't boast anything like this." He held up his prized fan letter.

"My mail comes from scholars, historians, and—" Richard looked away.

"Go ahead, Richard, tell him," Julianna urged. "It'll get around fast enough."

"And what?" Ned stopped chewing on his bar. "More ghosts?"

"Nay, and let's hope we're finished with ghosts since Margaret Beaufort's snagged a fancy man. I mean—eccentrics. They write to me. Me, as in King Richard the Third rather than my assumed identity. There are actually people out there who think I'm—me. They saw the film and are convinced I've come back to portray myself and set the world straight. Some even want me to give the keynote address at the next Annual General Meeting."

Ned let out a guffaw. "That would be precious indeed. Show up in that raiment you wore in the film, and convince them they're not bonkers. Better yet, just write and tell them to attend the next séance."

"Ned, let's not go there," Julianna warned. "We all made a pact. No revelations. And if Blabbing Brooke can keep her cave shut, we certainly can."

"Ah, but I can dream, can't I? To go on telly and proclaim to those unsuspecting—as well as the suspecting—masses who we truly are and from whence we came."

"Right. And spend the rest of our natural lives in Newgate's loony ward. Is that still there, Julianna?" Richard asked.

She shook her head. "Newgate's been and gone. They have much more modern loony wards now. And it looks as if Ned's clamoring for a chance to inhabit one."

Ned polished off the bar and licked the inside of the wrapper. "Our secret's safe with me. Only conditionally, that is."

"Conditionally how?" Richard persisted. "Giving orders again, Your Ex-Highness?"

Ned swallowed and licked his lips. "Nay, simply this—if someday the earth truly is in the path of one of those asteroids we keep hearing about, or if it's all going to come to an end in a cataclysmic catastrophe like I keep seeing on these daft telly shows, I'm going public. I intend to enjoy my final hours and die as I was born."

"It's a deal, Ned." Richard held out his hand to shake. "Whoever croaks last should tell the world about the others."

"Why are you talking about this? It's so morbid!" Julianna protested. "We should be celebrating life, not tempting death!"

"She's right." Richard stood, smoothing his trousers. "I'm going to celebrate life right now." He headed for the kitchen. "Life at its most effervescent."

"Champagne at this time of day?" Ned commented, heading for the bar. "Dickon, you surprise me, getting more like me each day. I'll join you with a celebration brandy. Julianna, you have any of those luscious truffles left? The ones with the nipples?"

Richard made his cabbage face. "Champagne is the farthest thing from my mind." He stopped at the writing desk and unsheathed his personalized dagger. "I'm going to cut myself a slice of my delicious banana-strawberry-caramel-corn-topped pizza. Care to join me?"

Ned shuddered. "Fetch the chopsticks, Julianna. We're ordering Chinese."

****

The film had been released only three weeks ago, but U.S. distributors were getting interested, courtesy of Jonathan Garrett, their American producer. He called Julianna to tell her to think about what she was going to wear to the Academy Awards.

"Nominations are in the air; I can taste it," he proclaimed, his voice confident and booming.

She'd be sure to pass that message on to the director; he was the one who needed to get outfits designed. She wondered if any French designers dressed chimps. After hanging up, she left for a speaking engagement at a local historical society.

She got back home that evening, pulled into the garage, and used the remote to close the door on the fans and reporters gaping at the house. Maybe they would have to build that moat after all.

But no one bothered them in the Hare 'n Hounds. So they went there for a pie-and-chips dinner. No one followed them there or back.

After dinner, Ned answered his ever-increasing inflow of e-mail, and Richard helped Julianna plan the next annual Ricardian tour. A huge map of England lay on the library floor between them.

Her doorbell disrupted her concentration. "Who can that be at this hour? It's after nine."

"Not another autograph hound or camera bug." Richard rubbed his eyes as he studied the map.

Now she checked first before opening the door.

She stopped short when she entered her living room. Her visitor was already on the other side of the door—inside!

"How—how did you get in here?" she asked the disheveled, rumply-haired bloke who looked like he was trying to find his way back home.

"I just—landed. On me feet." As he looked round, a spark of recognition lit up his eyes, as if he'd seen the place before, but knew not when. He scratched his head.

Richard entered the room and their collective gasps came at her from both directions, in stereo. "God's truth! What are you doing here?"

"You know this bloke?" Julianna turned to Richard, somewhat relieved the intruder wasn't a burglar, but not completely, now that she knew he was someone of Richard's acquaintance. That meant only one thing...

"You're from the fifteenth century?" she asked the visitor, still gaping at his surroundings.

His gaze finally landed on her. "Not quite. Well, most recently, yes, but not originally. Oh, it's a long story, Miss Hammond, and I don't want to bore you. I'm Ulch, the Grand Wizbar, who sent Richard's brothers and Lisbet here, and who sold George that amulet who gave it to Ned whom Richard took it from and wound up here—oh, dear! I just dropped in—pardon the bad pun—to see how you folk were getting on."

"How did you get here?" Richard came up, took him by the arm and sat him down. Richard sat across from him, hunched forward, as if preparing for an interrogation.

Julianna half expected him to shine the high-intensity reading lamp into the bloke's eyes.

"I'm actually from the future. The far, far future. Where we can physically travel through time, because we've evolved far enough. Luxurious space stations orbit Earth, humans are genetically engineered, there's no need for pesticides, because they've eradicated pests..." He threw his head back and shut his eyes. "Ah, what a life it is over there."

"That further begs the question, how did you get here?" Richard repeated.

"I was sent back to your time as punishment for committing a naughty deed," he replied. "Well, I've been released early on good behavior. Seems I reached my quota of good deeds—must've had something to do with you lot, eh?—and I'm free. I wanted to see how you were getting on, with your new-found fame and all. Seems you've settled in quite comfortably here, then." He emphasized the 'comfortably', patting the modern cushion he sat on. "Trousers still pinching you there,

Richard?"

"Nay, I got some that fit. Are you staying here—in this time, I mean?"

"I doubt it. I thought I'd have a go at Roman times. I can use a dose of decadence. Or maybe I'll just go to 90210."

"Lisbet and Ned are engaged, Brooke and George are married, and Julianna and I—" Richard counted on his fingers.

"I know all about it." He laughed, holding up his hand. "You needn't tell me. I've got the crystal ti—breast, remember?"

"And you've been observing us the whole time?" Julianna enquired. "I hope Margaret Beaufort and Shakespeare's ghosts going gaga over each other is the last weird thing I'll hear about in my lifetime."

"Just the good bits." He smiled and nodded. "I'm probably happier than the lot of you that it all worked out. Got me out of that plague-bitten era. Ugh!" He shuddered. An amulet round his neck caught the light and threw back colored rays. "No offense, of course."

"None taken." Richard gave him that half-smile.

"Don't you want to go to the far future and see your loved ones?" Julianna asked. "When did you get released?"

"Oh, about a fortnight ago. I've been back home already. Just came for a visit. There was nothing on telly tonight and me girlfriend's at bingo. Just felt obliged to ask if there was anything else I can do for you."

"You mean—like send us somewhere else?" A tone crept into Richard's voice that Julianna couldn't identify.

Ulch nodded. "If you wish. I know how adamant you were about changing history, going back and righting the cockups you'd made. I didn't think I'd ever get released in time to come forth here and give you the chance. Now that I'm here, I reckoned I'd extend the courtesy of asking."

Julianna needed to be near Richard at this moment. She went over and sat with him. Without looking up, he took her hand and squeezed it. This was the moment she'd been dreading—Richard facing the decision to go back to his own world or stay here with her.

Watching him sit and think about it, his fingers drumming on the chair, was more agonizing than if he'd suddenly vanished without warning. He was actually thinking about it—and that's what hurt the most.

Ned entered the room, his address book in one hand, a tankard in the other. "I need some—God's truth! How in bloody hell did you get here?" He looked neither pleased nor piqued—simply stunned.

"Greetings, your Highness." Ulch swept a low bow before Ned.

"Up with you, up. I'm no longer the king, you of all people should know that!" He turned to Richard. "My baby brother's the king in these parts, aren't you, Good King Dick? Or some loopy loons think so."

"Ulch was released on good behavior and came by to ask us if we—needed anything, Ned," Richard said, still clasping Julianna's hand.

She grieved as if their lives were about to end. She knew what was going to happen, and it was unthinkable.

"What could he possibly do for us, except send—"

Ned's eyes lit up, and he sat next to the wizard. "Are your powers intact?"

"As much as ever. I can send you wherever and whenever you wish. I trust you have unfinished business in your past you'd like to rectify? As do your brothers?"

Ned thought a minute and shook his head. "Nah. I made sure my affairs were in order before I departed. How fares the kingdom without me?"

"Thriving peacefully, sire. As per your orders, your nephew John took the throne," the wizard said, "The lass your brother George allegedly got with child came to me for a beauty spell and confessed that George isn't the father of her child after all. 'Twas a ruse to get him to marry her, but she's got another fancy man now."

"George will be glad to hear that," Ned replied. "Not that he'd have done aught about it anyhow."

"And, Richard, you'll be relieved to hear that Kate Haute is with child—but not yours. She admitted the child's true sire, the Duke of Buckingham."

"Well, dip me in ink and call me a nib." Richard expelled a relieved sigh. "This calls for a celebration. Banana-covered pizza for everyone!"

Then a long discussion about politics ensued, and Julianna excused herself. She just wanted to be alone, to relive the precious but pitifully brief time she'd spent with Richard, trying to understand the miracle that brought him here, having long talks with him, taking long walks with him, sharing her hopes, her joys, and and sorrows with him, falling in love with him.

She couldn't blame the wizard. Offering Richard the option to go back was the right thing to do. Neither would she hold him back if he wanted to go. He had a kingdom awaiting him and duties to fulfill. No, she wouldn't try to stop him. She wouldn't kick up a fuss or throw a tantrum. She had to let him go. His needs before hers. That's what love was all about.

He found her several hours later, sitting in her favorite spot by the stream, weeping quietly, her feet dug into the earth. Somehow it anchored her.

"Julianna, what are you doing out here? I've been looking all over for you. I thought you'd gone to bed, then when I peeked in—oh, never mind. What are you doing here?"

She took his hand and held it to her moist cheek. "Richard, I just want you to know that no matter what we talked about, no matter what plans we've made, sometimes life throws you a curve, and another one just hit us. If you must go back, I—" She couldn't go on. Sobs choked her.

He knelt beside her and brought her head to his chest, stroking her hair back from her face. "That's what upsets you so? Thinking I was going back?"

"You must, Richard. It's inevitable. I have no right to hold you back. I promised I'd never hold you back if you got the chance. You've got a life to finish there, the one you started."

"Nay. I started my life here when I met you. That's when my life began. On this past twenty-second of August." He lifted her chin with his finger and looked into her eyes.

He was a blur through her tears.

He wiped them away. "I wouldn't go anywhere without you."

"N—no?" Hic! Oh, bugger all! Now she had the hiccups!

"Never in a million years. Neither to fifteenth-century London nor twenty-first century London. Not unless you go with me."

Hic! "I didn't think you'd want me—hic!—there. You've got—well, you know."

"I'm inclined to go back, Julianna. To right the wrongs I'd done and to try to right the wrongs others are destined to do me. But you'd still be the love of my life. Just like in the film. That's why I'd go back. To do everything in real life just like I did it in the film. That's why I wouldn't go without you."

"But in the film I was Anne."

"That's right. You are my Anne. When I said I wanted you to be my Anne, I wasn't talking about Anne Neville. I was talking about Julianna Hammond. Will you marry me, Julianna?"

She felt the entire universe contained within her heart, and she was eternity. Time had no beginning, no end, no meaning. "Oh, Richard, of course I will! I'll go back and do it all again—for real this time!"

They sat in silence for a while. Finally her hiccups subsided. Fatigue muddled her brain. Her lids felt so very heavy.

"No indoor plumbing? No modern medicine? No *Star Trek*?" She smiled and he wiped away fresh tears. She could see the blue of his eyes, even in this much darkness.

He shrugged. "Everything's a tradeoff."

She slid her feet from the mud and stood. This was all too much to think about in one night, although her mind was made up. If he was going, she was going.

"Shall we go, Richard?"

"Yes," he said, "but remember, the fifteenth

century's a dirty, smelly—"

"I meant upstairs, Richard."

He gave her that smile. Hand and hand they walked back to her house.

Chapter Twenty-Two

Julianna watched as Lisbet clung to Ned. The intimate little gathering consisted of the five of them—the four time travelers and Julianna. Brooke couldn't get away from London that evening, so she sent George to Yorkshire in her private plane, which he said was more harrowing than the journey through time.

"I ain't going back that way no how," he'd declared as Julianna and Richard walked him across the tarmac to her car, his entire body atremble. "I'll crawl back to London on my bloody hands and knees before I go up in that tin can with wings again!"

Now they huddled by the fire in her library. She'd gotten extra bottles of brandy, wine, and lager, and even they were gone. It was a tense evening.

"So your mind's made up, then, Dickon?" Ned asked, once again; as it seemed, they'd gone round in circles several times. This was one decision that had to be verified over and over.

"Aye, Julianna and I are going back. But first we're going to marry in York Minster, and we request the honor of all you present. When I'm back in my time I need to right some wrongs, and do everything in my power to avoid dying in that battle. I'll begin by making sure the treasonous Stanley brothers are otherwise occupied—I'll ship them off to a monastery in the Shetland Islands. I'm fully prepared to die for my kingdom, but this time at least it'll be avoidable." His voice trailed off, and Julianna nodded, to signify that this had been her decision, too.

"I'm going back to precisely the moment I left," Richard added. "Not a moment before nor after. I'm not going to manipulate the powers of science to suit my own whimsy. That would be most cowardly. Something Tudor would do."

"I trust you intend to let things lie with Anne Neville as well, and you won't be chasing after her to beg forgiveness after that silly row," Ned spoke.

"I shall wed Anne to young Edward, the Prince of Wales, as she did in reality, but this time she lives out a full and complete life with him. I shall secure young Edward far from the Battle of Tewkesbury, so he'll be well protected. Better yet, for his protection, I'll ensure there *is* no Battle of Tewkesbury."

No one spoke for a while. The fire's crackling sounds filled the room.

"George, did you talk it over with Brooke?" Ned asked.

He nodded. It was a long time before he spoke. "We're staying here. As I don't have any fifteenth-century paternity suits to own up to, I have no reason to go back, and Brooke has a life she wouldn't trade for anything. I'm only glad she didn't drown me in a butt of Malmsey when she found out who I really was."

"But she wasn't all that surprised, was she?" Julianna said. "She had herself convinced beyond a reasonable doubt that Richard was a ghost."

"She wasn't surprised I'd come from five hundred years ago. What surprised her was who I am. I think that made up for it." George smirked and drained his glass.

"Well, we hope you'll all be very happy," Ned said, as Lisbet sighed and leaned against his strong chest. "I personally think you're all daft. The far future's the only place to go. Imagine how much more comfortable it is where Ulch is from. And I'm quite consistent with my motto *comfort et liesse,* am I not? Lisbet and I believe we've made the most sensible decision, where we're going. The wizard's extolling the future made up our minds. I can't wait to take that first-class odyssey to that space station that orbits Earth, with that new block of luxury highrises they just built. We're going to exchange wedding vows amidst our glittering galaxy. And genetically engineer our future children. They'll be geniuses, the lot of them. Gorgeous geniuses!"

"We don't need any engineering to have that, Ned," Lisbet cooed, running her fingers over his cheek.

"Do you realize we may never see one another again?" Richard broke the long silence, staring into his tankard. It seemed no one was making eye contact.

"Cobblers." Ned slapped his thigh. "We'll be in the far future; we can come back and visit any of you anytime."

"I don't know if that's possible, Ned," Richard replied softly. "I don't know where we'll be in a hundred years. Dead, I reckon. I'm not going to live forever, you know."

"I'll come get you," Ned assured him, in that big-brotherly tone that always melted Julianna's heart. "I came here to get you, I'll come there to get you, and bring you back to my time, in the future. Once you've accomplished your mission, why stay in that plague-infested time?"

"Yeah, Dickon, imagine what lager tastes like with a few thousand more years of perfecting!" George chimed in.

Richard lifted his head and looked at each of his brothers for a long moment before speaking. "I know where I belong, and that's where I'm going. And I plan on staying there. With my wife." He put a protective arm around Julianna. "Besides, I'm not that keen on lager, 'tis certainly not worth going thousands of years into the future for."

"We're even going to build this house, right here, on the same spot," Julianna said, "in the shadow of Middleham Castle. Our little sanctuary."

"Then that's it, then." Ned gave a single nod. "We've decided where we want to go. Let's just hope that lout doesn't bollocks it up."

Julianna flipped through the pages of the Richard III biography for the last time. "Let's hope this will all read differently some day," she said over a sigh.

****

Westminster Palace, 1473

After the midday meal, Richard and Julianna began making out their coronation guest list. Despite Julianna's endless practicing, she couldn't master the quill pen without smearing ink all over the parchment.

"How's this, Richard?" She held up her page covered with the alphabet, each letter a bit more legible than the one before.

"Splendid." He leaned over and they shared a warm kiss. "But you can always get a secretary to do your writing for you."

"I want to do something for myself around here.

Now, who else did I leave off the guest list?" She dipped the quill.

"Ned and George and their brides." Richard tried on his crown—for the tenth time that day. "But they have open invitations. They'll be here. George never passed up a free banquet."

She wiped ink off her hands. "I can't wait to see them. I wonder how they've been adapting to their new centuries."

"If their new centuries didn't meet every requirement of their exacting demands, they'd have come back. Trust me on that."

Richard and Julianna shared a secret smile, unseen by the hordes of servers scurrying around them.

"Tell the cooks that was a scrumptious lunch," she told the table server, making sure to compliment the staff, and deservedly so, every day.

"Was something amiss with it, milady?" The server's hands shook as she cleared the plates after their meal of spinach salad, steamed cauliflower, white carrots and cabbage in mushroom sauce.

"No, no…" Julianna placed a reassuring hand on the trembling lass's arm before she sent the stack of dinnerware crashing to the floor. "Scrumptious means good…" Another word that hadn't been invented yet. Oh, if only she could've brought her etymology dictionary along with her television, computer, electric blanket and indoor plumbing. "It's a word of Latin derivative, but it's been scrambled a tad."

"I'll have another helping of just the cauliflower," Richard ordered the server as he dabbed at his mouth with a serviette. "Please," he added, courtesy of Julianna's modern coaching.

"I'm so glad you guys...er, the folk in these times eat as many vegetables as you do. From what I always read about medieval fare, it seemed the standard diet was game, what you hunted down in the forests, and lampreys," Juliana said.

Richard shook his head, running his hands down his lean physique. "Could a gluttonous carnivore be this svelte? No, we always grew a great variety of veg in our various gardens along with the flowers we eat. I especially savor the fragrance of violets as well as the taste."

"Well, that's an acquired taste if you don't mind my saying so." The first time he got her to eat violets, she needed to dunk them in the honey pot.

Julianna sank into her plush velvet chair as a steward refilled her wine goblet halfway without even asking—they all knew she liked one and a half nips of malmsey after the midday meal. "Oh, yeah, I can get used to this," she sighed. Another steward placed a plate of three cheddar cheese wedges on the table beside it. "Thanks, gentlemen, and you can take the rest of the day off. Where I'm from, Sunday is a day of rest." She made it a point to thank everyone who waited on her.

But she knew the odds—reaching a ripe old tenth decade—or a ninth, eighth or seventh, was rare in this era of primitive medicine, open sewers, sudden death from plague, and no way to defend herself if some loon branded her a witch.

"This time period is nowhere near as horrific as I feared, Richard." She sipped at her wine—cellar temperature without the miracle of refrigeration, but it came close to chilling her tongue. "Most of these ways of life came as a pleasant surprise." By 'most of' she meant although the bread was soft and fresh, and the butter creamier than any she'd ever tasted, the bacon dripped with grease, and a skin of cream covered her morning milk.

He raised his goblet, and it touched hers in a delicate clink. "I knew you'd learn to roll with the punches, as you modern folk say. After all, royal life is rather pleasant even in these times, as long as I don't fritter the royal coffers on wars to keep those Welsh pillocks on their side of the line."

"It's not the Welsh pillocks that lost Bosworth for you the first time," she reminded him between sips. "It's your own two-faced countrymen who turned their backs on you."

"I know how to handle those bloomin' sods." A crafty sneer spread his kissable lips. "But let's not talk of war and betrayal so close to coronation eve. Have you calculated the final tally for the guest list? We need ensure everyone a bed—even though more than two guests have been known to share."

He'd rattled that off with such a casual air, she looked up from her latest attempt at quill penmanship. "People sleep three to a bed?"

"When they do finally sleep. They've been known to couple, triple and the more ambitious of the lot will indulge in a quad after an eve of festivities. That variety of sport didn't die with the Roman Empire, you know." He took another quaff of wine and sat back to read his Book of Hours, a daily ritual.

"Well, I'll be..." She didn't know why that surprised her, though. With Edward at the helm, the palace must've rocked and rolled every night he was in residence.

"Speaking of the royal coffers, Richard, I don't quite know how to ask this, but—how much can I spend on what you call royal raiment for the coronation? I'll need to be fitted for some new finery. I know all those ermine bellies and bogy shanks and gold threads are *de rigueur* for royalty, but I don't want to go overboard."

He lowered his book and shut it, marking the place with his thumb. "I'm not a bean counter, my love. You may choose the finest raiment—I do need my queen to reflect the splendor of my monarchy."

She let out a relieved sigh. "Thank you, I just haven't been here long enough to know all the house rules. Especially when it comes to finances. After all, I won't have an income of my own. Will you give me an allowance?"

He smiled, his sapphire-black hair catching the fireglow. "No, my dear, you spend as you see fit. I know you're not a wastrel as are certain Plantagenets who'll remain first-nameless, so I have no fear of you frittering beyond our means—or blowing through it as you say."

"Oh, that's a relief, because there are a few things I'd like to change round here."

Richard's thumb slipped from the book and he slid it over to the side. "Much as you desire it, I shan't summon Leonardo da Vinci here and commission him to invent the iPod. You'll have to settle for live music in the gallery and hear your Silver Thunder in your head."

Their second cauliflower helping arrived, and they dug in. "Hmm, not a bad idea," she said. "Although you must admit Leonardo has some innovative concepts that your people poo-poo as off the wall. I wouldn't mind getting him over here to put our heads together. At the very least we might get a helicopter out of it."

"Leave Leo where he is, Italy needs him more than we do." He drained his goblet and set it down, glancing around the chamber.

"I dismissed the stewards until tonight, sorry about that." She made it up to him by getting up and pouring him another gobletful of wine from the carafe on the sideboard.

"So what are the few things you wish to change round here?" He raised a quizzical brow.

"Let's start with the basics." She sat back down and settled in. "We won't even need Leo for this. How about having everyone bathe on a regular basis—say, once a day?"

He rolled his eyes. "Oh, the way you folk do back there?" He jerked a thumb over his shoulder. "I mean, forward there?" The shake of his head didn't look promising. "It's easy enough for us, with the means and incentive to practice meticulous personal hygiene, but common folk—that would be met with a great amount of objection. Of course you know some folk consider bathing dangerous."

"Yeah, out on the moors and in the peat bogs. But here—in the palace?" she asked. "If we start the ritual here, chances are it'll catch on other places. You never know, maybe it'll even reach France."

"Hmmpf." He scoffed. "You said a ritual, not a miracle." He spread his fingers, palms up. "Should you wish to order the court to bathe daily, make the attempt to implement it. But I'm not signing bathing into law like some despot. I'm going to be King Richard, not King Vlad."

"Awesome! I can convince our loyal subjects, starting right here at court, that bathing's been known to fend off disease." She dipped her pen and began scratching down notes on her parchment—*oh, to tap upon a tablet!* But she set aside her yearning and spoke as she formed the splotchy letters, "and regular hair washing rids it of lice and other vermin. Oh, yeah, I'll have them rubbing and scrubbing in no time. I realize not everyone has a tub. We can suggest daily sponge bathing. Just wait and see, Richard. By the time coronation day rolls around, you'll have the sweetest smelling court in Europe."

"Not a bad idea at that." He tapped his finger against his lips. "After living in your times, I do notice it's rather ripe round here."

"If you'll excuse me, Richard, I'm going to order a bath to be ready tonight for a nice long soak. Will you join me in a bath tonight before bedtime?"

"I shall. But keep the fire alive for a steady supply of hot water. I'm so spoilt from the twenty-first century I cannot even tolerate tepid water anymore."

"You got it." She stood and went around the table to give him a kiss and a warm embrace. "First I'm heading to the kitchen to speak with the cooks about this evening's meal. How does pheasant, brawn in comfyte, lampreys in galytyne, and strawberry tarts with cream sound? With a surprise side dish that I'm going to make myself."

He looked up at her with suspicious narrowed eyes. "Uh-oh. "If it's oysters you have in mind, don't bother. I don't need 'em."

She kissed him as his lips spread in a wry grin. "Nope. Nothing to do with enhancing libido. Just a tasty surprise dish. Then I'll look forward to your joining me at bedtime for some good clean fun."

****

She wound her way through the palace corridors to the royal chambers. The cold flagstones bit into her feet. They sure made these satin slippers thin.

She entered her bedchamber and summoned her chambermaid. "Please have that padded tub I like brought in here and have it filled with hot water at the bedtime hour, Jane."

Jane's nose screwed up in puzzlement. "Another bath, milady? But you had one yestermorn."

"Yes, I know, but I bathe daily. Good personal hygiene is akin to good health, and you're going to see that at court from now on. Every member of this court, no matter what position they hold, will be required to bathe daily."

"Daily, milady?" Jane blinked in surprise. "When King Edward was in residence, he bathed monthly, whether he needed it or not."

"Well, this is no longer King Edward's realm. King Richard the Third—and Queen Julianna the First—are going to change a few things, for the better."

"Very well, milady." She curtsied, backing out of the chamber.

"Clean the tub out first, please," Julianna added.

Jane looked at her with crossed eyes. "But I scrubbed it out just last Thursday fortnight. It's not been used since."

"Yeah, I believe it," Julianna muttered. "Now to the kitchen to see if I can invent pizza."

She invented pizza, all right, but not with tomatoes or bananas, which hadn't reached England yet. It didn't even take much effort—all she did was substitute other veggies for tomatoes—and watch the cooks try to hide their astonishment at this dotty new dish.

Julianna entered the kitchen and walked over to the rosemary, sage, mint and other herbs suspended from the ceiling beams. She closed her eyes and inhaled their fresh aroma,

Galfrid, the cook on duty, looked up from his dough-rolling and jumped at the sight of her. "Wha—wha—wha—is something amiss, milady? A problem with the noonday meal?"

"Not at all, Galf, my taste buds are still bursting." She reached into a bowl and plucked a few primrose petals to chew on. "I just want to see if I can whip up a rather peculiar delicacy our soon-to-be-king especially savored on our, uh—travels. It's called pizza, an Italian word, but virtually unknown round these parts."

"And what ingredients does this peeza—" He stumbled over the word and she helped him out.

"Pizza."

"—this pizza contain?" He leaned on the rolling pin, his eyes wide with questioning.

"Some veggies that you don't grow in these parts, but I trust we can whip up a reasonable facsimile. Now, please roll that dough into a circle and tell me where you keep the mushrooms, garlic, onions and vegetable marrows." A vegetable marrow pizza was better than none at all—and she knew Richard would devour it with gusto since he'd developed a taste for onions. They had onions only because she'd insisted they fetch some from the nearest yeoman's garden. Until she appeared at court, onions were considered peasant fare—blue bloods looked down their royal noses at the pungent bulbs.

She even set Richard straight about that age-old legend of Chaucer's—the ghastly Summoner in the Canterbury Tales did not become pockmarked, crooked and lascivious from eating onions. His horrendous breath—oh, well, so onions weren't perfect.

So onions came to court and stayed.

By the time the dinner hour rolled around, she astounded the cooks with her culinary knowledge—after all, how many future queens even set foot in a kitchen, much less get covered in flour up to their elbows and chop garlic till they reeked?

Richard squealed in delight at his custom-made pizza and didn't even mind that it lacked the finishing touch of bananas. "This is superb, my love, simply delectable, or as you say, scrumptious!" He chowed down with gusto and didn't quit till not a crumb remained on his plate.

"Then how about pizza at the coronation banquet?" She hoped her eyes cast a mischievous gleam. "And any time Tudor or his henchmen dare to cross the border, slaughter 'em with a volley of onions!"

****

The coronation of King Richard III was the most lavish in English history. When the king and queen retired to their apartments in the Tower of London to prepare for the feast, a page announced two visitors.

"Who are they?" Richard pulled off his shoes.

"Wouldn't say, sire," he replied, "Just relations of yours."

"Everybody's a relation when you're king,"

Richard grumbled. "Very well, send them in."

King Richard and Queen Julianna gasped in delight when their visitors entered. Ned and George, dressed in the raiment of plain folk, and their wives, Lisbet and Brooke, in the garb of peasant women. They embraced, over and over, and tears flowed.

"You look splendid, King Richard the Third," Ned said proudly. "Never thought I'd live to see my baby brother become king."

"That goes double for me," George echoed, fingering the ermine trim of Richard's robe. "This must've set the treasury back a few quid."

"How's the future treating you?" Richard asked as they all sat.

George found the wine supply and poured a tankard for everyone. "I'm Brooke's co-host!" George beamed.

"And I'm—" Ned hesitated, but Lisbet egged him on.

"Oh, go on, tell them!"

"I'm in a rather prominent position in the community in which we live, a lovely space station out in orbit between Earth and Mars." He smiled, more broadly now. "I'm the Mayor."

"So you're in your element." Richard smiled at his brother. "Looks like we all are."

"I brought you something." Ned dug into a pouch. He took out something that looked vaguely familiar to Julianna. "The amulet. Ulch said you should have it. It's still got the same powers it always had. I don't need it in our advanced times, so it's yours. Again." He slipped it over his brother's head, but it got a bit tangled. "Dickon, take the bloody crown off, will you, for the love of Pete? The world knows you're the damn king."

"Sorry, Ned." He plucked the crown off and placed it on its satin pillow. "Kind of grows on you, you know?"

Ned slid the amulet round Richard's neck. "Goes well with the robe, doesn't it?"

"This amulet still provides protection from any and all harm?" Richard held it twixt two fingers, lost in thought.

"As much as ever." Ned nodded. "He also wanted you each to have one of these." He handed Richard and George clear crystals, but without cords attached. "He assured me these crystals will enable our thoughts to reach each other across the time continuum. When either of you holds it and thinks of me, I'll know you're there, and vice versa."

Julianna couldn't stop the tears welling up. If it weren't for the protective amulet, she would never have met Richard; none of this would ever have happened. "That was so kind of him." She swiped at her moist cheeks. "Now your love for each other can transcend the vastness of time."

Richard held fast to the crystal, but he slid the protective amulet from around his neck. "Ned, if it's all the same to you, I'm giving it to George for protection. I no longer need it." He pressed it into George's palm and closed his fingers around it. "I will do everything in my power to avoid defeat in that battle. But if I am slain fighting for my kingdom, so be it. Some aspects of our destiny we cannot change. However, you, dear brother, staying in this century, in this dangerous world, you will need it. Besides, I'll not need any supernatural help for protection. I know how to do it right this time. And I've got all the magic I need right here." He gave his queen a loving hug.

"Aye, you've always thought with the head on your shoulders, I always admired you for that," Ned said, once again displaying that famous wink.

The brothers and their wives exited the chamber to attend King Richard the Third's coronation feast.

Epilogue

February 2013

George tuned in to Channel 4. "The King in the Car Park" blazed across the screen. A dozen Richard III Society members joined him in stunned silence as University of Leicester osteoarchaeologist Dr. Jo Appleby displayed a skeleton. She pointed out the missing feet and the severely curved spine. The skeleton, slender for a male, showed no sign of a withered arm. He'd lost several teeth before death; the rest showed some wear, with a few cavities.

George nodded. *He fancies his sweets.*

A halberd's blade had hacked away part of the battle-scarred skull. The thought of the pain from that damned blade pierced George's heart. "Those monsters, they took his helmet off him," he moaned, turning away.

The corpse had been subjected to "humiliation injuries" including a sword wound through the right buttock.

George shuddered. "Lord above," he whispered. He knew Richard's enemies slung his naked body over a horse, his arms and legs dangling over the sides, but why stab him in that hideous way? *Those heartless bastards.* He clenched his fists.

Although Richard had severe scoliosis and his right

shoulder may have been higher than the left, he wasn't the mangled humpback of Shakespearian lore. George's smile relieved his anguish.

As he viewed the documentary he told himself over and over, "Richard is living a happy life now. This will not happen to him. He changed his destiny." But that shred of doubt still haunted him. "Please, God, don't let this happen to my baby brother."

Finally, the moment they'd all been waiting for: the facial reconstruction. Expressive eyes gazed at the camera. Dark hair fell to his shoulders. A hint of a smile curved his lips.

George smiled back at his brother's image. Tears spilled down his cheeks. "Yep, that's my Dickon, I'd know that mug anywhere," he sobbed.

Needing to be alone, he excused himself and went out into the night. Taking deep breaths to clear his mind, he fought off the gruesome sight of the mangled skeleton.

"That's not Richard," he assured himself. To prove it, he slipped the wizard's crystal from his pocket.

The brothers used their crystals almost daily to connect over the centuries. George now pressed it to his lips. "Do you fare well, little brother? I just looked into your eyes on television. I'm thinking of you. Let me know you're thinking of me." As the amulet carried his thoughts, it grew warm and glowed in the darkness. Yes, Richard received his message.

Richard's calm voice filled George's mind as Richard's love filled his heart: "I'm fine, my brother. I've never been happier. I avoided that battle and peace reigns over my kingdom. We'll be together again someday."

"I will love you always," they both whispered at the same time.

****

George went online to see the latest on "The King in the Car Park" burial plans. He scrolled past the newest jokes and cartoons—a Leicester car park sign: "Short stay up to two hours, long stay up to 600 years." Richard at the pearly gates as one angel asks another, "Can you smell petrol?" A smirking Blackadder: "Really, Baldrich? Under a car park? That was your cunning plan?"

Grinning, George knew Richard would get a charge out of the Blackadder one. He slid the mouse over his "Richard III put the KING in parking" mouse pad and got to the serious business. When he read about the latest feud between opposing camps, his mouth fell open. Leicester wanted him. York wanted him. Westminster Abbey didn't have room.

Leicester's contention was that the remains were discovered under their car park, hence he should be reburied there. It seemed to George they'd said in so many words, "Sod off, York and Westminster. Finders keepers."

"Lord Jesú, this will be another Wars of the Roses," George muttered. "If this isn't resolved, they'll divvy him up like a bag o'sweets."

He read *The Independent*'s latest:

Row over burial site for King Richard III: Parliamentary petition calling for debate on final resting place misses target.

There is clearly a lot of interest in where he will ultimately be re-interred, a spokesman from the Plantagenet Alliance told the BBC.

"And it's sod-all what Richard wanted?" George shouted at the screen. "I've got a bloomin' Plantagenet alliance, too, I'm his Plantagenet brother!" He pounded his fist on the desk. He knew Richard's final wishes—to be interred on the grounds of Middleham Castle, his favorite residence. Not York Minster. Not Westminster. Not where his enemies slaughtered him. And certainly not under a bloody car park, even if the space did have an "R" stenciled into the asphalt—a weird coincidence, but there it was.

****

George sent e-mails to three of his closest Richard III Society friends, Trevor, Pippa and Dorothy. He carefully worded his proposal:

I will find a way to procure the bones so we can arrange the burial where he wanted. But I need your help—and your trust.

They replied within minutes, and not even by e-mail. They all texted him, one after the other. "We're with you all the way, George..." Pippa assured him. "If you can do it, count me in," came from Trevor. Dorothy texted and phoned, "No one ever has to know. This will be our secret, and we're delighted to share it."

He clutched the phone carrying his team's promises. Gazing out into the night, he squeezed his eyes shut. How to get the bones? "It'll be easier to pilfer them before they're put into the final coffin," he said out loud. "But where to get another skeleton?" His eyes popped open. "Or do I even need one?"

According to the latest bloggers, the bones would be transferred to a funeral home, then taken to Leicester Cathedral for the final burial. The ceremony would be televised and witnessed by a select group of lucky mourners.

Now how to get to the bones before that burial? He snapped his fingers. Aha! As a master of disguises in his former life—in a joke on Ned, he'd dressed like King Henry the Sixth on All Fools Day—he knew how to access the royal remains.

Instead of bribing the courier who'd transport them from Leicester University to the funeral home, he'd *be* the courier! Nobody had made the arrangements yet. He snickered as he cracked a smile; he knew looked bloody wicked. "Now *that's* a cunning plan!" he told an absent Blackadder.

****

Dressed in funereal black accented with a White Boar tie pin and a flat cap, he arrived at Leicester University's Admissions Office and announced himself as a Cromwell Funeral Home driver.

"They've assigned me to courier King Richard's remains to prepare for the reburial ceremony," he informed the secretary in his most somber tone. She gave him directions to the lab, and he fist-pumped himself as he sped away. "Yes!" he stage-whispered as he parked at the lab building and approached the front door. "One hurdle down, three to go."

But hurdle number one slipped back to square one as the lab technician gave George a puzzled frown. "No one from the funeral home told us you were coming today."

He thought fast. "Just call them. I can come back later," he rattled off, and half-turned to leave.

"Never mind, we knew you were coming, we just didn't know when. Wait here."

George let out a slow whistle as the tech vanished

into a back room. He returned with a box large enough for a dozen reams of A4 paper—but for an entire skeleton? Were the bones piled up in there like matchsticks?

The tech handed him the royal box, University cataloging labels slapped onto its top and sides.

George signed the receipt, but halted. "My dear sir, 'tis entirely apropos that we drape Richard's standard over this receptacle, as did the excavators before conveying these royal remains from the original grave to the van. After all, this is our king we've got here. Show some respect!"

The tech shrugged. "We do have it here. It's hanging in the lunch room. I'll go fetch it."

Left alone, George promised, "I'll get you home, Dickon. You won't spent eternity in Leicester if I can help it."

The tech returned with the cloth bearing the royal standard. He draped the box, smoothing the cloth over the top.

"Now that's more like it." George bowed his head and intoned Richard's motto, "Loyaulte me lie."

The tech cupped a hand to his ear. "What was that?"

"It's in deference to the king, but on behalf of those other folk." He turned to leave with a toss of his head. "They're bent on pomp and circumstance, you know how it is."

"I do now." The tech nodded a farewell to the king and his courier.

George tipped his cap and headed back out to convey Richard to his next temporary resting place.

****

He bowed to the round of applause as he displayed the standard-draped box to Trevor, Pippa and Dorothy. "Now we celebrate, and kill two budgies with one stone."

"You lost us, George." Trevor knelt before the royal box and ran his hand over the smooth fabric. "Catch us up."

George explained, "Whilst we celebrate, we'll fill a box with a reasonable facsimile thereof. But first how about some ribs on the barbie tonight?"

"Hey, ribs sound smashing!" Trevor rubbed his hands together. "I have a grill on my back porch. Anything else?" He glanced at the group.

"Grill whatever else you wish, but we really need ribs, and plenty of them. Trust me." George laid a hand on the royal box as his mouth watered. "Too bad you can't join us in this feast, Dickon."

****

"Did you find a proper receptacle for Richard's remains?" Pippa asked George as they gathered round Trevor's grill watching him apply rib rub to a rack.

"Absolutely. Something fittingly appropos. Just arrived today." George sipped at his wine. "He did like pizza fresh out of the box. But after all, he is the king. Ergo, he now reposes in an eighteenth century Northern Italy wrought iron safe, realized in ebony wood by an expert Italian artisan. Wait till you see the splendid front door with the original gold leaf details. He'll spend eternity under lock and key, in a repository fit for a king. He loved his hidey holes and his secret compartments, like the one under his bed where he stashed coins. He'd find it quite fitting—and fit he does. No need to pile him up in there. I carefully laid out and arranged the bones in as close to the proper order as I could. The reliquary cost me seven thousand quid, but nothing's too good for my baby brother. This time round anyway."

"Where did you buy it from?" Dorothy asked.

He displayed a satisfied smile. "Why, eBay of course." They all gave him approving nods.

"We should offer to chip in for it," Pippa suggested. "After all, you confided in us, and we're in this together." She looked at her companions. "What do you say, guys? How about donating to this worthy cause?"

They all agreed even though George waved a dismissing hand. "Don't feel obligated. Just give what you can. Meanwhile..." He wiped his mouth with a napkin and stood. "I'll go fetch a fitting receptacle for these remains—these ribs, that is."

George went out to his car and got the box that Leicester University had piled Richard in. He left the cloth with Richard's standard in the car for the real burial.

George returned to the backyard, propped the lids open, sat back and spread his arms. "Here's my cunning plan. There'll be no room for suspicion as to where Richard's bones really are when they're ready to reinter him. They'll be expecting bones. Hence we'll give 'em bones. In their very box nonetheless."

"You left no stone unturned, George," Dorothy praised him.

"Thank you, my dear, I'd have made a superb Sherlock Holmes had I lived in a fictional world."

They chowed down on the ribs, and George took the lead. He tossed his first gnawed rib into the

University's box. "Give 'em bones, lads and lasses!"

As they munched, they tossed their clean-picked rib bones into the box, laughing and making merry.

"As soon as we have a Richard-sized pile of bones, I'll courier them to the funeral home. Two hurdles down, one to go. And I do say, Trev, that was a fine stack of ribs that'll get a royal burial under that slab!"

****

After donning his most pompous raiment—tweed jacket with patch elbows, wire specs and pipe dangling from his lips, George drove the box of gnawed rib bones, draped in the royal standard, no less, to the funeral home.

"Leicester University sent me here with King Richard's remains. Is his new coffin ready?" he asked the funeral director.

Just as George heard at the University, the director said, "We're not expecting you, no one from the University called."

He gave a one-shoulder shrug. "Well, here I am, you want me to take them back?" He made that turning-to-leave move.

"No, no, give them here." The director held his hands out to take the box.

George took a quick step back. "Oh, no, sir, that won't be acceptable at all. As directed by the head of security at the University, I must ensure every one of these bones goes into the coffin and no one pinches a souvenir. We do not want to see Richard's ribs on eBay next week. I need personally put them into the coffin myself and witness you sealing it." He gave a resolute nod.

"Allowing clients to observe us carrying out our

work on remains is not our policy, Sir." The director rose to the balls of his feet and landed back down on his heels.

George rose to his own feet's balls. "I beg to differ, my good man. It's quite prestigious to bury Good King Richard the Third's bones. This is not some Jack the Lad we're interring, Sir. This is the burial of the century—of the millennium even. If you won't do it, I'll take it to someone who'll abide by the University's security rules." Once again he turned to leave with his precious cargo. "Your competitors will be happy to do business with His Royal Highness here."

"No!" The director nearly leapt on top of him. "We want the privilege! Follow me." He led George down the hall to a small room containing an open casket. "Here, I'll put the box in." Again he held out his hands.

George swiveled to his left, the standard's edges swirling around the box. "Sorry, my good man, but I need be alone. I cannot risk the chance any of these bones can go astray. I'll summon you when I'm through."

Holding the box with one hand, he shooed the director away with the other. Finally alone with his royally shrouded ribs, he emptied the box into the casket, spread the bones out and shut the lid. George called for the director and ordered him to seal the lid. Immediately and permanently.

****

Middleham Castle grounds

George stood over his brother's remains inside the magnificent, securely locked safe. He said a prayer as the men lowered it into the grave they'd dug earlier.

He thought of the "official" ceremony at Leicester

Cathedral earlier that day, with the clergy, selected guests and television cameras in attendance—the kind of media circus Richard hated. George and his trusted friends watched it live, smug in their secret knowledge, chowing down on another feast of ribs.

Now Trevor, Pippa and Dorothy joined him in paying their respects, George grasped his amulet. It grew warm—he knew Richard was listening. "We're giving you the burial you wanted, mate," he whispered to his brother across the centuries. "Here's hoping your next one is many decades from now."

The women dropped white roses into the grave. In a final gesture, George tossed his own offering to his brother—a pizza box and a banana peel. "Bananas on pizza forever." He stepped back to let Trevor fill in the grave.

Before departing, they placed a plaque upon the ground. It read:

On this spot King Richard the Third wished to be buried. May his mortal remains rest in peace...someday.

Author's Note

Because I wrote this as a romantic comedy, not a historical treatise, I took license with dates and events. This story is implausible, outrageous, and humorous. But at the same time I endeavored to maintain some semblance of reason. Therefore, my explanation below is an attempt to clarify the paradoxes wrapped in the conundrums inside the riddles that comprise the concept of time travel.

You may ask: if Edward travels from the fifteenth century to here, he changes what happened in the fifteenth century. I considered that paradox—when Richard went back to his own time after being here, he returned to an alternate universe, in line with the theory that time is an infinite continuum and 1485 is still "going on" just as our time is.

From our perspective, it "hasn't happened yet" but it's happening in that alternate universe, or other dimension, if you will. That's why there's some speculation that UFOs and aliens who visit Earth, if they truly do, may be time travelers from the future.

Theoretically, the universe is multidimensional, and "alternate universes" also exist, so in an alternate universe, your fate took the path you didn't choose in this one. Maybe you wanted to go to Hollywood to get into motion pictures but didn't. But in that universe, you did go to Hollywood, and might be a movie star in that universe.

It's all theory, of course; no one can prove it. Einstein did explore the concept of time travel. It may not be plausible to us, but it sure makes for great SciFi.

www.r3.org is the address of the Richard III

Yorkist History Server, sponsored by the American Branch of the Richard III Society. The Parent Society, located in London, can be reached at www.richardiii.net

A word about the author...

Diana has written several historical and paranormal novels set in England and the U.S., and two time-travel romances. She is the author of *Fakin' It* and *A Bloody Good Cruise*, both published by The Wild Rose Press.

Diana is a member of Romance Writers of America and the Richard III Society. In her spare time, she has been pursuing a Master's degree in archaeology and loves to visit historical sites all over the world. Diana and her husband own CostPro, Inc., an engineering business based in Cambridge.

Visit Diana at:

www.dianarubino.com

www.dianarubinoauthor.blogspot.com

www.facebook.com/DianaRubinoAuthor

and follow her on

Twitter @DianaLRubino

Thank you for purchasing
this publication of The Wild Rose Press, Inc.

If you enjoyed the story, we would appreciate
your letting others know by leaving a review.

For other wonderful stories,
please visit our on-line bookstore at
www.thewildrosepress.com.

For questions or more information
contact us at
info@thewildrosepress.com.

The Wild Rose Press, Inc.
www.thewildrosepress.com

Stay current with The Wild Rose Press, Inc.

Like us on Facebook
https://www.facebook.com/TheWildRosePress

And Follow us on Twitter

https://twitter.com/WildRosePress